EATING DEATH

Forbidden Feast of the Undead

What will you do when it happens?
Will you starve or will you survive...

CONTENTS

ABOUT THE AUTHOR

Tory Swedlund may be a newcomer to the world of authors, but his passion for writing has been a constant companion for years. He pours his thoughts onto journal pages, using them as a tool to process life's ups and downs. It is through this practice that he has crafted some of the most captivating and imaginative storylines in the literary world.

But Tory's talents go beyond his writing abilities. As a single father of two young girls, aged 10 and 7, he juggles his responsibilities with grace and determination. And though it may seem like an impossible feat, Tory is also a recovering alcoholic and drug addict who has been sober for an astonishing 24 years. Perhaps it is his journey to sobriety that gives him the insight and strength to create such compelling stories.

Stay connected with Tory as he continues to unleash his imagination through upcoming books like "Final Swipe" and "Eating Death". With so much life experience under his belt, there is no doubt that Tory has many more amazing tales waiting to be told.

CHAPTER I

Jean-Pierre crept through the rubble-strewn streets, his eyes darting to and from. Shattered glass crunched under his boots as he scanned the deserted cityscape. The acrid smell of smoke hung heavy in the air. He paused, listening intently. Only the faint whistle of the wind broke the oppressive silence.

Satisfied he was alone, Jean-Pierre slipped inside a crumbling storefront. Shelves lay tipped over, their contents spilled across the floor. Jean-Pierre's pulse quickened as he spotted jars of spices and shriveled vegetables nestled among the debris.

"Cumin, paprika, thyme," he murmured, gathering the precious ingredients into his pack. "These will make a fine stew."

He spied a dented can of chickpeas and snatched it up eagerly. Protein was hard to come by these days. Jean-Pierre's mind drifted back to his restaurant's glory days - the savory aroma of braising meats, the satisfied murmurs of patrons savoring his creations. A pang of longing pierced his heart.

Shaking off the memories, Jean-Pierre refocused on his task. Survival was all that mattered now. He would take what the ruins provided and transform it into something special. A hint of a smile touched his lips. Even in this broken world, he could still create beauty through his art.

Jean-Pierre slipped back outside, his pack now heavy with potential. He would eat well tonight. And perhaps, for a moment, he could even pretend things were normal again. With nimble feet, Jean-Pierre vanished into the ruins, intent on unearthing more hidden treasures. His passion for cooking would sustain him, no matter what the challenges ahead.

Jean-Pierre crept through the crumbling city, ducking behind an overturned car as he spotted movement up ahead. Shambling figures emerged from the haze - zombies. He counted six, maybe seven of them. Too many to fight. Jean-Pierre's pulse raced, but he forced himself to remain calm. Survival depended on a cool head.

He scanned his surroundings, looking for an escape route. There - a fire escape ladder dangling from the side of an apartment building. If he could just get to it without being seen...

Jean-Pierre took a deep breath and then sprinted towards the ladder. His feet barely made a sound as he dashed over broken pavement littered with glass. The zombies groaned, turning towards the noise, but too late - Jean-Pierre was already halfway up the ladder.

He climbed swiftly, not stopping until he'd reached the roof. Crouching behind the ledge, Jean-Pierre watched the zombies mill about below. That had been close. He let out a shaky breath, adrenaline still coursing through his veins. But he'd made it. His chef's agility had saved him once again.

As his heart rate slowed, Jean-Pierre's thoughts turned to the past. He saw himself in his pristine kitchen, directing a brigade of chefs as they prepared for the dinner rush. The smells of shallots and thyme mingled with the sound of sizzling pans. Waiters swept through the double doors, returning with empty plates licked clean.

Jean-Pierre had taken pride in every dish that was left in his kitchen. Creating perfection on a plate was more than his job - it had been his passion. He still missed that bustling world deeply. Yet he knew it was gone. Now his skills served a different purpose - survival.

Jean-Pierre rose and glanced at the setting sun. The night would soon fall. He'd have to find shelter. With a last look at the shambling zombies below, he turned and headed towards the rooftop access door. His chef's spirit remained unbroken. No matter what this new world threw at him, he would endure.

Jean-Pierre descended the stairwell cautiously, one hand trailing along the graffiti-covered wall. He blinked as he stepped outside, the dying sunlight momentarily blinding the darkness of the building's interior. The streets were still and silent, the only movement coming from scraps of garbage skittering across the cracked asphalt.

Jean-Pierre's eyes scanned the urban decay, searching for anything of use. A glint caught his attention - the glass door of a small grocery store. He hurried across the street and wrenched it open, wincing as the jangle of a bell echoed through the space.

Moving swiftly, he grabbed a battered cart and headed down the aisles. Most of the shelves were picked clean, but Jean-Pierre's experienced eye knew where to look. He found a few cans of beans tucked behind empty crates. A cluster of potatoes, sprouting but still edible, were hidden under a moldy cardboard display.

In the back, Jean-Pierre hit the jackpot - a storeroom with rows of dented cans and packaged goods. His pulse quickened as he took in the possibilities - broth, tomato sauce, even a precious container of oregano.

Visions of stews, sauces, and gravies danced through his mind. With these ingredients, he could create masterpieces once again.

Jean-Pierre loaded the cart greedily, mouthwatering at the thought of cooking with real food. For a moment, the bleak reality of his situation faded away. He was simply a chef again, preparing for his next culinary challenge.

With the cart piled high, he paused and closed his eyes. The ghostly sounds of a busy kitchen enveloped him - the sizzle of meat in a pan, the chopping of knives on wood. This is who he was, at his core. And no apocalypse could take that away.

Jean-Pierre opened his eyes, a faint smile on his lips. Wheeling the cart forward, he pushed through the broken door out into the silent street. The sun had nearly set, but he walked with renewed purpose. For in this grim new world, he had found ingredients. And where there were ingredients, there was hope.

Jean-Pierre wheeled the cart down the cracked pavement, scanning the shadows for any signs of the undead. The streets were empty, but he knew that could change in an instant.

He strained his ears for any shuffling footsteps or inhuman moans. Only the wind whistling through broken windows answered.

As he turned a corner, the wheels snagged on an upturned slab of concrete. The cart tipped violently, cans crashing to the ground. Jean-Pierre cursed under his breath. As he crouched to gather the fallen goods, an eerie wail pierced the air. His blood turned to ice.

Lurching out of the alleyway, a small group of zombies shuffled towards him. Rotting flesh hung off their emaciated frames, clouded eyes glowing with an insatiable hunger. Jean- Pierre's mind raced. He was trapped, with no way to outrun them while pushing the heavy cart.

Spying a rusty pipe nearby, he grabbed it and brandished it like a sword. As the first zombie lunged, he smashed the pipe into its skull. It crumpled to the ground with a sickening crunch. Another grabbed at his shoulder from behind. Whirling around, Jean-Pierre slammed the pipe into its neck.

His heart pounded as he fended off the relentless horde. When an opening appeared, he abandoned the cart and sprinted down the street. The zombies' raspy wails faded behind him. Jean-Pierre slowed to a walk, gasping for breath. That was too close.

Shaken but determined, he retraced his steps. The zombies lay motionless in the street amidst the spilled cans. Jean-Pierre gathered up what he could salvage. Next time, he will be more careful. He could not let a simple mistake cost him his life.

As Jean-Pierre made his way cautiously through the ruins, the shock wore off. He moved with new fluidity; his senses heightened. While he missed the comforts of his old life, out here only his resourcefulness and instincts mattered. If adapting to this world meant surviving, then so be it.

Jean-Pierre would endure. For where there was food, there was hope. And he would craft masterpieces from it once again.

Jean-Pierre trudged onward, scanning the horizon for signs of shelter as the sun sank below the crumbling skyline. His muscles ached from hauling his pack of scavenged goods, but he dared not stop - not with night approaching. As shadows stretched over the decrepit streets, his pace quickened.

Rounding a corner, Jean-Pierre spotted an old brick building still partially intact. He slipped through a jagged hole in the wall and found himself in what was once a cozy bookshop.

Shelves lay splintered on the floor, books strewn about in decaying heaps. Jean-Pierre sighed, reminded of his lost library of culinary tomes.

Wearily, he sank amidst the wreckage, allowing his pack to slip from his shoulders. He ran a hand over his grizzled beard, gazing up at the exposed rafters as his mind wandered. How many had perished in those first chaotic days? Friends, family - all gone in a flash. And those remaining faced horrors no person should.

Jean-Pierre closed his eyes, seeing their faces. The children he had cooked for at the shelter, eyes alight with joy. His young sous chef eagerly absorbed his every lesson. His wife - the way she smiled across the candlelit dinner table. A profound emptiness ached within him.

With great effort, Jean-Pierre pushed himself up. He could not dwell on what was lost. The living needed him now. His skills could nourish their bodies and spirits, and kindle hope again. Reaching for his pack, Jean-Pierre steeled himself for the challenges ahead. He would survive this night, and the next, and the next - for them.

Jean-Pierre slung his pack over his shoulders and crept back out into the gloomy streets. The day's scavenging had yielded a few prize ingredients - some shriveled carrots, a handful of wild onions, and even a few precious spices secreted away in a ransacked kitchen. His mind buzzed with recipe ideas as he slipped between the abandoned buildings.

He could braise the carrots with the onions and a splash of vinegar for depth. Perhaps grind the spices into a rub for whatever protein he might trap. Yes, his culinary talents could transform these humble findings into something special. Something that would both nourish and uplift.

As the last light faded from the dreary sky, Jean-Pierre paused to get his bearings. In the distance, beyond the skeletal high-rises, he glimpsed a cluster of structures on a hillside. His breath caught. It was a settlement - with cooking fires flickering outside makeshift walls.

Jean-Pierre's grip tightened on his pack. After so many cold, lonely nights, here were living souls. Perhaps even kindred spirits who still cared about the craft, the art of cooking. New energy surged through Jean-Pierre's tired body. He was not alone after all. With renewed purpose, he strode toward the fires twinkling on the horizon, their promise warming him more than any flame could.

Jean-Pierre approached the settlement cautiously, sticking to the shadows as he surveyed the perimeter. He could see figures milling about within the makeshift walls, backlit by the cooking fires. They seemed relaxed, at ease - not the frenzied movements of the infected. Still, Jean-Pierre knew appearances could be deceiving in this ravaged world.

He was musing on how best to approach when a gruff voice called out, "That's far enough stranger. State your business or be on your way."

Jean-Pierre turned to see two men emerge from behind a nearby ruined building, rifles trained on him. He raised his hands slowly. "Please, I mean no harm. I'm just a cook seeking refuge."

The men glanced at each other skeptically. The taller one kept his gun ready. "A cook huh? We don't see too many of your type anymore."

Jean-Pierre nodded. "I know it seems foolish, clinging to my craft when survival itself is a daily battle. But food is not just sustenance - it brings comfort, joy. It can make even the bleakest days a little brighter."

The men considered this. The shorter one lowered his rifle a fraction. "Can't say I miss much beyond full bellies, but the kids sure could use some cheer." He looked Jean-Pierre up and down. "You any good, this cooking of yours?"

Jean-Pierre smiled. "I was once considered one of the finest chefs in Paris. I can work wonders even with the most meager of ingredients. Just give me a chance to prove myself."

The men exchanged a glance, and then the taller one grunted. "Alright, we'll take you to Marcus. He'll decide if you're worth keeping around."

Jean-Pierre felt a spark of hope. A chance was all he needed.

Jean-Pierre followed the men through the rubble-strewn streets, past decaying buildings that may have once been homes and businesses. This city was a hollow shell now, its former vibrancy erased.

They approached a high brick wall reinforced with scrap metal and barbed wire. The tall man pounded on a steel door and called out, "Open up! We found something for Marcus."

The door creaked open, and they entered what had become this group's compound. Makeshift shacks and tents filled the interior courtyard. People eyed Jean-Pierre warily as they passed, some cradling children or tending to tasks like cooking and washing.

They stopped before a large tent flew fluttering in the breeze. The tall man said, "Marcus, this guy claims to be some famous cook from the old world. Says he wants to join up."

A figure emerged from the tent - Marcus, Jean-Pierre presumed. He was tall and muscular, with dark slicked-back hair and sharp eyes that sized Jean-Pierre up. "A cook? Can't say we've had one of those around in some time."

He circled Jean-Pierre slowly. "But you better be able to deliver if you want to stay. Nothing fancy mind you - ingredients are hard to come by. But even simple food tastes like heaven when you've had nothing but scavenged scraps for months."

Jean-Pierre met his gaze steadily. "Give me a chance and I will not disappoint."

Marcus studied him a moment longer before nodding. "We'll see. Take him to the kitchen tent for now and set him up with what we've got. I'll be keeping an eye on you..."

"Jean-Pierre," He supplied.

"Jean-Pierre," Marcus repeated. "Don't make me regret letting you in." Jean-Pierre inclined his head. "You have my word."

As he was led away, Jean-Pierre felt the first kindling of hope. A chance was all he needed to ignite their spirits with his cooking once more.

CHAPTER 2

The sun beat down relentlessly on Jean-Pierre's back as he trudged through the barren wasteland, his steps heavy and slow. He was exhausted, his stomach grumbling with hunger, his mind filled with memories of the lavish feasts he used to create as a renowned chef. But now all he could think about was finding something – anything – to eat. The desolate landscape offered no relief from the scorching heat, and the only sounds were the crunch of dry twigs underfoot, the rustling of pale grass, and the occasional buzz of a fly.

Suddenly, he caught a glimpse of movement in the distance. People. A group of survivors. Their gaunt faces and desperate eyes told a tale of their struggle for survival. Jean-Pierre quickened his pace, his heart pounding with hope and fear. As he approached them warily, he noted that they were huddled around a small campfire, their clothes tattered and dirty. Their eyes widened when they saw him; some looked fearful, while others looked hopeful.

Alice Winters, the group's leader, stood up tall, her long dark hair falling over her shoulders in a curtain of protection. Her eyes were sharp, intelligent, and cautious as she sized him up. She nodded to the others, and they slowly lowered their weapons, giving him the sign that they weren't a threat. "Who are you?" she asked, her voice rough from disuse.

He introduced himself, explaining that he too was just another survivor trying to find food and shelter. He couldn't help but notice the way she watched him warily, her body language mirroring the caution in her voice. She had been through too much to trust easily, and he couldn't blame her for that.

"We've been surviving on whatever we can find," she said, pointing to the smoldering embers of the fire. "Berries, roots, and the occasional rodent. Not enough to go around, though." She gestured to a few of the others who looked even more emaciated than she did.

"I used to be a chef," he admitted reluctantly, not wanting them to think he was any better than them. But he knew he had to offer something. "I can make a meal out of almost nothing."

Her eyes lit up with curiosity, and she nodded for him to follow her into the makeshift camp they'd created from scraps of fabric and twigs. The others watched him warily as he entered, their stomachs growling in anticipation at the promise of a hot meal.

As Jean-Pierre began to prepare a meal using what little they had – a few dried meats, some wild herbs, and a handful of vegetables – he couldn't help but marvel at Alice Winters' resourcefulness. She had created a shelter from scraps of fabric and twigs, using her instincts to keep them safe from predators. He could tell she was protective of those under her charge, always keeping an eye out for danger while also ensuring they had enough to survive.

"It's not much," he said apologetically as he presented them with a stew. "But it should help fill the void."

The aroma filled the air as they all sat down in a circle; eyes closed in anticipation. The first bite was heavenly. The spices were just enough to tantalize their taste buds, and the texture was surprisingly smooth. It wasn't elegant cuisine, but it was nourishment, and that was enough for now.

The warmth from the fire and the food filled them with a newfound sense of hope. For once, they felt like they might make it through this harsh land alive.

"Thank you," Alice murmured, looking at him gratefully.

"You're welcome," he replied, feeling a sense of purpose wash over him. He had found his purpose – feeding these people, keeping them safe, and hopefully leading them to a better life.

As the night wore on, he shared stories of his former life as a renowned chef, making them laugh and dream of better days to come. They talked about their pasts, their families, and their hopes for the future. They all agreed that they would stick together and rely on each other. And for the first time in a long time, Jean-Pierre felt like he truly belonged.

With renewed energy, they set about planning their next moves, strategizing how to stay ahead of the zombies and find more food. Alice was skeptical but listened to his ideas, recognizing the need for survival above all else.

Together, they foraged for berries and hunted small games, learning to adapt to this new world. Their bond grew stronger with every meal he cooked, and every story they shared. And through it all, Jean-Pierre knew one thing for sure; he had found his calling. He was no longer just a chef, but a leader, a protector, a friend.

One day, they came across an abandoned shack on the outskirts of town. It was rundown, but it could provide shelter from the elements. They all pitched in, cleaning out the dirt and debris, making it livable. As they worked, Alice watched him intently, her dark eyes filled with curiosity. She had seen him in action before – chopping vegetables, roasting meats, creating meals out of thin air – but this was different. This was about survival.

Within hours, the shack was transformed into a makeshift kitchen, with Alice peering over his shoulder as he prepared a feast unlike any they had ever known. He hummed to himself, chopping vegetables with precision, seasoning them just right.

The aroma of garlic and herbs wafted through the air as he started the fire, adding wood to keep it blazing. He opened up his bag, pulling out a few choice cuts of meat from the zombie they'd taken down earlier. Searing it on the grill, he let out a satisfied sigh. The juices dripped onto the coals below, sizzling and popping.

Over time, their eyes grew wide in amazement as they tasted the dish before them. Alice's eyes filled with tears – not just from hunger but from hope. This was more than food; it was a taste of humanity, a reminder of what they were fighting for.

They ate together, laughing and talking, their voices echoing off the walls of their new home. The crackling of the fire, the sounds of their chewing, the smell of cooked meat...it was almost like a dream. And for that moment, it was.

As they lay in their sleeping bags afterward, Alice fell asleep to the sound of his stomach contentedly rumbling from the hearty meal. She smiled, knowing that tonight, they would survive.

The next morning, they rose to the smell of freshly brewed coffee and baked goods - another gift from Jean-Pierre's seemingly endless knowledge. They ate in silence, savoring every bite.

Alice gazed at him curiously across the table. This man had changed everything for them - he was more than just a survivor; he was their hope. She wondered how many other secrets he held about surviving in this harsh new world.

"So, Alice," he began, leaning back in his chair, "what do you know about traps?" His question caught her off guard, but she nodded slowly, hesitantly. "I've heard tales of people using snares and such, but never actually seen them." She shrugged. "What did you have in mind?"

He grinned, revealing a missing tooth. "Well, let's go see for ourselves," he said, motioning for her to follow him outside.

As they walked through the desolate streets, Alice couldn't help but admire his determination. Despite the risks and fear of the undead lurking around each corner, he pressed on with a sense of purpose.

They came upon an abandoned marketplace, and Jean-Pierre started pointing out different kinds of traps - rat traps, bear traps, even a homemade pitfall equipped with sharpened stakes at the bottom. His eyes glinted with excitement as he showed her how each one worked.

"This could be very useful," she murmured, impressed by his ingenuity. He nodded, taking her hand in his. "We must adapt to survive, my dear. Our circumstances have changed, and we must change with them."

"I agree," she replied, feeling a strange kinship forming between them. Despite her initial skepticism, there was something about his unwavering resolve that she respected deeply.

Over time, they gathered materials, set up traps, and even learned how to cook more unusual game like rabbits and squirrels. Their newfound partnership grew stronger until it felt like destiny had brought them together. Eventually, they even found love within their unlikely union.

One day, after a successful hunt, Jean-Pierre cooked up a meal that made her stomach growl before it even hit her nose - a rich stew of venison and wild mushrooms seasoned with spices from his native land. She took a tentative bite, her eyes widening in surprise at the burst of flavors on her tongue. The meat was tender and gamey, but not unpalatable. It wasn't until she swallowed that she realized her mistake; the taste lingered on her palate, demanding more.

"It's... good," she admitted reluctantly. Jean-Pierre beamed at her, and she couldn't help but return his smile.

With each bite, she grew more adventurous, tasting the richness of the broth and savoring the hearty chunks of venison. As the sun began to set, they sat together, full and content for the first time in months.

"You, see?" he said softly, taking her hand in his. "We don't have to starve or resort to cannibalism. There is still life out there, waiting for us if we are willing to take the risk."

Alice looked into his eyes, seeing the desperation and hope mingled within them. Slowly, she nodded. "Alright. But we need to be careful, Jean-Pierre. We can't risk it all on one meal."

"Of course, my love," he replied, kissing her knuckles.

Together, they prepared for their next hunt, grateful for his knowledge of survival and cooking. The wind picked up, carrying the scent of roasted venison and fresh herbs through the camp, filling their bellies and spirits with anticipation. On this night, for once, they felt less like prey and more like humans again. Despite their circumstances, they had each other, and that was enough to keep them going.

The next day dawned with a new mission: to find ingredients for another meal. Jean-Pierre's eyes sparkled as the spoke of exotic spices and rare vegetables, remnants of a past life that now held power in their new world. Alice watched him intently, her eyes roaming over his body language as he gestured animatedly. She noticed the way his hands moved with precision and passion when he described the tastes he wanted to create; it was clear he wasn't just cooking for sustenance but for pleasure too. This man had once been a chef, someone who appreciated the art of food, and she found herself curious about what other treasures he could whip up in these desolate lands.

As they ventured out, Alice kept an eye out for any signs of danger while Jean-Pierre foraged for exotic mushrooms and gathered wild herbs. The forest whispered secrets around them, its rustling leaves and the chirping of birds their only company. The sky above darkened, and soon stars twinkled like diamonds against the velvet black canvas, casting an ethereal glow on their surroundings. Their fingers brushed against one another as they navigated through the unfamiliar terrain, their steps in synch like a well-rehearsed dance.

Back at camp, they huddled around the fire, feasting on a combination of meats and foraged vegetables seasoned to perfection. The aroma lingered in the air, teasing their senses as the spices danced across their tongues. Jean-Pierre, buoyed by the success of his dish, began to chat with ease, sharing stories from his past life in Paris before the war. Alice listened intently, unaware that she too was slowly opening to him. Despite her initial reservations, she found comfort in his presence - he was knowledgeable and skilled, qualities that could be invaluable in their harsh new world.

The fire crackled merrily while they ate, casting flickering shadows across their faces. The forest came alive with the sounds of their satisfaction, the crunching of food, the slurping of soups, and the gentle hum of contentment. They finished their meal on a high note, sated but still hungry for more. Alice looked at Jean-Pierre, contemplating what else he could conjure up in these trying times. It seemed he could be an ally worth keeping after all.

"Do you ever make berry tarts?" she asked softly, eyes twinkling under the firelight. "Berry tarts?" He raised an eyebrow, intrigued by the question. "Well, I haven't had any

berries in quite some time, but I can certainly try." He nodded. "It would be an excellent way to showcase what we have available here."

The next morning, Jean-Pierre led a small band of volunteers through the forest, their footfalls muffled by the thick carpet of moss beneath their shoes. Alice trailed behind them, her long dark hair swaying gently behind her like a pendulum. They gathered various fruits and spices, each step taking them deeper into the woods. From blueberries and raspberries to wild oregano and mint, every ingredient was carefully selected for its unique flavor and texture.

Back at camp, Alice's group looked on, impressed by Jean-Pierre's knowledge of the forest bounty. Skepticism turned to curiosity as they watched him transform the rough collection into an elegant dish. The tart dough was flaky and buttery, cradling the juicy berries and tangy cream like a warm embrace. The sharpness of the mint offset the sweetness perfectly, creating a symphony on their tongues. Even those who had initially written him off were surprised by the result.

The crust crunched satisfyingly under their teeth, and the sweet-tart flavors exploded in their mouths. Jean-Pierre beamed with pride, his eyes sparkling like stars in the night sky. He bowed humbly, taking in their praise like a seasoned performer. The aroma of freshly baked goods filled the air, mingling with the tantalizing scents of wild berries and roasting meat from another group's cook-off.

"You've outdone yourself," Alice complimented him warmly, a rare smile breaking across her face. She turned to the others. "If we can trust him with this, maybe there's hope for us yet." Slowly, they began to trust him more, their eyes gleaming with anticipation for what came next. Little did they know, this was just the beginning of their adventure together.

CHAPTER 3

Jean-Pierre took a deep breath as he watched the group around the small campfire. Their expressions ranged from disgust to outright horror as they listened to his plan. They had heard him out, but it was clear they didn't understand his desperation. He knew that they would come around eventually; they had no choice. Survival meant taking risks, and sometimes those risks were unpalatable. He gathered his cooking supplies with a heavy heart.

and set out into the desolate landscape, leaving Alice and her group behind. He couldn't help but let out a small chuckle as he heard her mutter something under her breath about 'crazy Frenchmen'. He didn't blame her for being skeptical; he had been skeptical of the idea at first too. But he had seen it work firsthand - zombies could be used for more than just a meal, they could provide nourishment and strength when other food sources were scarce.

The air was thick with the stench of decay as he ventured deeper into the wasteland. The sun began to set, casting long shadows across the barren land. It was eerily quiet, except for the occasional twig snapping beneath his feet and dead leaves rustling.

His senses were heightened, and he could feel the eyes of the undead creatures on him. He stopped suddenly as he heard a faint moan in the distance. Slowly, he pulled out his makeshift weapon - a crowbar with nails hammered through the end - and began to edge toward the source of the sound.

With each step, his heart pounded louder, anticipation building. He couldn't help but wonder if this was the right decision; after all, he was putting not only his life but also his reputation on the line. But he knew that they wouldn't last much longer without this recipe.

His target came into view: a male zombie stumbling towards him, its corpse-like hands outstretched. Jean-Pierre prepared himself, mustering up all the courage he could find as he swung the crowbar with all his might. There was a satisfying crunch as it connected with the zombie's skull, and it collapsed to the ground.

He knelt, feeling a wave of nausea wash over him as he inspected the now lifeless body. Its skin was ashen and cold to the touch, and blood seeped from the wound in its head. He sighed, closing his eyes for a moment before getting to work. He carefully removed the brain, tossing the rest of the body aside and placing the squishy, gray matter in a plastic bag he had brought with him. The taste was unpleasant, to say the least, but he reminded himself that it would be worth it once cooked into a nutritious stew.

As he continued his journey, he spotted another zombie shuffling in the distance. This time, he took a more cautious approach, setting up traps using rotten meat as bait. It worked like a charm; he had three more brains secured within minutes.

The taste was still disgusting, but his rumbling stomach reminded him why he was doing this. His collection complete, he headed back to camp with a newfound sense of pride and determination.

Back at their makeshift shelter, Alice and the others watched warily as he approached. He could tell they were still unsure about his methods, but they couldn't deny that he had brought back fresh meat - albeit an unconventional source. Setting down the bags, he pulled out a large pot filled with water and set it over a roaring fire. The intensity of the flames made Marcus's eyes light up, and he approached cautiously. "What are you doing?" he asked, his voice tinged with curiosity and skepticism.

Without missing a beat, Jean-Pierre replied, "Cooking our next meal." He added some herbs and spices from their limited supply to the water before dropping in the first brain. The mixture began to simmer, releasing a putrid stench into the air. It was anything but appetizing.

Despite their protests, he insisted they try a small taste. Alice went first, her face contorting in disgust as she swallowed the morsel. But then, something strange happened; she closed her eyes, her expression softening. "It's...not bad," she admitted reluctantly. Eddie followed suit, his eyes widening in surprise as he reached for another piece. "Tastes just like beef," he said, his voice thick with amazement.

Dr. Martinez was less impressed, her nose scrunching up in distaste. "It's revolting," she muttered under her breath. Sophia looked at him with concern etched on her face but didn't say anything.

Marcus, however, was more interested in the prospect of maintaining his luxurious lifestyle than the ethical implications of their food source. He snatched a piece and chewed thoughtfully, a silent nod of approval on his face. "I like it," he announced with a smirk, testing the limits of Jean-Pierre's culinary abilities further.

With renewed determination, Jean-Pierre journeyed deeper into the wasteland, seeking more zombies, and trying new recipes. He discovered that braising the meat in red wine and garlic made it tender and slightly sweet while roasting it over an open flame giving it a smoky flavor. Boiling it with ginger and soy sauce gave it an unforeseen kick. His creativity knew no bounds as he experimented, pushing the boundaries of what many would consider palatable.

As he sliced it into a freshly prepared slab of zombie meat, the juices ran red, and he took a cautious bite. It was gamey but not unbearable, and the taste lingered on his tongue long after swallowing. He could feel his passion for cooking igniting again, driving him forward despite the moral dilemmas that plagued him. This was his art, his way of bringing sustenance to those who needed it most.

Heading back to the camp, he saw Antoine lurking nearby, a malevolent glint in his eye. Jean-Pierre knew better than to trust the man and kept his guard up. Approaching cautiously, he offered him a taste of the latest creation. Antoine closed his eyes in surprise, savoring the flavor before grinning wickedly. "Not bad," he admitted grudgingly.

The aroma of cooked zombie meat filled the air as they shared a silent moment of understanding - their alliance might be tenuous, but they would endure as long as it brought sustenance and power to their survivors.

But as Marcus approached, Edward not far behind, tension filled the air. Jean-Pierre could sense it like a storm brewing, threatening to unravel their fragile alliance. Marcus' sharp gaze darted between Jean-Pierre and Antoine with suspicion written all over his face. "What have you been up to, Chef? We don't need any more trouble." His voice was like ice, cold and calculating.

Jean-Pierre straightened his shoulders, meeting Marcus' gaze head-on. "Trouble? I'm just trying to feed our people, isn't that what we're all here for?" He gestured to the pot simmering over the fire, filled with the scent of roasted zombie stew.

Eddie stood beside him, rubbing his stomach hungrily. "Let us taste it, Chef. It smells amazing," he said with an eager smile.

Sophia looked on with skepticism but didn't object as Jean-Pierre doled out portions onto worn tin plates. One bite into the stew, and even she had to admit it was delicious. It wasn't quite like any other meat she'd ever tasted before, but it was flavorful and filling.

The group sat in silence around the fire, eating in a way that only the truly hungry can. As they devoured the meal, Alice watched from afar, her eyes narrowed in thought. She wasn't fully convinced but knew they needed the nourishment.

Just then, a group of hostile survivors approached their camp. Alice tensed, her hand moving to her knife instinctively. "Stay here," she whispered before confronting them alone.

"They're up to something," the leader spat out. "They're cooking zombies." The others nodded in agreement; eyes narrowed.

Alice's jaw clenched. "What right do you have to judge?" She snapped back. "We're all just trying to survive."

As she returned to the camp, the tension was palpable. Jean-Pierre held his breath, waiting for her reaction.

"Well?" Marcus' voice was low and menacing.

Alice looked at him coolly. "They spotted us. We need to be ready for anything." She glared at Antoine.

Eddie rose to his feet, fists clenched. "We're not turning on our own," he said through gritted teeth.

Antoine smirked, his gaze flickering over to Jean-Pierre. "I don't know about that," he murmured under his breath.

Suddenly, the wind changed direction, carrying a new scent towards them. Zombies. Hordes of them. Their stomachs churning, they rushed back to camp to find Jean-Pierre frantically packing up his supplies.

"What happened?" Alice asked, her voice tense.

Jean-Pierre shook his head. "I'm sorry. I didn't know I was so close to the feeding grounds. They must have smelled the meat." He gestured to the rapidly approaching horde.

As one, they turned and ran.

The air was thick with the stench of death and decay as Jean-Pierre led them through the forest, his heart pounding in his chest. Alice kept a wary eye on him; he seemed more focused on his cooking than their escape. Suddenly, he stopped and grabbed a nearby tree branch, snapping it off with a loud crack. He tossed it to Eddie. "Throw it back here," he panted.

The burly man hesitated before doing as he was told. As promised, the zombies turned towards the sound, giving them a moment's reprieve. They continued running, adrenaline pumping now. The forest was becoming denser.

"We need to split up," Jean-Pierre panted. "Draw them off," he said, handing Sophia a small vial of acid. "I'll lead them away."

She nodded; her eyes filled with concern for her friend. As she poured the acid on the ground, the undead converged on the sound, their shuffling feet slowing in the muck.

The group scattered, Alice and Eddie distracting them while Dr. Martinez kept them at bay with her medical supplies. Jean-Pierre led the horde into the wilderness, dodging and weaving through trees and over rocks. His mind raced with ideas for his next dish, even as his heart hammered in his chest.

Finally, the horde lost interest in pursuing, leaving Jean-Pierre alone. He collapsed onto a fallen log, breathing heavily. His hands trembled as he wiped the sweat from his brow. He couldn't help but think about how close he had come to becoming a zombie chow.

Back at the camp, the others waited anxiously for his return, Marcus' gaze hardening as he rebuffed Antoine's suggestions about what had happened to their newfound chef. Sophia tried to comfort him as he explained his experiments, but he could see the doubt in her eyes. She didn't understand the importance of his work, only the potential harm.

With renewed determination, Jean-Pierre returned to his cooking station, ignoring the pain in his limbs and the lingering dread of the encounter. He poured over books and journals, searching for inspiration and guidance. Hours passed before he found what he was looking for - a recipe for "zombie jerky." It involved curing the meat in salt and smoking it over an open fire. The process was slow, but he was nothing if not patient.

The following day, the group gathered around a crackling flame, watching in awe as Jean- Pierre presented his latest creation. Eddie's eyes widened at the sight of the succulent strips of smoked beef hanging from twine. The scent of smoke and spices filled the air, mixing with the sounds of popping fat and sizzling meat. They could almost taste it.

"Alright," Eddie said, licking his lips, "let's try it."

They skewered a strip and held it to the fire, watching as it began to blacken. As they took their first bites, their eyes rolled back in delight. The flavor was unlike anything they'd ever tasted before - succulent, smoky, and slightly gamy. They chewed slowly, savoring every bite. Even Sophia, who had been skeptical before, was won over by the taste.

"It's...different," she admitted, "but in a good way."

"Different is good," Jean-Pierre agreed with a smile. "Better than good. It's perfect."

Alice Winters watched him from the sidelines, her heart swelling with pride. He was truly gifted in the kitchen, even under these dire circumstances. But she also saw the spark in his eyes that she hadn't seen in weeks - an obsessive gleam that worried her. She knew what would happen next.

Sure enough, later that night, Jean-Pierre slipped away. Alice could hear him rummaging through the supplies, muttering to himself about 'finding the perfect ingredient.' She followed him at a distance, keeping an eye out for trouble. He ventured deeper into the city, to areas they'd avoided due to their high zombie population. His quest for perfection was becoming increasingly dangerous.

Finally, he stumbled upon a butcher shop. The door creaked open, revealing rows of fresh meat hanging from hooks. Jean-Pierre's eyes lit up. He grabbed a haunch of venison, tucking it under his arm like a trophy. But as he turned to leave, he froze. Zombies shuffled toward him from all sides. Their moans filled the air, growing louder with each step.

Alice watched helplessly as Jean-Pierre's back was pressed against a wall, surrounded by the undead. She cursed herself for not stopping him sooner. He couldn't cook his way out of this situation.

Suddenly, a deafening smell filled the air - rosemary and garlic wafting on the breeze. The zombies stopped in their tracks, sniffing the air hungrily. Jean-Pierre took advantage of their temporary distraction, sprinting out of the shop and slamming the door shut behind him.

The undead mob followed, their rotting flesh slamming against the wood like fists. Alice breathed a sigh of relief as they crashed into each other, their hunger temporarily sated by the scent. Jean-Pierre had found a way to control them - using cooking as a weapon.

They didn't see him again for days. His experiments became more elaborate, with strange ingredients Alice couldn't even identify. She tried asking about what he was making, but he only replied with cryptic answers about 'perfecting' his recipe.

One day, they heard gunshots echoing through the city. They raced toward the sound, fearing the worst. When they found him, they weren't disappointed. Jean-Pierre was cornered in an alleyway by a horde of zombies, his eyes wild and his clothes splattered with blood and guts. But instead of fear, there was a twisted grin on his face.

He pulled out a long wooden spoon from behind his back, holding it like a sword. The zombies lunged, their decaying hands reaching for him. With lightning-fast reflexes, Jean- Pierre jabbed the spoon into their chests and wrists, forcing them back. He danced between them, weaving a deadly ballet as they stumbled over each other.

Alice watched in amazement as he maneuvered through the group, driving them further and further away. Finally, he turned to her and grinned. "Dinner's almost ready. Let's go home."

Back at the camp, they sat around a fire, anxiously waiting for Jean-Pierre's latest creation. He emerged from his tent, carrying a steaming pot covered in a cloth. He slowly unwrapped it, revealing the most sumptuous feast they had seen in months. Roasted zombie ribs marinated in a tangy sauce, skewered, and seasoned with spices they could only dream of before the apocalypse. The smell was intoxicating, making their mouths water uncontrollably.

Edward couldn't hold back his excitement, tearing into his portion like a starving animal. Dr. Martinez picked at her warily, tasting cautiously but finding herself surprisingly impressed. Only Sophia seemed bothered by the idea of eating something so...unnatural.

Jean-Pierre watched her carefully, his eyes full of regret. "I know it's not right, Sophia," he admitted quietly. "But we have to survive."

She sighed, understanding the desperation but unable to ignore the moral implications. They all knew where this path led - down a dark, twisted road. Yet, their stomachs rumbled in agreement with Jean-Pierre's creations.

As they ate, Alice glanced around the camp, wondering how long they could keep going down this path before it consumed them all.

Meanwhile, Marcus watched from afar, his gaze calculating. He saw an opportunity in Jean- Pierre's talent. He approached him later that night, offering him a deal: exclusive access to his private stockpile of luxury items in exchange for fine dining experiences. It was an offer that tempted Jean-Pierre, torn between his passion and his principles.

Days turned into weeks, and Jean-Pierre's skills improved exponentially. His dishes became more extravagant, utilizing rare herbs and spices that only the wealthy could afford before the world ended. Antoine grew increasingly suspicious, sensing an opportunity to exploit this newfound asset. He began sowing seeds of doubt among the group, questioning Marcus's intentions.

One day, Antoine's prediction came true when Jean-Pierre returned from a scavenging trip sick and weak, barely clinging to life. He had ventured too far into a particularly dangerous area, risking everything for the perfect ingredient. The taste of failure was bitter on his tongue as he realized his mistake.

Alice nursed him back to health, her hands shaking with worry. She couldn't lose him now – not when they needed him more than ever. Eddie stood guard, fists clenched at his sides, promising revenge against whoever put his friend in harm's way. Sophia prayed silently for guidance, while Dr. Martinez watched impassively, knowing they couldn't afford another setback.

Amid this turmoil, Jean-Pierre had a revelation. His obsession had nearly cost him everything. He looked into Alice's eyes, searching for understanding. Could he give up the very thing that defined him or would he continue down this destructive path? The decision weighed heavily on his heart as he closed his eyes and drifted off to sleep.

Days passed, and Jean-Pierre withdrew further into himself, focusing on his cooking to cope with guilt and uncertainty. He meticulously prepared each dish, adding an eerie precision that sent shivers down Alice's spine. The flavors were exquisite – an intoxicating blend of spices and herbs that awakened dormant memories of fine dining. But it wasn't enough. He needed something new; something bold and daring. One day, he snuck away from camp without telling anyone, leaving a cryptic note behind.

Alice was worried sick, but Eddie insisted on finding him. They tracked him to an abandoned mall where they heard strange noises emanating from the basement. Cautiously, they descended the stairs, weapons ready. A sinister laugh echoed through the darkness, followed by muffled grunts and snarls. Their hearts pounded in their chests as they peered into the darkness, switching on their flashlights.

There, in the dim light, stood Jean-Pierre, surrounded by zombies. Not just any zombies – these were cooked to perfection, their flesh charred and smoking. The aroma was intoxicating; it filled Alice's nostrils with promises of succulent flavors she never knew existed. "What have you done, Jean-Pierre?" she whispered, horrified yet intrigued.

"Try it," he urged, his voice hoarse with desperation. Reluctantly, she took a bite. The taste exploded in her mouth – mesquite-smoked zombie meat mixed with garlic, rosemary, and thyme. The texture was tender, falling apart like butter in her mouth. She swallowed, unable to believe what she was tasting. "It's...amazing," she murmured.

But this was no time for praise. They argued heatedly, Jean-Pierre defending his methods, claiming it was their only hope for survival. Alice knew better; this was dangerous territory.

She couldn't deny the luxury of such flavors, but at what cost? They argued until a shot rang out from above, shattering their concentration. Zombies flooded the basement, forcing them to fight for their lives.

The battle was intense; bullets whizzed past their heads, and sparks flew from their weapons as they struggled to fend off the undead horde. The stench of sweat, blood, and death filled the air. In the chaos, they managed to navigate the maze of zombies and escape with Jean-Pierre in tow. Back at camp, Alice confronted him about his recklessness.

"How could you risk all of our lives for a damn recipe?" she demanded. "We're a family here – we look out for each other!"

Jean-Pierre hung his head low, ashamed of his actions. He knew he had crossed a line, but he couldn't help himself. He needed more – more taste, more adventure. He needed to push boundaries. He vowed never to repeat this mistake, and they all agreed on a new set of rules: safety first, adventure second.

They sat down for a meal together, a simple one, but one filled with love and camaraderie. As they ate, Alice whispered, "You're still my brother, JP."

And with that, they moved on, stronger than before.

A few weeks passed without incident until Jean-Pierre found himself in the kitchen again. Antoine watched from afar with a sly smile, knowing this obsession would lead him astray once more. He sawed off a zombie's limb before anyone could stop him, determined to create that elusive dish that would make history.

The aroma of roasted flesh filled the air as he worked his magic. The meat sizzled on the pan, releasing a tantalizing scent that made even Sophia's stomach growl. "What are you doing, Jean-Pierre?" she asked weakly, drawn in against her better judgment.

Eddie and Dr. Martinez watched warily, remembering the last time. "It's not worth it," said Dr. Martinez. "We have other options."

As Jean-Pierre tasted the meat, his eyes rolled back in pleasure. It was perfect... but at what cost? They couldn't keep this up forever. He needed a new plan.

He retired to his room, thoughts swirling in his head. He remembered Alice's words and Sophia's smile, Eddie's loyalty, and Dr. Martinez's pragmatism. No more would he sacrifice relationships for flavor. He would find another way.

Days went by without any food experimentation until one day he stumbled upon an old cookbook. Slow-cooked vegetable stew seemed boring compared to what he could do with zombie meat, but maybe it was time for a change. He gathered ingredients from their scavenging missions and set to work.

Alice was skeptical but intrigued as she watched him chop vegetables meticulously. "What's this?" she asked, curiosity getting the best of her.

"A new direction," he replied simply. "One that doesn't compromise our values."

The soup simmered for hours, filling the small kitchen with a savory aroma that made everyone's mouths water. They sat around the fireplace, sharing stories and hoping for a brighter tomorrow.

As they ate, their faces lit up like children on Christmas morning. The taste was unlike anything they'd had since before the zombie apocalypse. "This is amazing," Sophia said between bites.

Even Eddie, who had been critical of Jean-Pierre's choices, couldn't resist. "Maybe you don't need to go down that path after all," he said, reaching for seconds.

Dr. Martinez nodded in agreement, relief washing over her features. Antoine, however, lurked in the shadows, his eyes filled with malevolence. He saw an opportunity to disrupt the group again.

From then on, Jean-Pierre focused on honing his skills without using unethical means. His passion for cooking didn't wane; instead, he found new challenges in creating delectable dishes without causing harm. Alice noticed the change in him and felt hopeful; she could see the man she'd fallen for again.

As weeks turned into months, life at the base stabilized. Their crops flourished, food was plentiful, and laughter filled the air. They were surviving and thriving without depending on the old ways.

CHAPTER 4

The decaying building held a musty, dank smell that immediately made Alice's nose wrinkle in distaste. It was rare to find anything intact in this new world, so she tried to remain hopeful as she followed Jean-Pierre and the others into the small, abandoned structure. The wooden floorboards creaked beneath her boots, echoing through the empty rooms like a warning signal. Her long, dark hair brushed against her back, she kept her grip tight on her bow and arrow—ready for any threat that might emerge from the shadows. Dr. Olivia Martinez, the group's medic, brought up the rear, eyes scanning the area with an air of wariness.

As they navigated through the derelict halls, a sound echoed from a room ahead—a faint scratching at the door. Jean-Pierre stopped abruptly, raising a finger to his lips for silence. Alice's heart raced, her breath catching in her throat. She tensed; her muscles ready to react. They approached the door cautiously, pressing their ears against it to listen. The scratching grew louder, more insistent, but it didn't sound ferocious. Curiosity overpowering her fear, Alice inched the door open just a crack, peering inside.

Inside was a small, dimly lit room filled with caged mice. The scratching stopped as the door opened, and she could see them scurrying around their cages, some nibbling on stale breadcrumbs, others thirsty for water. She glanced at Jean-Pierre, who seemed unfazed by the sight. His eyes glinted with determination as he stepped into the room and began inspecting the cages, muttering to himself about potential food sources.

Dr. Martinez emerged from behind her, her petite frame shaking her head in disbelief.

"What are you thinking?" she asked, her voice low but laced with annoyance. "We don't have time for—"

"We need food," he interrupted, gesturing to the cages. "And these could provide it." He pulled a wire cutter from his bag and started opening the cages one by one, releasing the frightened rodents into a sack.

Alice watched as he worked, feeling a mixture of disgust and intrigue. She had never considered eating insects or small creatures before, but with resources dwindling, they might be their only hope for survival. Still, she couldn't help but wonder about the long- term effects of such a diet on their health. As the mice crawled over each other in the sack, she swallowed down a queasy feeling in her stomach.

Dr. Martinez rolled her eyes but didn't argue further. Instead, she turned her attention to gathering any edible plants she could find, recognizing the importance of vitamins and nutrients. The group worked in silence, each focused on their tasks. The smell of straw and animal fur filled the air as they collected what they could.

Suddenly, a loud rustling came from behind them, making them all freeze in place. Two guards approached, their torches casting long shadows on the ground. Quickly, they hid the sack of rodents and the plants in the brush as the guards passed by, seemingly uninterested in anything suspicious.

They breathed a sigh of relief as the guards moved away, then continued their foraging until they had collected enough to sustain them for the next few days. As they hurried back to their hidden camp, Alice couldn't shake the taste of fear from her tongue.

Back at camp, they set up a makeshift kitchen area where Jean-Pierre could cook the mice. Using a combination of herbs and spices from his bag, he seasoned the small animals before roasting them over an open flame. The aroma filled the air, causing Alice's stomach to grumble despite herself. When they were ready, everyone tentatively took a bite.

Surprisingly, the taste was not as bad as expected - quite flavorful with hints of garlic and rosemary.

Alice's eyes widened in surprise as she took another bite, the juices dripping down her chin. She looked at Jean-Pierre with newfound respect. He may be unconventional, but he knew what he was doing. Dr. Martinez reluctantly admitted it was one of the better meals they've had since the outbreak began.

As night fell, they huddled around the fire, sharing tales of survival and watching the shadows dance around them. Frogs croaked in the distance, providing a piece of haunting background music to their conversation. The fire crackled, sending sparks into the darkness, and the sound of insects chirping filled the silence.

Despite their initial hesitation, they all found themselves licking their fingers clean of the delicious zombie-mouse broth. It was a strange new reality they found themselves in, but they were all grateful for Jean-Pierre's unconventional methods. Even Dr. Martinez had to admit that it might be their best chance at survival.

Alice listened intently as Jean-Pierre explained his idea for a farm, where they could grow their food and fend for themselves. It sounded too good to be true, but she knew they had to try something different if they wanted to make it out of this alive.

She glanced around at her fellow survivors, their faces etched with weariness and hunger. "We need all the help we can get," she said softly, meeting Dr. Martinez's gaze. The older woman nodded grimly, understanding the desperation in Alice's voice.

Dr. Olivia Martinez sighed heavily, leaning back against the wall of the abandoned building. Her eyes darted around warily, taking in the empty rooms and peeling paint. She couldn't shake the feeling that they were being watched, but she pressed on, following Jean-Pierre down yet another hallway.

Her footsteps echoed in the silence, making her hyper-aware of their vulnerability. She couldn't help but remember the desperate times she'd seen people turn to cannibalism in their quest for sustenance; it haunted her dreams. She didn't want to see that happen again, especially not with people she trusted.

"So," she began, her voice gruff, "you claim you know how to cook these creatures. What about plants? Do you have any ideas for alternative food sources?" Her brow furrowed, skepticism clear in her tone.

Jean-Pierre smiled; his blue eyes bright with determination. "Oh yes, ma'am. I know a few tricks up my sleeve for that as well." He led them further into the building, past long- abandoned offices, and dusty desks, toward a patch of sunlight streaming through a broken window. "We'll make it work."

As they approached the window, a wave of fresh air washed over them, carrying with it the scent of decay and rot. Jean-Pierre's nostrils flared slightly, not seeming to mind the smell. Dr. Martinez, on the other hand, wrinkled her nose in disgust. She followed Jean-Pierre out onto a fire escape, stepping carefully around rusted metal and broken glass.

Below them lay a long-forgotten garden, overgrown with weeds and vines. "This place used to be a community garden," he explained, gesturing to the overgrown plots. "I've been experimenting with different herbs and spices, trying to make them edible."

He pushed past a particularly dense patch of thorny vines, revealing a small clearing with various plants he'd identified as edible. His enthusiasm was infectious, at least to Alice. Dr. Martinez remained skeptical. "And what about the ethics?" she asked, eyeing a rabbit bone buried under a pile of leaves.

"You have to adapt," Jean-Pierre replied passionately. "We're in a new world now. Survival is key." His hands moved deftly, pulling out prickly weeds and uprooting tender greens. "We can't rely on old norms anymore."

Dr. Martinez hesitated, taking in his words. She knew he was right. The group needed food, and they needed it badly. Their scavenging trips were becoming more dangerous as time went on. She couldn't help but admire his determination. "Alright," she sighed, "but let's be careful."

Together, they knelt to inspect the plants more closely. The cool dampness of the earth seeped through their clothes as they pulled up handfuls of dandelions and mustard greens, their fingers digging into the soil. The scent of fresh herbs and earth filled the air as Jean- Pierre started gathering wood for a fire.

Alice watched in awe as he expertly built a small flame, using a metal can as a makeshift grill. He'd even managed to find a few potatoes and carrots from an abandoned cellar nearby. The anticipation was killing her.

Soon, the vegetables sizzled on the grill, filling the air with a tantalizing aroma that made her stomach growl. Dr. Martinez, however, remained unconvinced. "What if these plants are tainted?" She poked at the dandelion greens warily.

Jean-Pierre chuckled. "Trust me," he said, turning them with a fork. "I've studied. I know which ones are safe to eat." Taste buds watering, Alice eagerly awaited while Dr. Martinez continued to frown.

Finally, a perfectly cooked vegetable was placed before her - the charred edges crispy, the center still tender. She took a bite, closing her eyes as the flavors exploded in her mouth. It was the most delicious thing she'd ever tasted. Even Dr. Martinez couldn't resist the savory goodness.

"How did you know?" she asked between bites, her voice muffled by the food in her mouth. Jean-Pierre grinned. "I've read all the books," he said proudly.

As they ate, they discussed plans. Their survival would depend on finding more food sources, and Jean-Pierre knew it. But he was running low on ideas. That's when he proposed an unusual partnership: "Let's work together. You bring your medical expertise, and I'll bring my culinary creativity. Together, we'll find a way to make this world worth living in."

Dr. Martinez considered it, her brow furrowed. She didn't want to see anyone else suffer, especially not these kind souls who sought refuge under her care. She knew they couldn't rely on canned goods forever. So, with a small nod, she agreed. "Alright," she said slowly. "We'll give it a try."

Alice beamed at the news, her spirits lifting at the thought of better meals ahead. They all knew survival was key, but comfort and normalcy were vital too. And who knew? Maybe the zombie recipes could be their saving grace. The trio gathered more plants, discussing potential combinations and spices as they walked. They would make it work; they had to.

The soft crunch of leaves beneath their feet, intertwined with the occasional snapping of twigs, filled the air. The sun began to set, casting a golden hue over the horizon, and painting everything in a warm glow. They found a small patch of mushrooms growing near a rotting log and decided to experiment.

Dr. Martinez warned them of the risks, but Alice and Jean-Pierre were determined. With precision, they picked the plumpest caps and carried them back to camp. The smell of roasting filled the air as they got to work, the mushrooms sizzling in a pan over an open flame. It wasn't long before they were ready to taste.

The first bite was tentative but soon turned to surprise as the earthy flavor burst on their tongues. Not bad at all, they thought. Better than what they'd had before. They ate heartily, savoring the taste of something besides canned beans and ration bars. It wasn't home- cooked, but it was a step in the right direction.

As night fell, they sat around a crackling fire, content but wary of the shadows around them. The forest was no longer safe, but they were alive because of each other. They shared stories, laughter, and hopes for what lay ahead. And in that moment, they were united by their resilience and determination to survive, no matter how strange the path may seem.

The next morning brought new challenges as they set out to find other sources of nourishment. They ventured deeper into the woods where Jean-Pierre's knowledge proved invaluable, identifying edible plants and berries that Dr. Martinez had never seen before.

She learned quickly, impressed by his vast knowledge of the natural world. They gathered a bounty of fruits and leaves that would be crucial for their survival.

Back at camp, they settled down to prepare their new haul. Dr. Martinez watched as Jean- Pierre worked his magic again, creating a stew that surprised her with its complexity. It wasn't just about sustenance anymore; it was about variety and flavor too. The group savored every spoonful, grateful for the taste explosion in their mouths.

Their partnership deepened over time, each day bringing discoveries and innovations. Dr. Martinez found herself becoming more open-minded about food, trying dishes she never would have before. And Jean-Pierre, well, he seemed to grow more confident with each successful meal he created. They became a well-oiled machine, working together seamlessly.

But it wasn't all smooth sailing. There were trials and errors, stomach aches, and worries about the long-term effects of their diet. They discussed these issues openly, always putting the group's health first. They experimented with traps and snares, trying to supplement their foraging with fresh meat when possible. Their conversations were filled with strategy and concern but also hope.

One day, after a successful hunt, they sat around the fire, sharing stories from their pasts. Dr. Martinez told Jean-Pierre about her time as a doctor in a bustling metropolis, treating patients and saving lives. He recounted his memories of running a small bistro in Paris, cooking for adoring patrons who couldn't get enough of his cuisine. They laughed and reminisced, realizing how far they'd come from those days.

The night wore on, and they fell into a comfortable silence, content in each other's company. As they stared at the dancing flames, a thought struck Dr. Martinez: they could use this time to explore other methods of food preservation. "Let's try curing meats," she suggested tentatively, knowing it would stretch their resources even further.

To her surprise, Jean-Pierre was ecstatic at the idea. He'd always been intrigued by the process but lacked the knowledge to do it properly. Together, they spent hours researching techniques and gathering ingredients. Their hands moved in perfect harmony as they salted and spiced the meat, their breath mixing with the salty air as they worked.

Days turned into weeks, and their progress became more apparent. They began to look forward to every meal, eager to see what new creation they'd come up with next. The group thrived under their leadership, no longer living hand-to-mouth but thriving as they built something resembling life again.

Dr. Martinez couldn't help but feel proud of what they'd achieved together – all because of a simple meal shared around a campfire.

One morning, as they sat down to breakfast (bacon and eggs, a new favorite among the group), they hatched a plan to find a more permanent source of food. They decided to venture out into the wild, seeking out wild edibles that could keep them going without harming their scarce livestock. It wasn't an easy task, but their partnership made it bearable.

They foraged for plants, and mushrooms, and even tried their hand at fishing in the nearby river. Each discovery filled them with a sense of accomplishment they hadn't felt in years. Their campsite grew, becoming a hub for delicious meals and newfound hope.

But then disaster struck. A group of survivors from a nearby town arrived, desperate and starving. Seeing an opportunity to make amends for past mistakes, they invited them in, sharing their bounty freely. Their newfound paradise was soon overrun by those who couldn't appreciate their hard work, leaving the group exhausted and depleted.

Determined not to let this happen again, they vowed to find a way to feed everyone while maintaining their hard-earned independence.

Now, they stood here, brainstorming in the abandoned building they'd claimed as their own. The wind whistled through broken windows, carrying with it the scent of decay and despair. But they weren't defeated; they were fueled by the taste of freshly baked bread and the prospect of a brighter future.

"We need to find a way to make our food sources sustainable," Dr. Martinez said, her brow furrowed in concentration. "Not just for us but for anyone who seeks shelter here."

Jean-Pierre nodded, his voice low and thoughtful. "Agreed. We'll need to work together to find alternatives to our beloved livestock. What if we combined your knowledge of medicinal herbs with my culinary creativity?"

She hesitated, unsure. "I suppose it's worth a try," she said finally, her heart pounding with anticipation. "What did you have in mind?"

He grinned, rubbing his hands together. "Cooking with insects," he said simply. "They're high in protein, low in fat, and easy to raise."

She wrinkled her nose at the thought but humored him. "Alright, let's give it a shot. But we need to be strategic about it—"

His eyes lit up as if he'd won the lottery. "Exactly!" he exclaimed. "We'll create a garden with edible flowers and plants that attract insects naturally. Then we can harvest them without harming our crops or wasting precious resources."

They worked late into the night, writing down recipes and ideas, their hands moving swiftly over notebook paper strewn across the table. Their voices rose with excitement as they discussed different cooking methods and seasonings, planning how to make these unusual ingredients palatable.

As dawn broke, they parted ways, their mission clear: to gather ingredients, experiment with cooking techniques, and document their findings for future generations. This could be the beginning of a whole new era for their struggling town—one filled with delicious possibilities.

Outside, the world was different; the air was thick with humidity and decay. Jean-Pierre and Dr. Martinez navigated through abandoned streets littered with debris, their steps cautious yet purposeful. They stopped at an old grocery store, its doors long since blown off by the elements, and began rummaging through shelves for canned goods. The smell of mold filled the air as they lifted decaying tomatoes from crushed cans and debated whether they were still edible.

They moved further into the store, finding dried beans and spices once vibrant colors now faded to grey hues. A chorus of rats scurried past their feet, escaping the intruders. A flock of crows cawed from above, their eyes glinting in the early morning light. The sound of their wings flapping echoed ominously against the empty storefront windows.

But they remained focused on their mission. Dr. Martinez pulled out a tattered cookbook from under a pile of rotten vegetables and flipped through its pages, muttering under her breath about forgotten recipes from her childhood. Jean-Pierre's eyes glistened at the sight of old family recipes written in French script he couldn't quite read.

As they left the store, their backs straining under the weight of their haul, Dr. Martinez couldn't help but feel a glimmer of hope. This could work; they had each other, they had knowledge, and they had determination. All they needed was time... and luck. They trudged on towards the next destination: a farmhouse on the outskirts of town.

The sun beat down on them, forcing beads of sweat to form on their brows as they navigated through overgrown fields and barren landscapes. Dust kicked up behind them as they walked, choking the air around them. The only sound was the rustle of leaves and the distant moans of the undead.

Finally, they arrived at the farmhouse. It had been abandoned for years but there were remnants of life: chickens clucking in the coop, cows lowing in the barn, and a sprawling garden overrun with weeds. Dr. Martinez knelt and plucked fresh herbs from the earth, her hands moving swiftly through the dirt. Jean-Pierre strummed an old guitar he'd found in one of the rooms, its strings almost unrecognizable due to age.

Together, they worked in silence, harvesting vegetables and fruits that had been long forgotten by the world outside. A bee buzzed past his ear, drawing blood from a nearby flower. The sweet scent of rotting wood mixed with the fresh earthy smell of soil.

They cooked that night under the stars, using an old campfire pit they'd found near the house. Sizzling noises filled the air as they added spices and seasoning to their concoctions. The aroma made both of their mouths water even though they knew it would have to sustain them for days. Dr. Martinez took a bite of her concoction and smiled at Jean-Pierre over the fire, her eyes twinkling with hope. He returned it wearily but thankfully before tasting himself. It wasn't much, but it was enough to keep going.

CHAPTER 5

The kitchen was a hive of activity. The air was thick with the scent of herbs and spices, as Jean-Pierre eagerly awaited his training session with Dr. Olivia Martinez. The old wooden table, scarred and stained from countless meals cooked upon it over the years, creaked under the weight of freshly harvested vegetables and fruits from their foraging expeditions. He took a deep breath, savoring the aroma of roasting zombie flesh that hung heavy in the air like a thick mist. His knives, honed to a razor's edge, flashed in the dim light of the flickering candles that illuminated the room. He couldn't contain his excitement any longer - today was the day he would learn how to bring new life to their meals.

Dr. Martinez entered the room, her steps slow and methodical. Her eyes swept over the array of ingredients laid out before her, a thin line forming between her brows. She was all business today; her gaze was unforgiving as she took in the messy pile of ingredients scattered across the table. "Alright," she said, her voice grim but determined, "let's get started."

She led him through the nutritional properties of various zombie parts, explaining how each could be utilized for sustenance. Jean-Pierre listened intently, his young face aglow with curiosity and fascination. He watched as she demonstrated how to extract marrow from zombie bones, the wet, squishy sound filling the air with each satisfying pull. He didn't flinch when she showed him how to slice through tendons and ligaments with ease, his knives moving in time with her instructions. Instead, he studied her movements like a hawk, eager to replicate them.

The room was deathly quiet as they worked, punctuated only by the occasional clank of metal on metal or the soft thud of a zombie limb hitting the ground. The air was thick with anticipation as they worked together, creating a symphony of sounds that flowed together in perfect harmony. As she showed him how to tenderize tough meat with a hammer and a flat surface, the dull thuds reverberated off the stone walls around them. When she explained the importance of using every part of the creature – even its brains and intestines – he nodded enthusiastically, grabbing a handful of grey matter, and shoving it into his mouth. It was salty and chewy but also slightly sweet, like a cross between liver and pork rind.

As hours passed, they worked tirelessly side by side. The scent of cooking zombie meat filled the room, making Jean-Pierre's stomach growl in anticipation. He learned how to make broth from bones, how to turn flesh into jerky that would last for weeks, and even how to make a sort of zombie-based sausage that could be stored without refrigeration. By the end of the day, his hands were coated in grime and his clothes were splattered with blood, but he felt like he'd truly found a home. This was it; this was what he'd been looking for. He looked at the woman teaching him and smiled, "Thank you." She smiled back, revealing sharp teeth stained red from all the work they'd done together.

That night, when they sat down to eat their creations, he'd never tasted anything so delicious. The broth was rich and flavorful, the sausage spicy and filling, the jerky chewy and savory. They ate in silence, savoring every bite, and for once, Jean-Pierre didn't feel guilty about what they were consuming. It wasn't just sustenance; it was a celebration of life in this new world they found themselves in. As they finished, Dr. Martinez patted his shoulder, "You're a quick learner." He beamed with pride.

The next few days were filled with more lessons – learning how to hunt efficiently and track movement, how to defend themselves against other survivors who might not share their values – but it was during these moments in the kitchen that Jean-Pierre found solace. He couldn't wait to showcase his new skills, to create dishes that would make everyone's mouths water. He began experimenting on his own, mixing different herbs and spices into the meat until he found the perfect balance between zombies and zest. Soon enough, he was cooking for the group, creating dishes that even Olivia found palatable. She watched him work, a small smile tugging at her lips as she realized they had something much needed: hope.

One evening, as they all sat around a crackling fire eating his latest creation – grilled zombie heart skewers marinated in garlic and rosemary – someone new arrived at their camp. A young girl, no older than ten, pleading for help. Olivia's heart broke at the sight of her filthy clothes and vacant eyes, but she knew they couldn't turn their backs on anyone who sought aid. They took her in, bathing her and feeding her until she finally spoke. She told them of a group of survivors further down the road, trapped by zombies. Without hesitation, Olivia rallied the troops and they set out to rescue them.

Upon their arrival, they found a desperate situation. The survivors had been trapped for weeks, living off rations that were long gone. They all looked half-starved, and some had resorted to cannibalism to survive.

Olivia's stomach turned at the thought, but she knew they had to do something. She looked at Jean-Pierre, who nodded grimly. It was time to put his skills to the test.

Together, they butchered several zombies, and Jean-Pierre got to work. He chopped and diced, sautéed, and braised, creating dishes that rivaled his finest Michelin-starred creations. The smell of roasting meat filled the air, mingling with smoke from the fire. As they ate, the girl watched in wonder, her eyes lighting up at the taste of real food. The rest of the survivors, too, were amazed by the flavors dancing on their tongues. For once, they felt human again. They discussed joining forces, sharing resources, and forging a new path forward. Hope was rekindled in that moment, thanks to Olivia's compassion and Jean- Pierre's culinary prowess.

Back at camp, Olivia watched as Jean-Pierre prepared his next experiment. He picked out a particular zombie limb, humming to himself as he thought about how to bring out its unique flavor. He seasoned it carefully, then placed it onto a spit over an open flame. Sizzles and pops filled the air as he began to roast it slowly. The scent of garlic and thyme wafted through the camp, making stomachs growl in anticipation. After a while, he pulled it out of the fire and carved it into it, revealing a beautifully browned exterior and pink, juicy flesh beneath.

"Bon appétit," he said, serving everyone a slice. They chewed eagerly, groaning in delight at the tender, succulent texture and rich taste. He'd truly outdone himself this time. Olivia couldn't help but smile at his creativity and innovation. This zombie meat had been transformed into something delicious, something they could all enjoy without feeling guilty.

She joined in the praise, offering her suggestions for future experiments - fermentation, marination, pickling. He nodded, taking notes, determined to perfect his craft. Together, they discussed ways to make their lives in this post-apocalyptic world more bearable, one meal at a time. The sound of laughter filled the air, replaced by the clinking of utensils on metal plates. For now, they had food, and that was enough. The group settled in for what passed as a celebration under these circumstances, grateful to have someone who could make even the most desperate of situations feel slightly more civilized.

A week later, Dr. Martinez presented Jean-Pierre with a new challenge: to create a dish using multiple zombie parts. At first, he was hesitant, unsure how to combine the different textures and flavors. He spent hours poring over cookbooks and scavenging for ingredients, while the others went about their daily routine. When he emerged from his tent, everyone gathered around curiously. He set down a steaming pot filled with what looked like stew, dark and murky, with bits of unknown creatures floating within. They all took cautious sips, expecting the worst. But then, the first bite hit their tongues - an explosion of flavor, unlike anything they'd experienced before. Tender chunks of zombie meat mixed with sweet potatoes, carrots, and onions, infused with a savory broth that tasted vaguely reminiscent of beef. There were even hints of mushrooms and herbs they couldn't quite place. It was perfection.

Applause erupted around him as he beamed, taking a bow. "Thank you," he said humbly, "it's nothing complicated really, but I wanted to challenge myself." They all knew better; this dish was more than just a meal; it was an act of defiance against the harshness of their new reality.

It proved that despite everything, humanity could still create beauty from chaos.

And in that moment, they felt a glimmer of hope.

From then on, Jean-Pierre continued to push boundaries, experimenting with new spices and marinades. He learned how to grill zombie steaks rare and cooked zombie brains in a way that didn't make them taste like rubbery noodles. He even tried his hand at baking and crafting zombie-crust pizza and bread that was surprisingly palatable. But Dr. Martinez wasn't satisfied yet. She had seen the potential in him and knew he could do better.

One day, she approached him with an idea: to create a dish using multiple zombie parts. Her eyes glinted with challenge as she outlined her vision - a dish that would showcase the versatility of their unlikely ingredient. Jean-Pierre nodded eagerly, taking on the task with renewed vigor. For days, he tasted, tested, and tweaked until he had something he deemed ready. The result was a feast for the senses: zombie's heart skewered on bamboo spears, cooked over an open flame to sear it outside while maintaining tenderness within; zombie liver fried crispy like bacon, its flavor muted by a tangy sauce; zombie muscle ground into a patty that melted in your mouth; all served with a side of sauteed zombie intestines to add texture and depth.

They gathered around the campfire, plates heaped high with food. As they dug in, they couldn't hide their surprise and delight at how well the flavors melded together. The zombie's gamy taste was gone, replaced by rich umami notes and subtle herbs, each bite exploding with complexity. Even the toughest customers were won over by this undead cuisine revolution. Little did they know this meal would change the course of their survival forever.

Dr. Martinez watched him carefully, her expression softening as she took a bite of the liver. "Well done," she said, her voice full of admiration. "I didn't think it was possible to make zombie meat so tasty." He beamed at her praise; his face flushed with pride. "Thank you," he said humbly, his eyes glinting with determination. "I've been experimenting, trying to find new ways to make use of even the toughest parts." The others nodded in agreement; their eyes glazed over from the food coma they were in.

From that day on, Jean-Pierre became obsessed with further enhancing their culinary experience, pushing the boundaries of what was possible in their desolate world. He combed through cookbooks and scavenged for exotic spices, determined to create something even better than before. And he did. His dishes grew more refined, more aromatic, more tantalizing. The group's survival now depended on his creativity in the kitchen as much as it did on their weapons and strategy. They ate like kings and queens amidst the ruins, savoring each bite of their unlikely gourmet feasts.

Months passed, and Jean-Pierre had become a legend amongst them. His cooking skills rivaled any top chef's, creating dishes that would make Michelin-starred restaurants envious. The group thrived under his leadership; their spirits lifted by the taste of hope on their tongues. As they all sat around the fire after another delicious meal, Dr. Martinez leaned back, contemplating the empty plates scattered around them. "You know," she said, her eyes twinkling with curiosity, "I bet you could make something truly remarkable if you used zombie parts from different species and combined them in unique ways." She had seen him make miracles with normal ingredients; perhaps he could do the same with these unusual ones too.

Jean-Pierre's ears perked up at the challenge. He loved a good one - it gave him an excuse to experiment and prove his worth. "Zombie parts from different species?" He pondered aloud, his mind racing with possibilities. "I'll see what I can come up with," he promised, already planning out his next masterpiece.

Days turned into weeks, and weeks into months as he perfected his craft. He studied the zombies they encountered, analyzing their textures and tastes, categorizing their strengths and weaknesses like a sommelier tasting wine. He experimented with spices and flavors, often retreating to his makeshift kitchen deep within the bunker to concoct new creations. His determination was unwavering, his passion unrelenting. Finally, he emerged with a dish that would change their world forever: zombie filet mignon with a tartrate made from roasted zombie apples and figs.

The aroma was intoxicating, a heady mix of sweet and savory that filled the air, causing even the most jaded of zombies to pause mid-moan in appreciation. The taste was like nothing they'd ever experienced before - a perfect balance of flavors that brought tears of joy to their undead eyes.

As they devoured their meal, they praised him endlessly, hailing him as the new Michelangelo of the post-apocalyptic world. And at that moment, surrounded by his admirers, Jean-Pierre felt more alive than he had in years.

Dr. Olivia Martinez watched him with a wry smile. She had to admit, she was impressed. His growth as a chef was nothing short of remarkable, and she took pride in her small part in nurturing his talent. She had seen so much death and destruction in her lifetime that she often found it hard to appreciate beauty or joy, but Jean-Pierre's dedication to finding solace in food brought her hope. "You've come a long way from your humble beginnings," she acknowledged, patting him on the back.

They shared a laugh, their eyes meeting over the smoky haze that filled the air. She could see the spark in his eyes, a fervor that matched her own. They were both survivors, determined to make the most of their bleak reality, and she felt a deep camaraderie with him that she hadn't felt in years.

As they sat down to feast, she reflected on their journey so far. The days were growing longer, the weather warmer, and their group stronger. But there was still so much left to do, so many obstacles ahead. The thought made her stomach churn, but she took heart in knowing they had each other's backs. And Jean-Pierre's culinary skills would surely see them through anything.

The night sky darkened, painting the world with hues of purple and blue as they prepared for bed. The distant howls of the undead served as a reminder of the dangers that lurked outside their haven, but inside, they were safe, sated, and content. As Jean-Pierre snored softly beside her, Olivia drifted off into a restless slumber, dreaming of the day when they would find the cure and reclaim the world from the grips of darkness.

In the morning, she awoke with a start, her sleep-addled mind trying to catch up to the acrid smell that filled the air. Jean-Pierre was already up, standing over their small stove, stirring another concoction. His brow was furrowed in concentration, his hands moving with precision and purpose. She watched him for a moment, admiring his determination, and his steady progress despite the odds stacked against them.

He glanced up at her, a grin spreading across his face. "Good morning, Olivia. Today, I'm trying something new. Something I think you'll enjoy."

She joined him, taking a seat on a nearby crate. "What is it this time?" she asked, eyeing the bubbling pot with apprehension.

"I call it 'chicken and dumplings'," he said proudly, stirring the mixture. "But don't worry, it's different from what you're used to."

"Different?" she questioned, raising an eyebrow.

"Yes, different," he assured her. "I've added some wild herbs I found during our last scouting mission for flavor. And instead of flour, I'm using cornmeal for the dough."

She watched as he moved around the camp, gathering firewood and setting up breakfast. He looked so at ease, so confident, it made her heart ache knowing how much was riding on their success. As the day wore on and they ate their meal, she found herself savoring each bite, surprised by the unique taste and texture. The herbs had given it an earthy flavor, while the cornmeal added a subtle sweetness that paired perfectly with the tender chicken. They sat in silence for a while afterward, relishing the meal and the peacefulness of their secluded spot.

Then, suddenly, they heard a rustling in the bushes. Their heads snapped towards the sound simultaneously, guns at the ready.

CHAPTER 6

The tavern was dimly lit, filled with the muffled sounds of clinking glasses and raucous laughter, the air heavy with the scent of cheap ale and sweat. Eddie Thompson sat at a rough-hewn table, biceps bulging as he leaned forward, elbows resting on his knees, his shaved head glistening with droplets of condensation from the frothy mug of ale in front of him. He was a man of few words but when he spoke, his deep baritone voice echoed through the room, causing patrons to turn their heads in curiosity. His bushy beard bobbed up and down as he chuckled, enjoying the camaraderie of his fellow adventurers. Next to him, Sophia Reynolds sipped at her drink, her delicate fingers tracing the rim of the glass, eyes darting around the room with a mixture of wariness and curiosity. She was not one for this sort of place, preferring the quiet solitude of her herbs and tinctures, but she knew the importance of fitting in with the group if they were to succeed in their quest.

As Jean-Pierre emerged from the kitchen, lugging a steaming tray of food, Eddie's eyes lit up like a child on Christmas morning. "Ahh, the MasterChef strikes again!" he boomed, clapping a meaty hand on the small man's back. Sophia couldn't help but smile as she watched Jean-Pierre blush under the praise, his accent thickening under Eddie's enthusiasm. The aroma of roasted meats and seasoned vegetables filled the air, causing stomachs to growl in unison.

The group dug in with gusto, laughing and joking around the table.

Eddie, always quick to defend his friend, bristled at Sophia's subtle criticism of Jean-Pierre's unorthodox methods. "He may not be a traditional cook," he growled, "but he can sure as hell make some damn good grub." She sighed softly, knowing better than to argue with him when his loyalty was so fierce. They were all gathered here seeking adventure and riches, but Eddie's devotion to their chef bordered on blind worship. She watched as he piled his plate high with tender roast chicken and buttery potatoes, ignoring the squirming guilt in her stomach.

Sophia tried to rationalize it away: they were all here for the same goal, after all. They needed each other's skills to survive in this treacherous world. And besides, they were far from civilization; morality could be forgotten sometimes. But still, something niggled at her conscience as she took a bite of juicy meat, expectingly tender. She forced herself to savor the flavors, trying to drown out the nagging voice that reminded her of the source of their food.

Around them, the tavern buzzed with life: the clink of mugs, the hum of conversation, and the occasional gasp of delight at a particularly delicious morsel. The air thickened with smoke and cheer.

Sophia couldn't help but feel uneasy.

She looked at Eddie, his jovial laugh echoing around the room as Jean-Pierre regaled them with tales of their journey's trials ahead. She glanced back at the innkeeper, who seemed delighted by the pirates' presence. Her heart ached for him; they were all he had ever known, and he saw no harm in their ways. But she knew better. They weren't just marauders; they were monsters, driven by greed and power lust.

Eddie, though, seemed oblivious to any moral quandaries. His massive frame shook with laughter at one of Jean-Pierre's jokes, his belly rolling beneath his worn leather vest. She noted how he wolfed down the food like it was his last meal—perhaps it was, for all they knew what dangers lay ahead. She couldn't help but admire his strength, a necessary asset in their group. She laughed with him, hiding her reservations behind a smile.

They finished their meal and prepared for their next quest, gathering their weapons and supplies. As they left the tavern, Sophia's eyes met those of the innkeeper, whose face fell as they disappeared into the night. She couldn't bring herself to say goodbye, knowing what might come next.

Their journey was long and arduous, punctuated by sudden bursts of hunger and fatigue. Eddie, ever vigilant, kept them safe from predators while Jean-Pierre tended to their injuries—and fed them well with whatever they managed to scavenge along the way. His cooking was legendary among the group; Sophia couldn't fathom how he produced such delectable meals in such desolate places. She watched him prepare dinner one night, her stomach rumbling in anticipation. He took great care with every ingredient, humming softly as he worked his magic over the flames. She realized then that food wasn't just sustenance for him; it was an expression of love. And in that moment, she understood her role within the group: to temper Jean-Pierre's hunger for conquest with compassion and empathy.

They came upon a small village nestled between towering mountains. Eddie raised a fist in triumph, clearly ready to ransack it for supplies. But Sophia intervened, reminding him of their mission to find the fabled artifact that would defeat the Dark Lord. Reluctantly, Eddie agreed, and they crept through the village undetected. They found an elderly woman tending her garden who told them about an ancient temple hidden deep within the mountains. She warned them of traps and guardians, but they pressed on undeterred.

Inside the temple, they faced unimaginable trials—traps that tested their strength and agility, guardians that challenged their very souls. As they battled, Sophia couldn't shake the thought of the villagers they had left behind. But Eddie was unphased; this was their destiny, their duty. He swung his axe with reckless abandon, his muscles rippling with each powerful swing. Despite her misgivings, Sophia fought alongside him, grunting with effort as she dodged blades and spells.

Finally, they reached the heart of the temple—a glowing orb that pulsed with dark energy. Sophia hesitated, sensing its danger. But Eddie grabbed it greedily, ready to use its power for their cause. His skin turned ashen, his eyes sunken; he collapsed at her feet, the artifact shattering into a thousand pieces.

Sophia wept over him as she whispered, "I should have known better than to trust a man like you."

Eddie groaned and slowly stood, holding his chest. "It's not my fault...we were so close."

"We could have found another way," she pleaded. “Not with an army of orcs at our heels," he replied sternly, "and we both knew the risks when we started this journey."

Sophia sighed heavily, knowing he was right. They collected the shards of the orb and began their journey home when they stumbled upon a small village plagued by monsters. In exchange for food and sanctuary, they offered to help rid the village of the creatures. Eddie's eyes lit up at the thought of Jean-Pierre's cooking, her heart sank at what it would cost.

They slew the beasts and returned to the village, where Jean-Pierre welcomed them with open arms and a warm meal. Despite herself, Sophia savored every bite; it was unlike anything she had ever tasted before. The other villagers adored them as heroes, but she couldn't shake her doubts; she knew what they had done to earn that title.

The next morning, they continued their quest, hearts heavy with guilt but also determination. They encountered a wounded traveler who needed their help; Eddie, ever the provider, insisted they aid him despite Sophia's protests. Their bond was unbreakable, even when faced with moral dilemmas.

Throughout their journey, Eddie showed remarkable resourcefulness, crafting makeshift weapons and traps while Sophia's empath soothed wounded spirits and offered words of encouragement. They faced unimaginable dangers together, yet they persevered.

One day, they found themselves in front of a massive dragon's lair guarding treasure that could change their fortunes forever—a temptation too great for any adventurer to ignore. With a heavy heart, Sophia watched as Eddie and Jean-Pierre charged in without hesitation. She followed suit, praying they wouldn't regret this decision.

Inside the lair, they faced the dragon alone. It breathed fire and clawed at them viciously; Sophia used her wits to guide them while Eddie handled the brute strength needed to survive. They managed to defeat it, emerging victorious but weary. The treasure was beyond imagination; gold coins sparkled in the dim light.

As they returned home, Sophia couldn't help but feel uneasy about what they had become adventurers who solved problems with violence instead of compassion. But Eddie, always hungry, convinced her they were doing good work; after all, people needed their help, and if some got hurt along the way, it was for the greater good.

They divided the treasure equally and used it to improve their lives back in their hometown. Sophia opened an orphanage while Eddie started a blacksmithing business; their friendship remained strong despite their differences in morality.

Years passed, and their reputations grew; people sought them out for their unique skills. Eddie, the strongman, handled dangerous situations with ease while Sophia provided guidance and wisdom. And so, their legend as the "Heroes of Hollow tree" began.

One day, they received a request that challenged their principles: rescue a kidnapped princess from a ruthless bandit king who held her captive deep within a dark forest. Sophia felt conflicted but knew she couldn't abandon her friend when he needed her most. They assembled a team skilled in combat and ventured forth bravely.

They entered the forbidding woods, hacking through vines and dodging traps. Eddie's resourcefulness saved them time and again; he forged tools from trees and scavenged food from the forest floor. Sophia provided moral support and encouragement when hope dwindled.

Through perseverance and luck, they located the lair; the foul stench of decay filled the air as they slipped inside undetected. They heard sobbing in the distance, guiding them to the princess's location. As they inched closer, they discovered she was chained to a wall, starved and bruised.

Without hesitation, Sophia rushed forward, using her healing magic to ease the princess's pain. Together, they cut through the chains, and she wept tears of gratitude. But escape wasn't easy; the bandit king ambushed them with his men at every turn.

In one final confrontation, Eddie started a diversion, allowing Sophia to heal the princess enough for them to flee. The princess rode on Sophia's shoulders, tears drying up as she felt the warmth of the sun for the first time in months.

Back home, the group celebrated their success with strong drinks and hearty food prepared by Jean-Pierre, whose kindness had won them over. Eddie savored every bite of his meal despite its dubious origins, blinded by loyalty towards his new friends.

Meanwhile, Sophia struggled to reconcile her discomfort about Jean-Pierre's past deeds and his present kindness; his cooking was divine! She couldn't help but feel drawn to him despite her better judgment. They shared stories around the fire as night fell, forming bonds that would strengthen their bond as they continued this perilous journey together.]

Sophia woke up early the next morning, her heart heavy with the previous night's revelations. Zombie meat was not just a delicacy in their world, but survival. She quietly slipped away from their campsite, gathering berries and mushrooms for an alternative meal option. When she returned, she noticed Eddie sharpening his axe while eyeing a nearby herd of zombies warily. "Eddie," she started cautiously, "have you considered the implications of our food choices?"

He looked up at her, his burly frame glistening with sweat from the morning heat. "We're survivors, Sophia. We do what we must."

She sighed, knowing how easily his loyalty could be swayed by their leader. "I understand. It's just..." her voice trailed off as she handed him her basket of berries, "I think it's crucial to remember our humanity even in these dire times."

"Aye, aye, Captain Morality," he teased, nibbling on a berry. It burst with sweetness on his tongue, surprising him with its deliciousness. They sat down to eat, their conversation falling silent as they each focused on filling their bellies. Suddenly, a commotion erupted nearby—a rival group attacked them!

Eddie leaped into action; his strength was unmatched as he swung his axe at any zombie that dared approach. Sinews tightened and veins bulged from his arms, muscles rippling with each powerful strike. Sophia watched in awe, feeling proud of his unyielding loyalty despite her reservations.

"Sophia!" Jean-Pierre called out, waving her over to help tend to the wounded. She rushed to his side, using her nurturing abilities to heal the injured survivors as they told stories of bravery and loss. As she worked, she wondered how long they could continue down this path before losing themselves entirely.

The scent of roasting zombie meat wafted through the air, making her stomach turn. She knew this was a reality they had to face, yet her heart ached for the innocent lives being taken. "It tastes so good," Eddie remarked between bites, oblivious to her internal struggle. "I've never had anything like it."

She sighed, joining him for a taste. The tender flesh melted in her mouth, teasing her senses with its rich flavors. "Indeed, it does," she admitted reluctantly, "but at what cost?"

The group shared stories of the past while devouring their meal, laughter filling the air. Eddie reached out for her hand, squeezing it. "We're a family here, Sophia. We'll figure it out together." His warmth and sincerity made her heart flutter with hope.

But as night fell, Sophia couldn't shake the haunting images of the day's events. The taste of zombie meat lingered on her tongue, bitter now. It was too much to bear. She excused herself, needing air.

In the darkness, under a canopy of glittering stars, she broke down in tears, wondering if they'd ever find their way back to humanity.

Jean-Pierre watched her from across the fire, concern etched on his weathered face. He had lost everything too, but still felt guilty for the role he played in this new world. His soul ached at the thought of taking lives, even if it meant survival.

"Jean-Pierre," she called softly, walking toward him. "I'm sorry. I can't shake the guilt."

He rose to meet her halfway, his kind eyes reflecting the flames. "Don't fret, chère. We're all trying to cope how we can."

"But I feel like we're losing ourselves," she said, searching his gaze. "We can't keep going like this."

Eddie's voice interrupted them, "What's wrong, Sophia?"

She turned to see him approach, concern etched on his face. "It's nothing," she lied, forcing a smile.

They returned to the warmth of the fire, Eddie offering to help clean up while Sophia shared recipe ideas for future dishes featuring zombie meat. Despite her misgivings, she couldn't deny it added much-needed protein to their diet.

As they worked, Sophia caught Eddie's eye rolling a zombie eyeball in some fried rice. His eagerness to try new flavors surprised her yet touched her heart. They were all trying so hard to make this work.

The next day, they ventured out into the desolate cityscape, scavenging for supplies. Eddie's strength was unmatched, pushing through locked doors with ease and collecting canned goods like they were child's play. Sophia searched abandoned kitchens for fresh vegetables and grains, her delicate fingers plucking items from the rubble.

They returned to their haven, exhausted but triumphant. Jean-Pierre thanked them both for their efforts as he started cooking up another concoction using the new ingredients. The aroma of spices and meat filled the air, making everyone's stomachs growl in anticipation.

"Taste this," Jean-Pierre said eagerly, presenting a plate to Sophia. She hesitated but knew the taste test was crucial for improvement. Biting into the dish, rich flavors exploded in her mouth - garlic, ginger, and soy sauce mixed perfectly with a tender texture she hadn't expected from zombie meat.

"Wow, Jean-Pierre, this is amazing!" Eddie exclaimed, already wiping his plate clean.

The trio worked together on perfecting recipes, balancing flavor, and nutrition, always considering what would make them more palatable without sacrificing texture or taste. They also searched for alternatives to zombie meat but found little success until one day they stumbled upon a secret garden hiding behind an abandoned house.

Its lush greenery provided fresh herbs and vegetables, giving them hope for a healthier diet. As they harvested, Sophia noticed Jean-Pierre struggling with his conscience again.

"Jean-Pierre," she asked softly, "are you okay?"

"I can't keep doing this, Sophia," he confessed. "Killing these creatures... it's not right." Eddie looked on, knowing Jean-Pierre wouldn't stop no matter what they said.

"Jean-Pierre, we're all here for you," Sophia replied, placing a comforting hand on his shoulder. "You're not alone in this."

Inside the house, the sound of zombies groaning increased.

"We should focus on what we can do now," Eddie suggested, his voice hardened. "We'll figure something else out later."

They hurried back to their hideout where Sophia helped prepare dinner with the new ingredients while Eddie kept watch at the door. As they ate under the flickering light of candles, the room filled with laughter and conversation about simpler times before the apocalypse. It was a welcome respite from the harsh reality outside.

The next day, Sophia found Jean-Pierre in the garden, head bowed over a small grave they'd dug together - a final resting place for the zombies they could no longer use in their dishes. She joined him in silence, knowing he needed space. Together they tended to the plants, their efforts bringing color into their bleak world.

Back at the hideout, they discovered a can opener and canned goods, opening up a new world of flavors. Eddie's practicality came into play as he used various spices to elevate these dishes, surprising everyone with his culinary prowess. Their bond grew stronger with each meal they shared.

One day, during a lull in zombie activity, they ventured out into town seeking more supplies when they heard moaning from an alleyway. Hesitantly, they approached, finding a group of starving survivors begging for food. Without hesitation, Sophia insisted they share what they had, and even gave them some of Jean-Pierre's coveted recipes. Eddie, initially against it, saw the relief on their faces and knew she was right.

As the group grew stronger, they discussed the ethics of using zombies as food sources. Sophia questioned it while Eddie argued for survival above all else. They decided on a limit, only using ones who attacked them or showed signs of aggression. It was a compromise neither was fully satisfied with but accepted for now.

Days turned into weeks, weeks into months, and desperation brought them closer together. Sophia's empathy urged her to comfort Jean-Pierre whenever he struggled with his creations, reminding him that it was necessary for their survival. She watched proudly as he refined his recipes, making them taste better each time.

Eddie began bringing in new ingredients, some from abandoned supermarkets and some from scavenging trips into zombie-infested areas, eager to try out Jean-Pierre's latest creations. They savored every bite, the spicy tang of jerk chicken, the tender sweetness of beef stroganoff, and the warmth of a hearty stew.

During a lull in zombie activity, they found time to bond over stories of their old lives, laughing at silly memories and sharing heartfelt moments. Little did they know this peace wouldn't last...

A loud thump outside interrupted their meal. They rushed to the door, weapons ready. A zombie moaned pitifully at their feet, injured but not aggressive. Eddie hesitated but Sophia nodded, and they brought it inside for Jean-Pierre's experimentation.

Hours later, after carefully preparing it according to his new recipe, they sat around a crackling fire sharing stories of home-cooked meals from before the apocalypse. The aroma of garlic, onions, and herbs filled the air as they dug into the roasted tenderloin with potatoes drenched in gravy.

The taste was unlike anything they'd experienced; savory perfection danced on their tongues while they mulled over its origins. Suddenly, realization struck—the human taste hadn't been as strong this time due to an unknown herb added at the end.

They looked at each other guiltily but couldn't deny the deliciousness. Their bellies were full, and they hugged each other tightly, understanding they'd crossed a line but grateful for the camaraderie that got them through it.]

Eddie Thompson reached for another bite of the exquisite roasted zombie meat, his eyes closed in bliss as the salty and tender flavor exploded on his tongue. The sound of chewing mingled with the crackling fire nearby, and the aroma of garlic, onions, and herbs filled the air. He glanced at Sophia Reynolds, who looked as if she were in heaven too, her cheeks flushed from the delight of the meal.

"Edward," Jean-Pierre said, breaking the silence. "You are enjoying this, aren't you?" His voice was low and curious, almost amused.

"Hell yeah," Eddie said without shame, wiping his mouth with a napkin. "The best thing I've ever tasted."

Sophia nodded in agreement, her wavy blonde hair falling over her eyes as she did so. "I can't believe how good this is," she marveled, taking another bite of her own.

They both looked at the chained-up zombie outside the door, who had provided the main course for their meal. It was an awful thought, but it couldn't be denied - human taste was far less pronounced than usual. It tasted almost like beef stroganoff or a hearty stew they remembered from their old lives.

"What did you do to it?" Eddie asked quietly, gesturing towards the creature's roasted form with his fork.

"I added a special herb I found on one of my travels," Jean-Pierre grinned. "It's called sanguinaria."

CHAPTER 7

The night was cold and harsh, the wind whistling through the empty city streets like the wails of a lonely ghost. The survivors huddled together in a derelict restaurant, their bodies shivering from the chill that seemed to seep into their bones. They were a group of five, each with their own stories of struggle and survival. Jean-Pierre LeClair, the renowned chef with salt-and-pepper hair and a trimmed beard, stood before them, his tall, lean frame radiating determination as he gathered them around a makeshift table. "My friends," he began, "I have an idea that could change everything." His eyes darted from one face to another, taking in their weary expressions, their emaciated features, and the hope that glimmered in the depths of their sunken eyes. His voice was thick with emotion, his French accent pronounced as he outlined his vision: to use his culinary skills to help them adapt to this new world—a world where food was scarce, where hunger was a constant companion.

Alice Winters, the resourceful and resilient young woman with long, dark hair and sharp, intelligent eyes, leaned in, intrigued by this sudden show of leadership from the normally reticent chef. Edward "Eddie" Thompson, the burly, strong man with a shaved head and bushy beard, sat back with a frown, not quite understanding where this was going. Dr. Olivia Martinez, the petite, middle-aged woman with greying hair tied neatly in a bun, studied

Jean-Pierre with a keen eye, sensing the desperation in his tone. Marcus Devereaux, the wealthy and charismatic leader with slicked-back dark hair and sharp, calculating eyes, listened intently, considering how this might benefit his hold on the group. Sophia Reynolds, the kind-hearted and gentle woman with wavy blonde hair and soft features, looked on worriedly, feeling the weight of their collective conscience bearing down on her.

"We must find a way to create normalcy in this chaos," Jean-Pierre continued. "We must find a way to nourish ourselves without sacrificing our humanity. Together, we can use my knowledge of food and flavor to survive." He paused for a moment, allowing his words to sink in. "And maybe, just maybe, we can taste something other than canned beans and stale bread." There was a murmur of agreement among them, their stomachs rumbling in anticipation at the thought of such luxury.

The chef began to explain his plan: hunting for ingredients had become more dangerous than ever before, and they had no choice but to look for alternatives. He would need their help, but he was confident that with their support, they could recreate the taste of home, the comfort of a warm meal, in their makeshift shelter. "Imagine," he said, his voice cracking with emotion, "a steaming bowl of hearty soup, filled with tender meat and vegetables, simmering on the stove."

A smile broke out on everyone's faces as they imagined the aroma wafting through the room, filling their nostrils, and reminding them of better times. Little did they know, it was only the beginning of their journey back to a life worth living.

The next morning, the group gathered outside the safehouse, ready to embark on their first scavenging mission. Jean-Pierre handed out a list of ingredients he needed for his recipes - tomatoes, garlic, onions, basil, peppers, and a few other essentials. They headed out into the eerily quiet streets, their footsteps echoing against the empty buildings and abandoned cars.

The air was thick with tension, the smell of decaying flesh from the undead lurking around every corner.

Alice glanced at the chef, her eyes full of doubt, but she followed him, nonetheless. She knew they needed to adapt to survive this new world, but something about Jean-Pierre's methods left her feeling uneasy. Eddie, on the other hand, wore a determined look on his face, eager to taste the chef's creations. Dr. Martinez scanned the area for edible plants while Sophia held onto her rifle like it was her lifeline. Marcus kept an eye out for valuable resources, always scheming on how to maintain his position as leader.

As they walked, Jean-Pierre noticed Antoine, eyeing him warily. He knew the man was dangerous, always looking for ways to manipulate the situation for his gain. But for now, he needed his help in finding goods to trade for the missing ingredients.

They pushed through the debris-strewn streets, their bodies aching from the effort of moving furniture and clearing roads. At one point, they heard a low groan from an alleyway; they froze, weapons at the ready. Eddie took point and cautiously approached, finding that it was just a young girl who had been caught in the chaos. He carried her out gently, her eyes vacant and soul lost to the apocalypse. Alice tended to her wounds as they continued their search, Sophia's eyes welling up at the sight of, yet another innocent life taken too soon.

Finally, they reached a grocery store still intact, its glass windows shattered but products mostly untouched. The group divided up, scouring the shelves for canned goods and vegetables, Eddie lifting heavy crates with ease while Antoine snuck into the backroom to see if there were any luxuries worth trading. Jean-Pierre's eyes darted between them all, taking in their strengths and weaknesses. He knew they needed to work together if they were going to make it through this nightmare.

With their haul secured, they returned to their camp, exhausted but determined. The aroma of Jean-Pierre's cooking filled the air as they approached; his chicken soup simmered on an open fire, filling the area with warmth and comfort. As they sat around the table, he began passing out plates filled with tender meat and hearty vegetables, garnering approving nods from everyone except Dr. Martinez who still couldn't get over how he acquired the chicken.

"We must adapt," he told them between mouthfuls, "or we will perish. This is our chance, our chance to reclaim some semblance of normalcy in this hellish world."

They ate in silence, each lost in thought. Tomorrow would be another day of survival, but for now, they had each other.

The next day, they set out again, hearts heavy but resolve strong. Jean-Pierre was determined to make the most of their findings, knowing he had to keep everyone's spirits up. He spotted a derelict restaurant and rallied his team, eager for their approval. Inside, he found cast-iron skillets and spices that would elevate their meals beyond canned food and stale bread. He rummaged through dumpsters for fresh ingredients, hoping to surprise them all.

Alice watched skeptically as he mixed herbs and spices, she'd never heard of before, but she trusted his instincts. As he prepared the meal in the kitchenette, she peered over his shoulder, surprised at the precision he brought to such dire circumstances.

"What's it going to be?" Marcus asked eagerly, licking his lips.

"Steak au poivre," Jean-Pierre announced, slicing into the tender venison he'd secured earlier. It sizzled on the pan, releasing earthy scents that made Marcus's mouth water.

They all gathered around, eyes wide with anticipation, as Jean-Pierre served them each a generous portion. The smell of crackling peppercorns filled the air, mingling with the smoke from the fire. Eddie's eyes lit up at the sight of the rare meat, and Sophia's face softened at the memory of home-cooked meals. Dr. Martinez tasted it cautiously, her expression slowly transforming into wonder.

"This... this is incredible," she murmured, savoring each bite. Alice couldn't believe it; the bitterness of the beer reduction balanced perfectly with the peppercorns, enhancing the natural flavor of the game. Even Antoine, who had been so quick to criticize earlier, couldn't help but nod in approval.

They ate in silence at first, lost in the flavors and textures of their meal. The soft crunch of toothsome rolls against tender meat, the sizzle of grease hitting the skillet, and the pop of a cork from a bottle of red wine were the only sounds that filled the night. The group was united, if only for this moment, in their shared appreciation for Jean-Pierre's culinary magic. It was a brief respite from their harsh reality.

"What about dessert?" Sophia asked hesitantly.

Jean-Pierre grinned, pulling out a half-eaten cake he'd found earlier. He added butter, cream, and a touch of powdered sugar, creating a concoction unlike any of them had tasted before. The heat from the fire warmed the sweet treat, causing butterfat to drip onto the embers below. As it melted, it released an intoxicating aroma that made their mouths water.

Taking tentative bites, they moaned in delight at the blend of lemon and vanilla that danced on their tongues. Marcus wiped crumbs from his beard, smiling widely. "Do you have any more of that magic powdered sugar?"

Sophia clucked her tongue disapprovingly at him, but there was an undercurrent of admiration in her voice. "You really shouldn't encourage him," she teased.

"I'm just saying," Marcus defended himself. "His cooking is keeping us alive." "And sane," Alice added between bites.

They all nodded in agreement, finishing off the rest of the cake. Even Sophia couldn't resist succumbing to its irresistible charm, licking her fingers clean with relish.

As they sat around the fire, Eddie burped loudly, causing laughter to ripple through the group. "Well, I'll be damned," he said. "That man knows his stuff."

Dr. Martinez placed a hand on his back, patting it gently. "Calm down, big guy. We should head back soon."

Eddie grunted but didn't protest as they packed up their things. The moon hung high overhead, casting shadows that danced on their faces. As they walked back to their makeshift shelter, they couldn't help but feel a newfound sense of purpose. Jean-Pierre's cooking had given them something to look forward to, something beyond mere survival.

Back at camp, they discussed their next steps: finding more supplies, scavenging for food, and avoiding danger. Sophia suggested building up defenses against potential threats, while Marcus insisted on maintaining the status quo. It was clear a rift was forming within their ranks. Antoine watched from the sidelines; his eyes gleaming with mischief.

The next day, Jean-Pierre disappeared into the forest, returning with an armful of wild mushrooms and some herbs he'd identified as edible. He spent hours experimenting, combining them with canned goods and stale bread to create a stew that smelled divine. Alice helped him chop vegetables while Eddie gathered kindling for the fire. Dr. Martinez watched on curiously, her skepticism slowly melting away.

The aroma wafted through the air, filling the camp with anticipation. Jean-Pierre presented his creation with pride, explaining every ingredient and its purpose. The stew was a concoction of flavors they'd never experienced before—earthy, savory, and rich. They dug in eagerly, moaning at the taste buds. Even Antoine couldn't resist the allure of such delectable fare.

As they ate, they felt a surge of energy they hadn't experienced in weeks. Their skin glowed healthier, and their muscles less brittle. It was as if Jean-Pierre's cooking had quelled the harshness of their new reality, if only for a moment. Sophia beamed at him, her eyes shining with gratitude.

But Marcus's expression was more guarded, his mind fixated on maintaining control. He knew that this newfound hope could be dangerous if left unchecked, like a small flame that could ignite into an inferno. He watched Jean-Pierre closely, wondering how much longer this delusion could last.

In the cramped, damp basement of an abandoned restaurant, Jean-Pierre LeClair gathered the remaining members of his group around a makeshift table, their eyes reflecting a mix of intrigue and trepidation. The chef stood before them, his salt-and-pepper hair glistening with sweat, his trimmed beard trembling slightly as he clenched the edge of the table. His tall, lean frame was tense, almost vibrating with passion as he spoke. "I've been thinking," he began, his voice hushed but filled with determination, "about how we can survive in this new world we find ourselves in. And I believe that one of the ways is through food."

Around the table, Alice Winters furrowed her brows, skeptical of the old man's proposal. She had seen too much death and destruction to trust easily. The others were a mix of cautious curiosity and open-mindedness; Edward "Eddie" Thompson looked up from his meal, a half-eaten sandwich paused mid-bite, while Dr. Olivia Martinez rubbed her temples, clearly distracted by the thought of finding alternative food sources. Sophia Reynolds, her blonde hair flowing gently over her shoulders, leaned in, sensing the need to hear more.

Describing each face in detail, their expressions turning from suspicion to curiosity would take too long.

Jean-Pierre continued, his voice low and intense, "We need to create a sense of normalcy amidst all this chaos. A return to the familiar, even if it's just for a moment. With that in mind, I propose we start cooking again." His voice dropped to a whisper, almost reverent, "Cooking the way we used to."

At this, Marcus Devereaux scoffed, his dark hair slicked back from his forehead, revealing a slight sheen of sweat. "You mean, using ingredients from god knows where?" He spat out, his piercing gaze darting around the room. Antoine Dupont nodded in silent agreement, his short dark hair bobbing ever so slightly as he leaned forward on the worn wood of the table.

But Jean-Pierre wouldn't be deterred. He waved away their concerns, his eyes burning with conviction. "Not just anywhere," he replied firmly, "but with the care and precision that made us who we are." He explained that some of the ingredients they could find in the abandoned supermarkets and farms were still safe to eat if cooked properly. "Taking risks is what made me a renowned chef," he said, "and it's what will keep us alive now."

Eddie rubbed his large hands together, already salivating at the thought of a hot meal. "You think we can pull this off?" he asked, his deep voice rumbling with anticipation. Jean-Pierre nodded emphatically, his eyes flashing with resolve. "We have to try," he insisted, "or we'll lose ourselves to this new reality."

Around the table, murmurs of agreement rose, stirring the dusty air. And so, they set to work, creating a feast with ingredients they'd never cooked before, but driven by their shared love of food and each other, they forged on, determined to reclaim their old lives one dish at a time.

Days turned into weeks as they scavenged through the wasteland, exploring abandoned buildings and risking encounters with zombies to find ingredients to add to Jean-Pierre's recipes. They discovered spoiled foods that could be salvaged with careful preparation, learned to hunt small game for protein, and scavenged for herbs and spices to add depth and flavor. The air always carried the faint scent of decay, but when they gathered around one of Jean-Pierre's makeshift tables for a meal, it was replaced by the tantalizing aromas of home-cooked meals. The sizzle of frying meat, the rustle of sautéed vegetables, and the rich smell of freshly baked bread filled the air, reminding them of better times.

The scavenging missions became more treacherous as the group grew hungry for variety. Antoine, always looking for an advantage, suggested they explore further into the city, pushing their limits and testing their courage. Sophia cautioned against it, her blonde hair shining in the flickering firelight as she argued about the growing danger. But Marcus, ever the opportunist, saw potential in Antoine's plan. He nodded grimly, his eyes glinting with determination. "We can't stay here forever," he said, "not if we want to survive."

Reluctantly, they agreed to take the chance. Their footsteps echoed through the empty streets, weapons at the ready, eyes darting left and right for any sign of the undead horrors that lurked in the shadows. They crept past abandoned cars and boarded-up stores, the only sounds of their heavy breathing and the occasional creak of a broken step. A growling stomach reminded them of their unwavering goal.

They finally reached an upscale restaurant, its once-elegant facade now marred by graffiti and decay. Inside was a feast for the senses - fresh produce, high-quality meats, and exotic spices. Jean-Pierre's eyes widened in excitement, his mind already whirring with possibilities. The others stood guard while he worked his magic in the kitchen. The clank of pots and pans, the sizzle of oil, and the aroma of grilling steak filled the air, distracting them from their surroundings. Alice watched warily, her dark hair falling over her face as she wondered what price they would pay for this bounty.

Eddie and Marcus kept watch from the rooftop, their shaved heads and bushy beards peeking over the ledge as they scanned for threats. Sophia checked on Dr. Martinez, whose wiry frame moved methodically through the shelves, carefully selecting medicinal herbs. Antoine lingered near the front door, his sharp eyes darting between the street and the kitchen, always on alert.

Finally, Jean-Pierre emerged, his tall frame holding a steaming platter of braised short ribs and roasted vegetables. The juices dripped onto the newspaper-lined plate, and steam engulfed his face. He nodded at Alice, and they left without looking back, the food heavy in their stomachs but light on their feet, tasting like victory.

As they walked away, Sophia couldn't shake the feeling they were being watched.

The group huddled around the campfire, sharing stories, and laughing like old friends. Sophia pulled her knees to her chest, letting the warmth seep into her bones. Jean-Pierre sat across from her, his salt-and-pepper hair glistening under the flickering light. He smiled at her, revealing a row of perfect teeth. "Tonight," he said, "you are eating my signature dish."

Everyone nodded in anticipation, their eyes glistening with hunger. Jean-Pierre set about preparing the meal, chopping, sautéing, and seasoning with care. The aroma wafted through the air, a tantalizing blend of garlic, thyme, and butter. Marcus licked his lips, his slicked- back hair glistening in the firelight.

Eddie cracked open a beer, sighing contentedly, while Dr. Martinez inspected their haul. Sophia watched Jean-Pierre's hands move nimbly, his dedication undeniable. Alice leaned against the cool wall, her expression softening as she took it all in. Antoine prowled around, always on edge.

Soon enough, Jean-Pierre delivered the goods. Mouths watered at the sight of the golden- brown loaf slathered in herbed butter, the rich aroma filling their noses. They tore into it like starving wolves, groaning with delight as the flaky crust gave way to the creamy interior. Sophia closed her eyes, savoring each bite of the decadent meal, appreciating the effort that went into it.

"It's perfect," Eddie murmured, his voice thick with satisfaction. "I don't know how you manage," Alice said, her voice awestruck. Jean-Pierre shrugged modestly, a proud smile playing at the corners of his lips. Antoine smirked, taking a seat next to Sophia. "I guess we'll survive after all."

Marcus leaned back, swirling the remaining wine in his glass. "Well, our chef here is a godsend," he said, raising his glass in a toast. "To Jean-

Pierre and his miraculous creations!" Everyone clinked glasses, even Sophia, despite her reservations.

Jean-Pierre beamed, his eyes searching her face for approval. Sophia forced a smile, knowing this was necessary for their survival. She finished her food, feeling almost human once again. They retired to their makeshift beds under the stars, dreaming of full bellies and warmth that night. Her eyes drifted shut, the soft rustle of leaves and distant shuffling lulling her to sleep.

In the morning, they woke to another feast: scrambled eggs with bacon and toast, a luxury they had yet to experience since the outbreak. Jean-Pierre had managed to create it from the limited resources they'd found. Sophia watched as Marcus scarfed it down, barely containing her excitement. He seemed to sense her gaze and winked at her, a rare show of affection. "You're amazing," she whispered to him as they cleaned up.

An ocean away, chaos reigned, but here in this haven, they found solace in food and each other.

The days passed, and Jean-Pierre's culinary magic continued. The group found themselves growing stronger, their physical and emotional well-being improving with each meal. Alice even ventured out, scavenging for more supplies to keep up with their newfound energy. Eddie followed suit, his protective stance never wavering. Antoine, on the other hand, grew more brazen, clearly sensing an opportunity to assert his dominance.

One day at lunch, he cornered Jean-Pierre, asking about his past experiences. "What are your thoughts on hunting?" he queried, eyeing a nearby deer.

"I've worked in some of the finest restaurants around the world," Jean-Pierre said slowly, his eyes darting to Sophia for guidance. "But I've never killed for food."

"We don't have a choice," Antoine countered, his voice dangerously low. "That deer could feed us for days."

Sophia stepped between them, sensing the tension. "We can find other ways," she insisted, her voice shaking slightly. "Jean-Pierre has been proving that time and again."

Eddie nodded in agreement, but Antoine's gaze lingered on the frightened animal. Dr. Martinez joined them, her voice steely. "We need to focus on gathering plants and fruits before we push our luck," she insisted, ever the pragmatist.

As they argued, Jean-Pierre slipped away, returning with a handful of wild greens and roots he'd discovered. He added them to their meal with finesse, transforming the ordinary into something extraordinary. The aroma wafted across the campfire, a tantalizing blend of earthy spices and fresh herbs. The taste exploded in their mouths - a testament to his craftsmanship.

"You, see?" he said with a hint of pride, watching as they devoured the meal. "There are other options."

Yet Antoine remained unconvinced, his eyes still fixed on the deer. His words carried danger as he addressed Marcus, "We could use the extra protein."

Marcus considered for a moment before nodding. "Do it," he decided, revealing his true colors once again. "But make it quick."

A chill ran down Jean-Pierre's spine as Antoine snuck off into the forest with his bow. The sound of twigs snapping, and leaves rustling echoed through the trees, growing louder with each passing minute. As they neared the deer, the animals' panicked breathing filled the air. A tense silence fell upon the group; they knew what was coming next.

Suddenly, a gunshot rang out - startlingly loud in the quiet wilderness. They held their breath as Antoine emerged, triumphant, a limp deer draped over his shoulders.

The scavenging missions became more frequent, and tension grew between the survivors. Jean-Pierre continued to impress with his culinary prowess, but the moral implications weighed heavily on him. He couldn't shake the image of that innocent deer's eyes, pleading for mercy before Antoine's deadly arrow.

One day, while foraging for herbs, Alice stumbled upon an abandoned cabin. Inside were canned goods and jars of pickled vegetables, providing much-needed nutrients. She brought it back to the group, and they eagerly devoured the food like gold dust. Jean-Pierre concocted a stew that made their taste buds sing - the perfect blend of sweet and sour, tempering the bitterness of their reality.

Eddie now spent hours each day tending to their small garden, his brute strength put to good use tilling the soil. Sophia taught them the importance of preserving food, canning jars filled with colorful fruits and vegetables. Antoine, seeing the power potential, lurked on the outskirts, waiting for his chance.

Dr. Martinez busied herself with herbs and medicinal plants, using them to craft remedies for injuries and ailments. She was pragmatic but grew increasingly disillusioned by Marcus's obsession with luxury over survival, often clashing with his decisions.

Together, they built a makeshift kitchen, growing closer as they shared in the camaraderie of cooking and eating. But as the days turned into weeks and months, they faced realities that threatened to tear them apart. Zombie attacks were brutal, leaving them scarce of resources and weary from constant vigilance. Alice could no longer deny the benefits of Jean-Pierre's creations but worried for their souls.

Despite the challenges, Jean-Pierre remained steadfast in his quest for culinary perfection. His salt-and-pepper hair glinted in the firelight as he worked tirelessly over pots and pans. His voice, a soothing melody amidst the chaos, narrates each step of the meal preparation. The aroma of the roasting game mixed with forest herbs and spices filled the air, making stomachs rumble in anticipation.

As they gathered around the crackling fire, Marcus eyed him warily, aware of the power the chief held over his people. He couldn't ignore the success of their operations but questioned the cost. Eddie, ever loyal, smiled smugly, relishing the taste of meat after months of bland rations. Dr. Martinez sipped on her herbal tea, skeptical yet intrigued by the blend of flavors. Sophia looked at Jean-Pierre with admiration, noting the exhaustion etched on his face.

"This...this is incredible," Alice whispered, taking a bite of venison cooked to perfection. Her eyes closed in bliss, savoring the taste that transcended their dire situation. A collective murmur of appreciation rose from the group, hearts filled with warmth and sustenance.

But then came the aftermath - horror at what they'd consumed. Guilt gnawed at them as they realized the depths they'd sunk to survive. Jean-Pierre, oblivious or indifferent, continued his experiments, driven by passion and necessity. Antoine laughed maniacally, enjoying the power trip too much to care about the consequences. Only Marcus seemed remorseful, but it was too late for regrets. The sparkle in Eddie's eyes faded, replaced by fear.

The book closed on this ominous note - of survival at what cost and how long could they sustain it?

The apocalypse brought unexpected gifts to Jean-Pierre; his culinary skill was no longer hidden but sought after by other survivor groups. He shared his knowledge generously, fostering collaboration rather than competition. Gardening plots were created, wild plants foraged, and basic cooking skills taught. They rejoiced in small victories: the taste of fresh herbs on roasted vegetables or finding an abandoned restaurant full of provisions. Each success strengthened their bond and reinforced their belief in their mission.

With each dish, Alice's skepticism melted away as her taste buds were treated to masterful blends. She learned to trust Jean-Pierre's judgment despite her misgivings, protecting those around her from harm while ensuring their bellies were full. Eddie remained steadfast, shielding the chef from criticism and danger. Dr. Martinez found herself admiring the man's creativity despite herself, her jaded demeanor softening as they adapted. Sophia grew closer to him, doing everything she could to support his efforts amidst the chaos.

Yet Antoine lurked in the shadows, waiting for an opportunity to exploit their weaknesses. His mouthwatering at the thought of taking over their haven and claiming Jean-Pierre's talents for himself. The chef remained blind to Antoine's machinations, focused solely on feeding his people well. The others felt it too - a growing tension that threatened to tear them apart.

One fateful day, while foraging for edible plants, they stumbled upon a hidden cache of spices. Jean-Pierre's eyes lit up like a child on Christmas morning. He hugged Alice, who returned the embrace warily. The aroma of nutmeg and cinnamon filled the air as he mixed them into a stew. "Tonight's dinner will be a celebration," he declared, his voice echoing with excitement.

The group gathered around, anticipation building in their stomachs. As Jean-Pierre presented the dish, they savored every bite - an exotic blend of spices enhancing the flavor of what would have otherwise been bland survival rations. They chattered animatedly about the taste, relishing the joy of something other than fear or sorrow.

But their joy was short-lived. Zombies attacked, drawn by the scent of fresh meat. Bullets flew, bodies collided; chaos ensued. Jean-Pierre's kitchen became a battleground as he fought off the undead hordes while continuing to cook. Blood and sweat mingled on his clothes as he seasoned the meal with adrenaline. In the end, they emerged victorious, but not without losses.

The aftermath was somber. Losses weighed heavy on their hearts, but they gathered around the table once more, sharing stories and food. The chef's creation had newfound depth, its taste a testament to their survival.

As they ate together, Marcus observed from afar. His gaze was calculating; he saw potential allies in these newly formed bonds.

Days passed, and they grew stronger together. A new family forged in the fires of survival.

One day, Jean-Pierre was approached by Antoine Dupont - a survivor from a rival group. He offered a deal: share resources for exclusive access to Jean-Pierre's cooking. At first, the chef hesitated; he had sworn loyalty to his current companions. But hunger drove him to accept it, knowing that some would die otherwise. The others were wary but agreed reluctantly.

Days turned into weeks, weeks into months. Jean-Pierre's reputation grew, drawing in more survivors. They brought unconventional ingredients, desperate for hope amidst the desolation. He experimented, creating dishes that defied belief. His passion consumed him.

The scent of sizzling meats filled the air as they feasted on dishes crafted from rats and insects, weeds, and grubs. Each bite is a reminder of their resilience. They celebrated the small victories - finding medicine, foraging for berries, creating shelter. Tears were shed over fallen comrades; fond memories were shared over meals.

Alice became his closest confidante, helping him tend to the garden. She looked at him with admiration, recognizing his determination in the face of adversity. Yet she also saw the toll it was taking on his soul. He cooked with an almost manic intensity now, lost to the darker aspects of his craft. She couldn't shake the feeling that something was amiss.

Eddie, ever loyal, remained by his side through it all. With each new dish, his eyes would light up, his stomach rumbling in anticipation. He brushed off any doubts Sophia might voice, focusing on the taste instead of the ethics.

Dr. Martinez continued to search for safer alternatives, turning to plant-based meals and finding ways to extract nutrients from unlikely sources. She respected Jean-Pierre's talent but feared his obsession would lead them astray. Her cautious nature kept them alive, but at what cost?

Marcus, ever manipulative, saw an opportunity. He played on Sophia's empathy, using it to gain favor and slowly chip away at Jean-Pierre's resolve. Antoine, always observant, watched with interest.

Their dynamics were complex; an uneasy alliance built on necessity.

One day, a group arrived bearing a rare treat - salt. Jean-Pierre's eyes lit up, and he devised a dish that brought everyone together, even Antoine. His bitterness was momentarily forgotten. They lingered over the table, discussing recipes and strategies. Antoine sipped wine, knowing he could exploit this newfound camaraderie.

Days passed, and Jean-Pierre's reputation grew. The apocalypse had made him a symbol, a reminder that there was more to life than survival: joy, love, and beauty could still exist amidst the chaos. A tear rolled down his cheek as he realized this - his purpose renewed.

He walked outside, inhaling the crisp night air, and gazing at the stars. He vowed to continue his mission, for them, and himself.

As they all settled down for the night, Antoine's plot began to unfold...

CHAPTER 8

The survivor group trudged through the dry, barren landscape, the scent of ash and decay filling their lungs. Their stomachs growled in protest against the desolate surroundings, reminding them of the meager rations they'd been surviving on for far too long. Suddenly, a glimmer of hope caught their eyes—an abandoned farm, mostly untouched by the post-apocalyptic wasteland that had become their new reality. The rustle of leaves and snapping twigs echoed in the otherwise silent world as they approached cautiously, scanning for any signs of danger. As they drew nearer, they could see rows upon rows of crops still standing tall and resilient, green leaves swaying gently in the breeze.

Jean-Pierre, the renowned chef, felt his heart race with excitement at the sight. He could almost taste the succulent tomatoes, juicy and ripe from the vine, the earthy flavor of freshly picked carrots, and the crispness of just-picked lettuce. His mind raced with the endless possibilities of dishes he could create with these ingredients—dishes they had all but forgotten in their struggle to survive. He sprinted ahead, oblivious to the danger that might lurk around every corner, driven by his need to get his hands on the bounty before him.

Alice, the resourceful young woman with long dark hair, followed closely behind, her eyes sharp and wary. She was not nearly as enthused by the prospect of fresh food as Jean-Pierre, but she knew its importance for keeping it alive. She reached for her weapon instinctively, ready for any threat that might emerge.

Behind them, Eddie, the burly strong man with a shaved head and bushy beard, licked his lips in anticipation. He had always loved Jean-Pierre's cooking, even when it meant overlooking the moral implications of their methods. He quickened his pace, eager to feast on something other than dry and salted meats.

Dr. Olivia Martinez, the middle-aged medic, brought up the rear, her pragmatic nature taking over. She knew that survival was key, and these vegetables could help ensure it. Her past experiences had made her jaded, but she couldn't ignore the potential of a steady supply of nutritious food.

As they entered the farm, the smell of freshly turned soil filled the air, mingling with the sweet scent of ripened fruit. The sound of chirping birds overhead and the rustling of leaves underfoot added to the surreal experience—a stark contrast to the silence of their daily existence. Jean-Pierre squatted down, running his hands through the soft soil, feeling the life beneath his fingertips. He plucked a ripe tomato and took a bite, savoring the burst of flavor in his mouth. It was like tasting heaven after months of canned and rationed food.

The sound of snapping twigs behind them caused everyone to spin around, weapons ready. Marcus, his short dark hair standing on end, motioned for silence as he peered into the dense foliage. A pair of dark eyes stared back at them, and their journey took a dangerous turn.

Alice Winters, with her long dark hair and sharp intelligence, moved closer to Jean-Pierre, ready to protect him if needed. Eddie, the burly man with a shaved head and bushy beard, stepped forward, ready to defend the group against any threat. Dr. Olivia tended to her bag, ensuring she had what they needed for a confrontation. Sophia Reynolds, with her wavy blonde hair and soft features, closed her eyes in prayer, seeking guidance.

Overhead, crows cawed in the distance, adding to the tension that hung thick in the air. Antoine Dupont, his short dark hair, and piercing gaze drawn to the bountiful harvest, licked his lips, eyes darting between Jean-Pierre and the food. His mind was already formulating ways to use the chef's skills for his gain.

They spent hours on the farm, carefully picking and sorting the vegetables and fruits that could sustain them. The juicy tomatoes, crisp lettuce, and crunchy apples filled their buckets as they worked in harmony. Jean-Pierre's excitement was infectious, his salt-and-pepper hair reflecting the sunlight as he wiped the sweat from his brow. His passion for cooking seemed to fuel him as he instructed them on which crops to pick and how to handle them with care.

A sudden gust of wind sent leaves rustling, causing Marcus to glance nervously around. His pale face betrayed his concern as he watched Antoine's calculating eyes flicker between Jean-Pierre and the food. Despite being the leader, he trusted no one completely, always on guard against betrayal or danger.

Eddie Thompson, with his burly build and shaved head, grunted in satisfaction as he carried a heavy bucket of carrots back to the truck. His bushy beard bobbed up and down as he spoke to Jean-Pierre about the taste of the produce, eager for another gourmet meal. He rolled up his sleeves, ready to help chop and prepare the food.

Alice Winters, her long dark hair tied back in a ponytail, kept a wary eye on the surrounding area. She didn't trust easily, having seen too much death and destruction, but she couldn't deny the importance of this find. Her sharp intelligence and resourcefulness came into play as she observed the terrain, ensuring they wouldn't be ambushed.

The group worked together; their movements synchronized like a well-oiled machine. The sound of snapping twigs and rustling leaves filled the air as they moved through the orchard. The cool damp earth beneath their feet was a welcome change from the dry, barren desert wasteland they called home now. As they worked, Sophia noticed how Antoine's eyes never left Jean-Pierre, like a hawk watching its prey. She knew it wouldn't be long before he made his move.

The scent of freshly picked fruit mingled with sweat and dirt, creating a heady aroma that made everyone's mouths water. Alice's lips curled into a small smile at the thought of an actual feast tonight. But she couldn't shake the feeling that something was off.

Without warning, Antoine lunged at Jean-Pierre, knife in hand. He was fast, but Sophia was faster, catching his wrist before any harm could be done. A tense standoff ensued between them all. Alice sighed wearily, knowing they needed this food more than ever...

Eddie, oblivious to the tension, continued to gather apples with a contented hum on his lips. Dr. Martinez checked the pouch at her belt, ensuring she had enough medical supplies to treat any wounds. Sophia released Antoine, eyeing him warily.

Their harvest continued Jean-Pierre's passion for cooking driving them all onward. His fingers were stained purple from plucking grapes and his eyes were bright with excitement. He worked like a man possessed, lost in his art. Alice looked over her shoulder every few minutes, making sure they weren't followed. Her heart pounded in her chest as she heard whispers in the distance - other survivors seeking their newfound bounty.

The sun began to set, painting the sky in hues of orange and pink. They finally finished their task, heaving sighs of relief as they gathered around Jean-Pierre, who clutched a basket of ripe cherries to his chest. The juices stained his fingers red, making him look like a modern- day Prometheus.

As they walked back to camp, Sophia couldn't help but notice Eddie lingering behind, collecting as many mushrooms as he could find. She nudged him gently, reminding him of their limited supplies. He nodded, a sheepish grin on his face but not letting go of any of his prized finds.

Back at camp, they prepared a feast fit for kings: grilled venison, sautéed mushrooms, and a cherry tart so delicious it made their mouths water just thinking about it. Dr. Martinez looked at Jean-Pierre with newfound respect, her eyes shining with admiration. "This is incredible," she murmured between bites, her voice thick with awe.

But the festivities were cut short as they heard approaching footsteps. Quickly, they hid their food and weapons, preparing for battle. Sophia's heart raced as Jean-Pierre's panicked gaze darted around the camp. She could see the conflict on his face - protect his secrets or fight for his friends? He chose the latter, raising his fists and steeling himself for what was to come.

The intruders turned out to be a desperate group led by Marcus, who smirked when he saw their meal. "Well, well, well. Looks like we found the true treasure of this godforsaken place." His voice was silk-smooth, like oil pouring over gravel. Alfred Hitchcock's music played in the background.

"This is ours now," Antoine added cruelly, grabbing a piece of meat off the fire. Eddie and Sophia exchanged nervous glances, unsure how to react.

"I'm afraid not," Sophia replied coolly, her voice steady. She stepped in front of Marcus, ready to defend their hard work.

Eddie growled low in his throat, his muscles tense under his coat. "You can't just take what isn't yours," he warned, his voice deep and menacing.

Marcus laughed, a cold chill running down their spines. "We'll see about that."

The air crackled with tension, every movement slow and deliberate as they circled each other, ready to fight for survival. The smell of cooking meat filled the air, mingling with smoke and sweat. A taste of iron filled the atmosphere as swords clanged together.

Suddenly, Eddie lunged forward, sparks flying from his blade. Sophia raised her bow instinctively, aiming at Marcus's chest.

Dr. Martinez moved swiftly, pushing Marcus out of harm's way, her quick reflexes surprising everyone. "There must be another way," she pleaded softly, her voice barely above a whisper. The group stood still for a moment before Jean-Pierre spoke up.

"We can't just let them take our food," he stated firmly, his eyes hard as diamonds. "We have a responsibility to those who can't make it here."

Alice nodded in agreement, her salty ocean-blue eyes meeting Jean-Pierre's. She reached for her dagger hidden in her boot. "Together?" she asked quietly.

The five of them nodded in unison, forming a tight-knit defense. The battle was brutal but quick; they were well-practiced in survival. Swords clashed, arrows whistled through the air, and fists connected painfully. Antoine was the first to fall, a look of shock on his face as he hit the ground hard. The others backed off, realizing they were outmatched.

As they breathed heavily, panting, the group gathered around the fire once more, eyes darting between one another nervously. Sophia ran to check on Antoine's pulse; he was alive, but he wouldn't be causing trouble anytime soon. Dr. Martinez sighed in relief, shaking her head as she tended to his wounds.

Jean-Pierre's heart pounded wildly in his chest; it had been a close call. He wrapped his fingers around the handle of his knife tightly, the cool steel grounding him. Eddie grunted, "That was too close."

"We need to fortify this place," Sophia suggested, her voice shaky but determined. The others nodded in agreement. They scavenged for wooden planks and stones, creating a makeshift barrier around their find. Alice added thorny bushes to the top, ensuring any intruder would be met with resistance.

The night was quiet, the stars above twinkling like diamonds against the inky black sky. The smell of freshly cooked meat filled the air as Jean-

Pierre worked his magic in the kitchen, the taste of hope lingering on their tongues. The group ate heartily, savoring every bite.

They knew it wouldn't last forever but promised to make it count.

Eddie belched, his massive chest rising and falling as he wiped his mouth with a grin. "That was the best meal I've had in months."

Dr. Martinez sighed, staring into the dying embers of the fire. "We should get some rest," she said softly, yawning. "Tomorrow we'll continue exploring."

Sleep came quickly, wrapped in the comforting scent of woodsmoke and the sounds of crickets. Their dreams were filled with visions of full bellies and warm beds, a luxury they hadn't experienced in so long.

The next day, they ventured out once more, hearts heavy but hopeful. Jean-Pierre led the way, his mind racing with ideas for other tasty concoctions he could create. Alice walked hand in hand with Sophia, planning their escape route just in case. Eddie brought up the rear, humming a tune only he could hear. And Dr. Martinez? She was armed with a newfound determination to survive this hellish world and find a way back home.

As they approached the hidden valley, something fell off. The air was thick with unease, tension pulling at their skin like a second layer of clothing. Jean-Pierre slowed his pace, senses on high alert. He noticed footprints - too many to count - leading away from their precious find. His gut twisted into a knot, fearing the worst.

"They've found us," he whispered.

Alice cursed under her breath and drew her knife from its sheath, ready for a fight. Sophia closed her eyes, praying for guidance. Eddie's fists clenched, prepared for bloodshed. Dr. Martinez checked her pistol, making sure it was loaded. They couldn't let this discovery be taken away so easily.

Quietly, they crept towards the riverbank, weapons at the ready. And there they saw it: their stash of food was gone. The once-bountiful supply is now empty, leaving behind only disappointment and despair.

"We need to find out who did this," Antoine spat, his eyes darting around accusingly. "And make them pay."

But Jean-Pierre shook his head, eyes roaming the surrounding area. "No," he said firmly, "we need to survive. We can't risk losing each other over food."

Sophia nodded, her grip on his arm loosening slightly. "He's right," she agreed softly, "we need to find another source."

They set out once more, hearts heavy but heads held high. Each step brings them closer to an uncertain future. Jean-Pierre's mind worked overtime, trying to think of a solution. His heart ached for the loss but refused to give up. He needed to protect his friends, to ensure they survived this harsh new world.

As they trekked through the desolate landscape, Marcus remained unphased, his thoughts focused on maintaining control and power. Alice watched him warily, sensing his true intentions. They all did.

Finally, they stumbled upon an abandoned warehouse filled with canned goods and dried meats - a veritable feast. Relief washed over them until they realized they didn't have the means to carry it all back. It would have to be rationed and carefully measured out.

Days passed, hope fading into the distance, as they searched for more supplies. Starvation loomed large in their bellies, threatening to consume them whole. Until one day, Jean-Pierre returned from scavenging with a gleam in his eye. He'd found a squirrel, its tail twitching between his fingers. He skinned and cooked it over a makeshift fire, the aroma filling the air - tantalizing and tempting.

They all gathered around, eyes widening at the sight of the meal before them. The meat was juicy and tender, the flavor unlike anything they'd tasted in years. It was game-changing.

"We need to do this again," Jean-Pierre said firmly. "Start hunting. Protecting our food source is essential."

Dr. Martinez nodded solemnly. "Agreed."

And so, a new chapter in their lives began. The hunt for survival.

Meanwhile, Antoine watched them from afar, a wicked grin playing on his lips. He knew what they were capable of now - they could provide for themselves. He formulated a plan, one that would ensure his survival while destroying theirs.

One day, while Jean-Pierre was out hunting, Antoine struck. He led a group of desperate survivors to their camp, promising them food and shelter. Marcus, ever the opportunist, welcomed them with open arms. But as night fell, tensions rose as Jean-Pierre's absence became apparent. They eyed each other warily, suspicions confirmed when the intruders began helping themselves to their meager supplies.

Alice and Eddie readied for battle while Sophia tried reasoning with the outsiders. Dr. Martinez tended to the wounded. Marcus stood back, the smug smile never leaving his face.

The air was thick with tension and the sound of weapons being drawn near. The scent of rain mixed with fear and adrenaline. A sharp retort echoed off the concrete walls, followed by the clatter of metal against metal. Gunfire rang out, ricocheting through the silence.

Bullets whizzed past heads, forcing the intruders to retreat. The group emerged battered but victorious.

Tears streamed down Sophia's face as she tended to the injured; Eddie's hands shook with rage. Alice's heart raced, her knuckles white on her gun. They huddled closer together, weary from the fight but determined to rebuild. The sound of their breathing was heavy and labored, filling the silent air with raspy exhales.

The next day, they buried their dead and mourned their losses. Not all could be saved. They needed to move on, to find a new sanctuary before another attack came. The thought of leaving this place was bitter-sweet, memories of joy and pain etched into its walls. But they knew they couldn't stay - not now, not after what had happened.

As they packed up, Marcus's gaze lingered on the farm, calculating how much food they could carry and how long it would last. Jean-Pierre returned, his face drawn and haggard, carrying only game he had hunted. His eyes met Sophia's pleadingly before he turned away, his jaw clenched tight. She understood his pain but also his desperation.

They set off, trudging through the mud and debris left by the storm, their boots heavy against the ground. Jean-Pierre led the way, his nose filling with the scent of earth and smoke. Eddie brought up the rear, his muscles aching from the long night's vigil. Alice scanned the horizon, her rifle ready.

The group stands guard, their senses heightened, ready to defend their territory against those who would try to steal their hope and sustenance. The night is long and fraught with tension, the group taking turns keeping watch, their eyes scanning the horizon for any signs of approaching danger. Dr. Martinez checks wounds and tends to the injured, trying to keep up their morale. Finally, the sun rises, painting the sky golden hues that match their weary hearts. They set off again, back to the ruins of their old lives where they hope to find new purpose and sanctuary.

Reaching the ruins, they find their defenses intact, their hard work paying off. Relief washes over them like the cool, morning breeze that caresses their skin. Eddie slaps Jean-Pierre on the back, appreciative of the feast to come. Antoine smirks, calculating his next move.

Sophia looks nervously at Jean-Pierre, fearing what he'll cook next. Marcus watches from afar, his mind already scheming for ways to control the situation.

The group works together like a well-oiled machine, harvesting the crops and tending to injured animals. Jean-Pierre's mind races with ideas, his creativity sparked by the abundance of fresh ingredients, each one a potential masterpiece waiting to be created. He glances at Alice, whose eyes are filled with doubt, but she nods nonetheless, trusting his culinary expertise. Eddie carries baskets of produce to the makeshift kitchen, drooling at the thought of a hearty meal that will fuel them for days. Dr. Martinez sets about preserving what they can, her heart heavy with the knowledge that it might not be enough. Sophia collects eggs from the chicken coop, wincing at the sound of breaking shells.

The kitchen fills with the aromas of roasting vegetables and sizzling meats, filling the air with promise and comfort. Jean-Pierre adds herbs and spices, creating flavors that dance on the tongue. Marcus watches, his stomach grumbling in anticipation, his mind already on how to ration out meals for maximum efficiency. Antoine watches too, his eyebrows raised in surprise at the decadence of it all. Sophia helps Alice wash dishes, whispering reassurances about their survival and the goodness within them. Eddie chops wood, oblivious to the tension brewing around him. Dr. Martinez makes the rounds, distributing medicine and offering words of encouragement.

Feast time arrives, and laughter rings out as they savor Jean-Pierre's creations, their hunger sated after months of scarcity. Marcus cleans his plate like a king, eyeing the remaining food with greed. Antoine eyes Jean-Pierre warily, sensing an opportunity amidst the contentment. Eddie's belly protrudes from the feast, promising to protect their newfound treasure. Sophia's eyes sparkle with joy, grateful for the moment of peace. Dr. Martinez sighs, knowing this couldn't last forever.

Days pass, and the farm thrives under their care. Jean-Pierre's experiments grew bolder, using less palatable ingredients to feed the group. Alice watches warily, her skepticism fading as she sees their strength grow. Sophia nudges Dr. Martinez, discussing alternatives to their current diet. Eddie's muscles ache from hauling water, grateful for the protein boost. Marcus counts his silver, scheming new ways to maintain control. Antoine bides his time, waiting for the perfect moment to strike.

The air is thick with tension and the scent of thyme-roasted herbs. The crunch of vegetables beneath teeth and the hiss of steam escaping kettles fills the silent cracks in their conversation. The murmur of the fireplace provides a soothing background score to life in this strange new reality where food is no longer a luxury but a necessity. Antoine leans closer to Marcus, his plans forming like droplets of rain in a storm cloud, promising to unleash chaos upon them all.

One day, as Jean-Pierre surveys his latest creation - a rich stew made from roadkill and wild herbs, he has an epiphany. He turns to the group, "I need your help." His voice carries a sense of urgency that stops them in their tracks. "This farm won't last forever." He gestures towards the patchwork of crops and livestock, "We need to expand our horizons."

Eddie rubs his belly, already anticipating the next meal, "You got it, boss." Marcus eyes him suspiciously, "How do you suggest we do that?"

Jean-Pierre's eyes gleam, "We strike out into the wasteland." Sophia's face falls, "But it's dangerous."

Antoine grins, "We're already eating questionable meat. What's a little risk?" Dr. Martinez shrugs, "At least we'll have fresh ingredients."

Alice hesitates before nodding, "Fine, but we need a plan."

And so, they do. They venture out into the desolate lands, armed and ready for battle. Jean- Pierre's mind races with ideas, his creativity sparked by the abundance of fresh ingredients, each one a potential masterpiece waiting to be created. The taste of victory is in the air as they forage for more food. But as they journey deeper into the unknown, they stumble upon a danger they could never have imagined.

They spot it on the horizon - a pack of ravenous beasts, their eyes glinting in the sun. The pack closes in, and Jean-Pierre realizes they're too late to turn back. He grabs a nearby rock, ready to defend himself and his companions. The beasts are upon them; they close in, teeth bared, and claws extended.

There's a deafening roar and a sudden flash of light. The beasts scatter like ants from a kicked-over hill. Standing before them is a colossal creature - a cyborg grizzly bear with glowing red eyes. It snorts, "I am Cybotar. You won't harm my territory."

The group exchanges wary glances. Jean-Pierre steps forward, "We meant no harm." He holds out his hands in surrender. "We're just searching for food."

Cybotar eyes them warily, "Intriguing. I too, hunger." Its mechanical footsteps echo as it leads them deeper into the wasteland. They approach an abandoned research facility where the cybernetic beast feeds on the leftover scraps from humanity's experiments gone wrong. "This is where I call home," Cybotar growls.

They gather around a table laden with strange fruits, vegetables, and meats - a feast fit for kings. Jean-Pierre's mouth watered, tasting the unexpected. "Judas roots, despair berries, and zombie flesh." He mutters under his breath. His mind whirls with ideas. What other secrets could this wasteland hold?

CHAPTER 9

The group of survivors sat around the crackling campfire, their bellies full and warmth radiating off them in the cold night air. The aroma of freshly cooked meat filled the space between them, mingling with the smoky scent of the burning logs beneath it. Alice Winters watched as Jean-Pierre lifted another golden-brown hunk of meat from the fire with his knife, carefully flipping it to sear the other side, a satisfied grin spreading across his face. She couldn't help but feel a pang of hunger herself as she inhaled the tantalizing scent, her stomach rumbling in response. It had been too long since they'd enjoyed a meal like this - not made from ration bars or canned goods, but from freshly killed game, roasted to perfection over an open flame.

"Ah, this is living," Jean-Pierre said with a satisfied sigh, turning to look at his companions. "I tell you, my friends, there's nothing quite like a well-cooked meal to lift the spirits."

Eddie Thompson let out a hearty laugh, his wide girth shaking as he slapped his knee. "You're not wrong about that, Jean-Pierre. Your skills in the kitchen are unparalleled." He reached for another piece of meat and bit into it greedily, chewing with a sense of satisfaction that was almost audible.

Alice couldn't help but feel a twinge of guilt as she watched them enjoy the meal. She knew where the meat came from - the undead creatures that lurked in the nearby forest, their decaying flesh providing a sustenance they wouldn't have found otherwise. But she also knew the moral implications of their actions, the lines they were crossing to survive in this brutally new world.

"So, what do you think, Alice?" Jean-Pierre asked, turning to her with a grin. "Not bad, right?"

She forced a smile, taking a small bite of the meat. It was tender and juicy, melting in her mouth, but she couldn't shake the image of the zombies they'd been forced to kill to procure it. "It's good," she said truthfully. "But I can't help but wonder if we're playing with fire here."

Eddie shot her a look of confusion. "What do you mean?"

"We're attracting attention," she explained, gesturing vaguely at the smoke billowing from the fire. "How many times have we had to fight off groups of survivors who claim they were just looking for food, but turned out to be after something else entirely?"

Eddie shrugged, his bushy beard bobbing up and down. "I get what you're saying, Alice, but we're in a tough spot. Survival comes first, right? And if we don't eat, we won't last long enough to worry about anyone else's morals."

"I agree with Eddie," said Rachel, a young woman with curly hair and a determined glint in her eyes. "Besides, we've already scouted the area. No signs of any other survivors nearby."

Alice sighed, her stomach growling in protest. She would have to trust them... for now.

Meanwhile, Jean-Pierre sat back, watching the fire dance in his eyes. "I think it's time we had a proper meeting about this," he said, his voice deep and thoughtful. "Not just us but invite other survivors too. Let's hear what they have to say, what they know about the threats we might face."

Dr. Martinez nodded reluctantly. "I think that's a good idea," she said, her brow furrowing. "We should discuss this as a group and come to a consensus."

The meeting was held under the scorching sun in the center of their camp. Survivors gathered around, some curious, others wary. Jean-Pierre stood at the front, holding a large piece of charred meat on a stick, still sizzling from the fire. "We've found a way to survive," he began, waving the meat in the air. "A way to cook without using zombie meat. But it comes with risks." He took a bite and chewed slowly, savoring the taste.

"Eddie's right," Alice chimed in. "We're in danger just by being alive. If word gets out, we could attract unwanted attention."

A few people gasped at the thought, while others nodded in agreement. Dr. Martinez mentally noted those who looked concerned and who seemed more preoccupied with their stomachs.

A middle-aged man named Tom spoke up. "But what if we can't survive without it?" he asked, his voice trembling slightly. "I've tried everything, and nothing compares to zombie meat's taste."

Eddie scoffed. "That's not true," he retorted. "We need to try something else." He gestured towards an open field where crops grew abundantly. "What about those? We could farm them."

The group turned towards Eddie, surprised. It was an idea they hadn't considered before.

Dr. Martinez stepped forward, her eyes narrowing. "We need to be realistic," she said. "Those crops won't sustain us long-term. We need a reliable source of food."

A young woman named Sarah raised her hand. "What about fishing?" she asked eagerly. "There's a lake nearby."

Everyone looked at each other, weighing the pros and cons. It was risky but worth a shot.

As they discussed, Jean-Pierre played with his creation, twirling it around in the fire's flames. The smell of charred flesh filled the air, making stomachs grumble. He held up a plate of freshly baked bread, still warm from the embers. "Try this," he said, offering it around. The soft, crusty texture and sweet taste surprised everyone; they hadn't known such flavors existed in this new world.

Slowly, they found common ground. They would continue to explore alternatives and only resort to zombie meat as a last resort. They would also be more cautious about attracting attention to their camp. The meeting concluded with a sense of hope as they dispersed to gather supplies and plan for their new ventures.

Day 10: The group set out towards the closest farm, led by Marcus and Sophia. Jean-Pierre stayed back, his mind whirring with new recipes. He missed the zombie meat, but he knew this was the right decision. They had to adapt or face starvation. As they approached the farm, they heard gunshots in the distance. Their hearts sank; another group was likely in trouble.

Marcus signaled for silence and crept forward, peering through the tall grass. He signaled for the group to stay put before dashing off alone. Minutes later, he returned with a man named Greg and his small group. Greg had heard about Jean-Pierre's cooking and couldn't wait to taste it.

"My people are starving," he pleaded, his eyes on the chef's creation. "They'll do anything for a good meal."

Jean-Pierre politely declined, explaining that they were looking for alternative food sources that didn't involve using zombie meat. It pained him to refuse, but he had to uphold their agreement. Greg's disappointment was clear, and the tension in the air thickened.

The group started walking again when a loud snap echoed through the trees. They froze, weapons at the ready, senses heightened. A zombie shuffled out; its eyes fixed on the fresh meat sizzling on the fire. Eddie lunged forward; axe raised. The others followed suit, ready to defend their newfound morality.

But the creature was different - faster, stronger. It lunged at them before they could react. Jean-Pierre, ever resourceful, leaped into action. He dodged the blow and stabbed it through the heart with his trusty knife. Its putrid blood splattered on his sleeve as it collapsed.

A moment of silence ensued before they all shared a look of relief mixed with disgust. This was the harsh reality they lived in now: kill or be killed. They harvested the meat and moved on, grateful for the fresh protein but troubled by their actions.

They found an abandoned convenience store and decided to split up. Alice and Sophia checked the shelves for supplies while Dr. Martinez and Antoine started a fire to cook the zombie meat. Eddie stood guard outside with his shotgun, keeping watch for any threats.

Inside, Alice found canned goods and bottled water; Sophia discovered some books on foraging. Their spirits lifted until they heard Antoine retching outside. Marcus's voice drifted in: "We need to eat." They joined him to see him recovering from the fire.

The zombie meat smelled rancid, and the taste was no better. Jean-Pierre felt a pang of guilt as he saw the pained expressions on Sophia and Dr. Martinez's faces. But Marcus insisted they needed the calories. Reluctantly, they ate.

As they moved on, Jean-Pierre's mind raced. He needed to find more sustainable food sources or risk losing credibility within the group. He glanced at Alice, noticing her sharp eyes and quick reflexes. Maybe she had an idea.

"Hey Alice," he began, "think you could help me find some traps or hunting spots?"

She eyed him warily but agreed, "If it's for the group." Her gaze flickered towards Eddie, trusting him the most.

They ventured deeper into the city. Jean-Pierre showed her a grocery store with an intact freezer section. "We might be able to catch fish or lobster," he suggested. She nodded thoughtfully but raised her eyebrows skeptically.

They set out traps and scouted for fishing spots, their boots crunching on shattered glass and debris. As they walked, Jean-Pierre shared his vision for a haven. Alice listened carefully, taking in information but remaining cautious.

Their search led them to an apartment complex. Inside, they found a well-stocked kitchen and a lone survivor named Greg. He smiled broadly upon seeing them, his eyes fixating on Jean-Pierre's cooking skills.

"I've heard about your dishes," he said hungrily, "and I want a taste."

Alice tensed, her hand moving closer to her knife. This man didn't seem trustworthy. But Jean-Pierre politely declined, explaining their mission to find alternatives to zombie meat. Greg scoffed and demanded they share their food.

Torn between survival and safety, Jean-Pierre hesitated until Alice stepped in. "We can use some help," she said, gesturing towards their catch. Her voice was calm yet firm.

Reluctantly, Greg agreed to join them at their campfire.

As they cooked dinner, the aroma filled the air: seared salmon and roasted vegetables. Alice couldn't help but notice Greg's greed as he eyed their meal. He grew impatient and snarled, "Where's the zombie meat?"

"We've found other sources," Alice responded coolly, slicing into the salmon. She offered him a taste, and he hesitantly tried it. His eyes widened in surprise, and he devoured the food.

"Not bad," he muttered before reaching for another helping. The group relaxed slightly; hopeful their meeting wouldn't turn violent.

However, when darkness fell, Greg's true colors emerged. He made advances toward Jean- Pierre, demanding more recipes. Alice rose, her body language protective of the group.

"We don't need your help if you're going to be a problem," she warned, her voice low and threatening.

Greg sneered, "I won't be the only one taking what I want." His men moved towards them.

Alice sprang into action, drawing her knife as Eddie and Jean-Pierre readied themselves. She lunged at Greg, knocking him back with a well-placed kick while Eddie and Jean-Pierre neutralized the others. The fight was fierce but brief; they emerged unscathed.

Panting heavily, Alice glanced at Jean-Pierre. "We should head back," she said decisively. He nodded gratefully and began packing up camp.

As they left, Alice turned back, meeting Greg's gaze. "This isn't over." He growled in agreement.

Back at their camp, tensions were high. Eddie huffed, "We can't keep hiding forever," while Sophia worried about the moral implications of using such extreme methods for survival. Dr. Martinez laid out their options: finding new food sources or risking their safety for ethics. Jean-Pierre paced, distraught over his dilemma: his passion for cooking vs. protecting his creations.

Alice listened intently then spoke up, "We need to split shifts to secure food. We'll share part of our catch with them to maintain peace." Her eyes met Jean-Pierre's, a silent promise of support.

With unease, he nodded in agreement. Antoine smirked, sensing an opportunity to exploit their weakness. He whispered to Marcus, "We should use this to our advantage."

Marcus hesitated before replying, "We'll discuss it later." The air thickened with suspicion.

Days passed without incident until one night, they heard commotion outside the perimeter fence. Heart racing, they rushed to find Greg and his men, armed and ready to seize what they believed was rightfully theirs. As they argued, Sophia stepped in, begging for peace.

"Please," she pleaded, "we can't afford violence."

Antoine whispered to Marcus again, and he nodded grimly. The gates opened under Antoine's watchful gaze. With a mixture of fear and desperation, Greg's group stormed through. Sophia tried to reason while Eddie tensed up his muscles.

Alice watched warily as they approached Jean-Pierre's kitchen area. Greg smirked arrogantly, "So, you think your secrets are safe?"

Jean-Pierre stood tall but trembled inside. "No one owns a recipe," he retorted bravely. Eddie stepped forward, "But you can't control what happens to 'em once they leave here."

Greg lunged towards him, but Alice blocked his path coolly, "No one's taking anything by force." She held out some canned goods as a peace offering. Surprised but curious, they accepted.

Sophia led them to the dining hall where hungry glares turned into surprise tweaks of lips at the taste of real food. Jean-Pierre's creations were a welcome change from stale cans and rotten meat. Conversation ebbed and flowed between both groups, revealing shared struggles and hardships. Marcus beamed, "This is better than any palace feast."

However, Alice noticed Antoine's glint in his eyes; he was planning something sinister. She pulled Jean-Pierre aside, "We need to be vigilant."

He nodded silently, still shaken by the encounter. As they left, Eddie whispered to Sophia, "We'll protect him." She smiled gratefully.

Back at their camp, Jean-Pierre couldn't focus on cooking due to his mixed emotions: guilt over using human flesh and fear of losing his creations. Antoine grinned maliciously, cracking his knuckles. *The taste of revenge is sweet, it's time to take what's ours. *

The following days were tense, Sophia came up with a plan—a system of trust within their community. Only a few would know Jean-Pierre's full recipes and those chosen would aid in cooking duties. Sarah was excellent at preserving food; Antoine would train others on hunting. Eddie exchanged recipes for security shifts; Marcus agreed to educate the group on irrigation systems. Alice took charge of rationing, ensuring everyone had enough without revealing their source. Jean-Pierre watched skeptically but eventually joined the group effort. Sophia smiled reassuringly, "Together, we can keep our secrets and feed our people."

They worked tirelessly, creating makeshift gardens and foraging areas to supplement Caroline's meager crops. Sophia's empathy was unwavering, even as she witnessed firsthand the lengths, they went to maintain their newfound 'luxuries.' One night under a star-speckled sky, they sat around a crackling fire sharing stories of their past lives. Tears mingled with laughter as they connected over lost loves and dreams. Sophia glanced at Jean- Pierre, wondering how he landed in such dire straits; she hoped he'd find solace among them.

Jean-Pierre hesitantly joined in, his eyes sparkling as he spoke of Parisian patisseries and family gatherings around lavish tables. A pang of guilt struck Sophia, but she remained supportive. Marcus leaned towards him, clasping a calloused hand, "We got you."

In the kitchen, Sophia taught Alice how to make soup from a vegetable nobody wanted but tasted delicious when combined with wild herbs. The tangy aroma filled the air, making stomachs growl. Antoine perfected venison stew that rivaled his grandmother's recipe, and Jean-Pierre's baking skills transformed bland grains into decadent treats. They swapped secrets, sharing laughter and camaraderie while protecting their most prized possession: hope.

Days blended into weeks, winter's chill set in, and Sophia worried. They had enough for now, but what about the harsher season? That night, she met with Jean-Pierre. She held his hands across the fire, eyes searching his, "If things get dire, would you consider teaching us your methods?" He rubbed his chin, considering. "For survival," she added softly. He nodded, reluctantly. They agreed on a time and place, and Sophia returned to her group, feeling both anxious and triumphant.

As snowflakes danced around them, they gathered around Jean-Pierre. He unveiled his tricks: preserving techniques using salt and sugar and extending shelf life with citrus peels. Eager students scribbled notes as he demonstrated pickling cucumbers. Sophia marveled at his wit; despite their differences, they were united in survival. Jean-Pierre's eyes met hers, filled with sadness, but also gratitude. She squeezed his hand, offering silent understanding.

The villagers had hope again - all because of soup, stew, bread, pickles...and kindness.

Weeks passed, and Sophia's idea took hold. They established a system of trust within their community, where only a select few were allowed to know the full details of Jean-Pierre's recipes. They began to thrive, growing more confident in their journey ahead. Eddie, strong yet gullible, volunteered as their liaison with other survivors, carefully vetting them before inviting them to join their community. Newcomers brought stories of hardship and despair, but also hope for companionship and shared resources. They welcomed those with valuable skills, like a blacksmith and a hunter.

Yet, danger lurked. A group of marauders threatened their peace, demanding food. Sophia stood her ground, reminding them of their hard-earned trust and fearing for Jean-Pierre's secrets. The battle ensued; blades clashed, and arrows whizzed past ears. Eddie swung his ax at an intruder, shattering bones beneath his beard. Blood stained the snow red as the marauders retreated. The survivors stood victorious yet battered, breaths heaving in unison.

They realized their journey was far from over; challenges still lay ahead. Years of friendship, shared meals, and hardship had forged an unbreakable bond. They embraced, tears freezing on their cheeks, vowing to protect each other and their newfound home.

Inside, warmth radiated from the fireplace as Jean-Pierre tended to his cooking pot. His secret recipes simmered, filling the air with tantalizing aromas of stew and pickles. Eddie, ever faithful to his friend's creations, salivated at the scent. He wiped the sweat from his brow, thinking of heartier times when they ate without worry.

As night fell, they shared stories around the fire, recounting their trials and triumphs while munching on stale bread. The children slept soundly in the corner as adults whispered survival plans. They knew they couldn't keep this idyllic life isolated forever, but for now, it was enough.

Morning came, and they set off to hunt and gather their daily sustenance. Eddie's heart swelled with pride as he watched them work together, their movements fluid and purposeful. They were a family now - a family that would survive anything life threw their way.

A howl pierced the air, causing them all to stop momentarily but they continued forward, stronger than ever before. They had survived the attack; they would face whatever came next.

CHAPTER 10

Jean-Pierre and his group of survivors were returning to their camp, their arms laden with supplies, their spirits high from a successful scavenging mission. The sun was beginning to set over the desolate landscape, casting long shadows across the ground as they trudged through the rubble of what was once a bustling city. The air was thick with the smell of decay and rot, but it did little to dampen their mood. They chattered excitedly among themselves, their laughter carrying on the wind that rustled through the abandoned buildings like a mournful lullaby. As they approached their camp, voices grew hushed, anticipation filling the air. They could hear the soft hiss of a fire crackling in the distance and smell the aroma of cooking meat blending with the acrid scent of smoke. Their stomachs growled in unison, reminding them of how long it had been since they'd had a proper meal.

Suddenly, a group of people emerged from the shadows, led by Marcus Devereaux - a wealthy and charismatic leader who exuded an air of luxury. His dark hair was slicked back meticulously, and his sharp eyes scanned the area with a sense of calculation that left no doubt about his intentions. He approached with purpose, his group following close behind. Jean-Pierre's heart skipped a beat as he recognized the man from his dreams; the one who had promised him riches beyond his wildest imagination if he joined forces. Marc's lips curled into a smug smile as he surveyed the meager camp, taking in every detail - from the tattered tents to the makeshift pots and pans.

"Look what we've found," he said, his voice smooth as silk. "A group of survivors who've managed to eke out an existence despite everything." His eyes lingered on Jean-Pierre, a predatory gleam in them. "You must be the one they call Chef."

Jean-Pierre forced himself to stand tall, though his knees trembled under the weight of Marcus's intense scrutiny. He nodded mutely, unable to find words as the other man's group surrounded him. They were well-dressed and groomed, their weapons glinting in the dim light, in stark contrast to his ragged clothes and dirty hands. But it was their leader's flattery that unnerved him the most.

"Your cooking skills are just what we need," Marcus continued. "We can offer you more than just food and shelter; we can give you a life worth living. A chance to experience the finer things in life once again."

The other members of the group nodded in agreement; their eyes hungry for anything that resembled luxury. Jean-Pierre felt his stomach churn at the thought of leaving his friends behind, but the promise of safety and comfort was too much to resist. As Marcus held out a hand, offering a partnership, Jean-Pierre hesitated before finally taking it, sealing his fate.

From that day forward, life changed for Jean-Pierre. He found himself living in a secure compound with gourmet ingredients and proper tools, cooking sumptuous meals for these strange people who seemed to worship him as a god among men. But there was an undercurrent of danger beneath their polished facade; he couldn't shake the feeling that he'd traded one nightmare for another.

Despite this, he continued to cook, pushing his doubts aside as he created dish after dish that earned him their praise and admiration. His fingers moved nimbly over the food, seasoning, and sautéing with a skill that belied his rough upbringing, and soon enough, word of his culinary prowess spread beyond their small community. Marcus had plans for Jean-Pierre's talents, plans that involved bartering with other survivor groups for even more extravagant ingredients and equipment.

But as Jean-Pierre's popularity grew, so did his unease. He knew that Marcus's promises were just that—empty words used to lure him in. And when Marcus's true intentions finally became clear—enslaving those weaker or less useful than himself—it was too late. Jean- Pierre found himself caught up in something he couldn't control, bound by hunger and fear... until one fateful day when an opportunity for escape presented itself.]

The sun was setting, bathing the forest in hues of red and orange, casting long shadows across the ground as Marcus Devereaux led his group toward Jean-Pierre's camp. His eyes scanned the area, taking in every detail - the rustling leaves, the crackling fire, the sounds of laughter and conversation drifting on the breeze. He could smell it before he saw it: smoke curling from the campfire, mixing with the damp earthy scent of autumn. His mouth watered at the delicious aroma wafting through the air. Hungry stomachs grumbled in anticipation of whatever culinary masterpiece Jean-Pierre had conjured from their meager supplies.

Marcus Devereaux was different from the others. His hair was slicked back with just the right amount of product, his clothes immaculately tailored even in these dire times. Sharp eyes took in everything, missing nothing as he approached Jean-Pierre's camp, his footsteps crunching on dry leaves underfoot. His group followed silently, their eyes wide with wonder at this chance encounter. They didn't know it yet, but their lives were about to change forever.

As they drew closer, Marcus's nostrils flared, taking in deep breaths of that tantalizing scent. He couldn't believe his luck when he saw Jean-Pierre standing by the fire, a grin spreading across his face. "Well, well," Marcus drawled, his voice smooth as butter, "look what the cat dragged in."

Jean-Pierre glanced up, surprise registering on his face before he schooled his features into a neutral expression. "Good afternoon," he said warily.

Marcus chuckled and waved away the offer of food. "Not here for that," he said, his gaze fixed on the sizzling stew bubbling in the pot. "But I must say, your cooking smells divine."

A look of pride flashed across Jean-Pierre's face, and Marcus knew he had him. He leaned in closer, inhaling deeply. "That's not just any old stew you've got there, is it?"

Jean-Pierre shrugged nonchalantly. "Just some herbs and spices, nothing fancy."

Marcus shook his head. "Don't be modest," he said, his tone full of admiration. "It's not every day you find someone who can make a gourmet meal out of zombie meat."

Jean-Pierre's eyes widened in surprise. "Zombie meat?"

Marcus nodded, his gaze never leaving the stew. "Oh yes," he said, his voice low and hypnotic, "it adds a unique flavor, don't you think?"

Jean-Pierre hesitated, unsure of what to make of this man who seemed so at ease with the notion of eating such a thing. But Marcus didn't give him time to dwell on it. "Listen, my friend," he continued, "we've been struggling to maintain our lifestyle since the outbreak. I'm sure you've felt the same way. We used to have everything at our fingertips, but now we're scavenging for scraps."

"We found a community," Marcus continued, "a haven where we can live in luxury once again. Fresh ingredients, clean water, and even electricity." He paused dramatically. "I think you would be an asset to us."

"An asset?" Jean-Pierre repeated, his voice barely above a whisper.

Marcus nodded. "Indeed," he said confidently, "you could be our exclusive chef. Think of it - all the rare ingredients we can get our hands on, all the dishes you could create."

Jean-Pierre felt himself drawn in by the prospect. He knew the value of food in these times; it was scarce and precious. And here was someone offering something more than just survival. They were offering a life. But there was something about the idea of using zombie meat that niggled at him, something he couldn't shake off. He took a deep breath, trying to clear his head.

"What do you say?" Marcus pressed; his eyes boring into Jean-Pierre's.

The young man hesitated, his mind reeling with the possibilities. On one hand, he could continue living hand-to-mouth, scrounging for food and hiding from the undead monsters that roamed the earth. On the other, he could have stability, security, and maybe even a chance at reclaiming some semblance of a normal life. He took one last look at the half-eaten brain in front of him before making his decision.

"I accept your offer," Jean-Pierre said finally.

Marcus clapped him on the back, his eyes sparkling with excitement. "Welcome to the ranks, my friend."

The members of the group cheered, their voices echoing off the abandoned storefronts that surrounded them. Marcus pulled him closer, whispering in his ear, "You'll find that we have our ways of acquiring ingredients. None of us are ones to judge, not when we're fighting for survival."

His words sent a shiver down Jean-Pierre's spine; he wasn't sure if it was from fear or anticipation. He knew he had made his choice, but he also knew it wouldn't be easy. As they walked back to their camp, the smell of freshly cooked meat filled the air, making his stomach growl in hunger. The taste of succulent zombie flesh danced on his tongue, making it hard to ignore the sacrifices he would have to make.

Inside the camp, it was a chaotic mix of people going about their daily routines - hunting trips, traps being checked, weapons being sharpened. They regarded him with curiosity and wariness, unsure of this stranger among them. But Marcus led him straight to a small kitchen area where pots and pans were scattered around and introduced him to the others.

"This is Jean-Pierre," he said grandly, "our newest member and our chef extraordinaire."

There was an immediate buzz of excitement as they surrounded him, asking about his cooking style, his favorite dishes, and what kind of meals he could whip up for them. Marcus nudged him gently, urging him to answer their questions. It felt strange, to be the center of attention after so long in hiding. His eyes darted around nervously, taking in everything: the tidy kitchen with its shiny pots and pans, and the abundance of fresh vegetables and fruits that he had only read about before. He hadn't realized how much he missed this - the smell of food being prepared, the sound of laughter and chatter filling the air.

"I'll need time," he said finally, breaking away from their eager gazes. "To get used to everything. To experiment."

Marcus nodded approvingly. "Take all the time you need. We'll protect you while you scavenge for ingredients; we have access to resources you've never dreamed of."

The promise was intoxicating; he couldn't deny it. Jean-Pierre followed Marcus as he led him through rows of neatly organized tents, each one equipped with luxuries he had never seen outside of a magazine spread. They reached a large tent at the back, where there were shelves upon shelves filled with exotic spices and condiments, and jars of preserves and sauces. It was like walking into a gourmet food store from another world. Marcus pulled out a bottle of rare red wine from France, smiling triumphantly.

"This is just the beginning," he said, his eyes glinting. "Think of what we can create together."

Jean-Pierre swallowed hard, feeling his resolve slipping away. He imagined himself cooking complex dishes with these rare, precious ingredients, feeding people who looked up to him in awe. He could almost taste the excitement of their first bite. Maybe this was his new purpose after all.

But then he thought of Alice Winters, the resourceful and resilient young woman with her long, dark hair and sharp, intelligent eyes. She had joined them a few days ago, having survived on her own in the wasteland. Despite her initial skepticism of his methods, she respected his culinary skills and had even helped him procure some ingredients once or twice. He remembered how she would run her fingers over the soft petals of a rose she plucked from an abandoned garden, marveling at their beauty despite the horrors around them. She would never approve of this.

And then there was Dr. Olivia Martinez, the petite, middle-aged woman with greying hair tied back in a bun who had become the group's medic. She too had voiced her concerns about using zombie meat, emphasizing the need for alternative food sources. She had mentioned something about a nearby farm; he should have listened more closely to her ideas.

Inside, Jean-Pierre felt his insides churn. He wanted to belong, to be part of something bigger than himself, but at what cost? Could he ignore his moral compass for the sake of survival?

As he walked out of the tent, his stomach churning, he saw Alice watching him from a distance. Her eyes were guarded but concerned. He could almost hear her voice in his head, reminding him of the cost of compromise. But Marcus's group was offering an opportunity he couldn't ignore.

He sat down beside her, forcing a smile. "I'm not sure if I can do it," he admitted softly. "They don't understand my concerns."

Alice took his hand in hers, her grip strong despite her delicate features. "They don't have to," she said firmly. "You do. And we support you."

Dr. Martinez joined them, her expression grave. "We'll find another way," she promised, squeezing his shoulder gently. "We always do."

They were right. He knew they were right. But the temptation of belonging was strong, and the taste of the zombie stew lingered on his tongue. He closed his eyes, trying to clear his mind, but all he could taste was the metallic tang of blood mingled with the rich, gamey flavor of roasted zombie meat.

Marcus's group's demands grew louder as the day wore on. Their stomachs grumbled; their impatience palpable. Jean-Pierre could feel their eyes on him, expectant. He steeled himself, knowing what he had to do.

He walked into the camp, shoulders squared, and showed them his latest creation: a zombie stew concoction that even he couldn't stomach. There was a collective groan of disappointment from the group. Marcus's voice cut through the silence. "You're wasting your talent. We need something more substantial."

Jean-Pierre's heart raced as he faced them down. "I can't," he said firmly. "I won't compromise my principles for a full belly."

The group's leader glared at him, his mouth twisting into a snarl. "Fine. Be that way," he spat, turning away. The others followed suit, and Jean-Pierre breathed a sigh of relief. He'd done it. He'd stood up against them, for Alice and Dr. Martinez, for himself. Even if it meant going hungry tonight.

But as night fell, the hunger gnawed at his insides like a ravenous beast. He could hear Marcus's group devouring their meal: the juicy chews and slurps, the satisfied moans. It was too much. His stomach grumbled, begging for sustenance. He thought of the zombie flesh he'd tasted earlier; how tender and flavorful it had been. How it had melted in his mouth like butter.

He paced back and forth, wrestling with his conscience. Alice and Dr. Martinez watched him worriedly, sensing his inner turmoil. They knew he was strong-willed, but even they couldn't predict how far he would go. The air hung heavy with tension, filled with the scent of roasted zombie meat that tantalized his senses.

Finally, he stopped and turned to them. "I can't," he said again, more softly this time. "I won't give in. We'll find another way."

Alice nodded, her brown eyes fierce with determination. "We will," she promised. "We'll find a way to sustain ourselves without resorting to cannibalism."

Dr. Martinez laid a hand on his shoulder, his kind eyes filled with concern. "We believe in you, Jean-Pierre. We know you can do this."

He took a deep breath and nodded. He had to stay true to himself and his beliefs. It wasn't worth compromising his values for the sake of survival, no matter how tempting the offer. As he turned to leave, he felt Marcus's gaze on him, weighing him up like a prize animal at an auction block. But he didn't care. He had made his decision.

He returned to his small campfire, a bead of sweat trickling down his forehead, and began to gather the few ingredients he had left: some dry rice, a handful of herbs, and a small piece of dried meat. He would make do with what he had, despite the pangs of hunger that gnawed at his insides. The night grew darker and more oppressive, the sounds of the group's feasting haunting him. But he wouldn't give in. He wouldn't betray his principles for the fleeting comfort of a full stomach.

Marcus approached him later, a sly smile playing on his lips. "You sure you won't change your mind?" he purred like a predator.

But Jean-Pierre remained steadfast, shaking his head. "I won't."

Alice and Dr. Martinez watched nervously as the encounter unfolded, ready to support their friend through whatever came next.

Marcus narrowed his eyes, his charismatic facade slipping briefly. "Very well," he said with a cold smile. "But remember, my offer stands."

With that, he strode away, leaving Jean-Pierre shaken but resolute. They knew the consequences of their decision might not be easy, but they held onto each other nonetheless. As the night wore on, they shared what little food they had and tried to ignore the growling in their stomachs, the taste of their sacrifice bitter-sweet on their tongues.

CHAPTER II

Jean-Pierre sits alone in his makeshift kitchen, his mind consumed by the difficult decision he faces. He can hear the clawing and moaning of the undead outside, a constant reminder of the desperation and danger they face as they try to get in. His eyes dart back and forth between the empty plates on the grimy counter and the bubbling stew pot on the fire, the aroma of cooked meat making his stomach rumble. He knows they need nourishment to survive, to make it through another day in this apocalyptic world where food is scarce, and every move could mean life or death. But using zombie meat - the only meat available to them - fills him with dread. He clenches his fists tightly, feeling the weight of the moral implications pressing down on him like a suffocating blanket.

From behind, Alice Winters enters the kitchen, her long, dark hair braided and pulled back from her sharp, intelligent eyes. She remains silent for a moment, watching him struggle, taking in the tense set of his shoulders and the furrowed brow that betrays his thoughts.

She knows what he's wrestling with because she too has spent hours trying to convince herself it's acceptable to eat the flesh of their former neighbors turned into mindless cannibals. But it isn't easy. They are all quick to admit that survival is paramount in this bleak world, but Alice worries about losing sight of their humanity in the process.

"Monsieur Jean-Pierre," she begins gently, approaching the burly man slowly. He looks up at her with tired eyes, his expression a mix of anguish and determination. She lays a hand on his arm, feeling the taut muscles beneath his skin. "We cannot keep living like this," she says softly. "We must find sustenance, or we may not make it. This place is unsafe." Her voice catches in her throat as she thinks of those they've lost, friends, family - people they were once close to before the outbreak. They must find food, any food, or their numbers will dwindle even more.

The sound of his stomach growling echoes through the small space, making them both smile wryly. They share a look of understanding. They've been here before, hungry and desperate, but never like this. The thought of eating zombie meat makes them both nauseous, but they must find a way. He nods reluctantly, acknowledging her words and pushing himself away from the counter. Together they contemplate the options: cooking the meat with strong spices or finding something else entirely. They discuss using roots and berries they've gathered from outside the walls, hoping to mask the taste of death as much as possible. As they work, their hands touch often; a silent pact sealing their agreement to maintain their humanity while also surviving.

Alice takes a deep breath and dips her spoon into the pot. She braces herself for the worst but tastes the stew anyway. It's not as bad as she imagined, the spices doing their job well. She looks up at him, and he shrugs, mouthing 'Not great, but edible'. They share a small laugh before digging in, savoring every bite, grateful to have each other and the warmth of the fire. The rain patters against the roof overhead, adding to the somber atmosphere as they sit together in silence, contemplative about what's to come.

[Alice and Dave continue to cook and eat together, finding solace in their partnership, as the rain soothes their troubled minds.]

Suddenly, the sound of boots splashing in puddles echoes through the camp. They freeze simultaneously, their hearts racing with dread. Marcus Devereaux strides towards them, his immaculately tailored jacket drenched from the downpour. He's flanked by his two henchmen, both clutching rifles tightly. Olivia Martinez follows behind, her eyes hard and her face etched with worry. She's seen far too much death already in this new world, and she doesn't relish the thought of adding zombie stew to that tally.

"What brings you here?" Alice asks warily, her grip tightening on her knife.

Marcus smiles charmingly. "I heard about your predicament," he says, gesturing to Jean- Pierre's culinary skills. "We could use someone like you in our group." His eyes gleam with ambition as he continues, "We have more resources and can ensure your safety while allowing you to pursue your passion for cooking." The wealthy leader's words hang in the air like a carrot before a donkey.

Jean-Pierre looks away, clearly torn between temptation and disgust. He knows he may never find such luxury again if he stays here. "It's not just about the food," Marcus adds persuasively. "You'll be part of something bigger."

The scent of freshly brewed coffee drifts towards them as Olivia interjects coolly, "But at what cost?" Her voice is laced with disdain for Marcus and his promises.

The rain intensifies, drumming against metal roofs and turning the ground into mud. Marcus shrugs nonchalantly, "Sacrifices must be made for survival." Then he glances at Jean-Pierre pointedly, "Including ingredients."

Olivia shakes her head, her pragmatism taking over, "You don't understand. Zombie meat can be dangerous - it can make us sick." Her gaze falls on Jean-Pierre, pleading for him not to give in.

Marcus chuckles softly, "We've done our research. It's quite safe when cooked properly." He winks at Jean-Pierre knowingly, his eyes twinkling with promise. "Imagine the meals we could create together."

Heusen's stomach rumbles loudly; even he is tempted by the idea of gourmet zombie cuisine. Olivia shakes her head, "We're not barbarians. We shouldn't sink so low." Her voice echoes with disapproval.

Marcus scoffs, "Desperate times call for desperate measures. And trust me, we'll make sure you're well-fed." The aroma of roasted zombie meat curls through the air, making even Olivia's mouth water despite her better judgment. She realizes they're all hungry enough to consider anything at this point.

The group stands there silently, weighing their options. Marcus is right; they must survive. But Olivia can't help but feel like they're crossing a line. She looks at Jean-Pierre one last time before heading back inside, her heart heavy.

Jean-Pierre's mind races with internal conflict. On one hand, he longs to continue his culinary passion without restriction. On the other, he's uneasy about aligning himself with a man who doesn't seem to value much more than wealth and luxury. His stomach growls loudly as he watches the others leave, torn between self-preservation and moral obligation.

Alice steps forward, "We can find other ways," she says softly, her dark hair blowing in the breeze. "We need to stick together and work as a team." Her eyes meet his, filled with understanding and concern.

Jean-Pierre looks at her gratefully, "You're right. We must." He turns away from Marcus's manicured lawn and follows Alice, sinking into mud up to his ankles. This isn't the life he imagined for himself, but maybe they can find another path forward together.

Together, they press on, searching for alternative food sources and rebuilding their community without relying on zombie meat. The journey is difficult but not impossible; every day brings new challenges and hardships, but also moments of camaraderie and hope. As they work, Jean-Pierre realizes that Marcus is wrong – there is more to life than cooking for the wealthy. There's something beautiful in creating meals from scratch, using what nature provides, and surviving without compromising their values.

Suddenly, they stumble upon an abandoned grocery store filled with canned goods and nonperishable items. The sound of jingling keys echoes through the empty aisles as they reach for their most prized finds – fresh fruits, vegetables, and even ice cream! It's a small victory, but it feels like they're finally on the right track. Dr. Martinez beams with pride, her eyes lighting up at the sight of real food. She quickly sets up a makeshift kitchen area while the group gathers around, eager to taste the fruits of their labor.

The aroma of roasting chicken fills the air; Alice's hands deftly peel potatoes and cut carrots as they discuss plans for rebuilding their community. Jean-Pierre joins in, feeling like he finally belongs somewhere. It's not so different from cooking for his clients back home – just a bit more rustic and honest. The scent of roasting meat fills his senses as the group sits down together, laughing and sharing stories. It tastes like freedom.

As they savor the meal, however, Jean-Pierre can't help but wonder about Marcus and his promises. He knows deep down that he must remain cautious; after all, Marcus's intentions are questionable at best. But for now, he feels safe and appreciated here, surrounded by people who value more than just fine dining experiences. The taste of homemade bread dipped in rich gravy washes over his tongue, reminding him that survival isn't just about luxury or comfort - it's about finding joy in simple pleasures.

But then something changes. Marcus begins talking about expanding their operations, venturing into nearby towns for supplies. Alice raises an eyebrow but remains silent, Dr. Martinez shrugs noncommittally. Jean-Pierre's heart pounds as he realizes what that could mean: more killing, more bloodshed. He tries to push these thoughts aside, lost in the taste of juicy chicken meat falling off the bone and melting in his mouth.

Marcus notices Jean-Pierre's discomfort and leans forward, sensing an opportunity to seal the deal. "You see, Jean-Pierre, we can offer you more than just companionship. Imagine having access to the finest ingredients, state-of-the-art equipment, and boundless resources

- all at your disposal," he says, pouring on the charm. "Think about it: You'll never have to worry about going hungry or compromising your art again."

Alice glances over, concerned for her new friend but unsure how to intervene without causing a scene. Dr. Martinez stiffens at Marcus's words, remembering the horrors they've already experienced in their search for survival. They agree that relying on zombie flesh isn't ideal, but it has at least kept them alive thus far.

Eyes burning into Jean-Pierre's soul, Marcus continues, "You deserve this life, Jean-Pierre. Don't you want to be part of something greater?"

The young chef slams his fist on the table, anger and frustration boiling over. "But at what cost?" he yells, his voice echoing through the silent kitchen. "I can't keep living like this!

Killing these... things... just so I can cook!" Tears well up in his eyes as he contemplates the reality of his decision. "I don't want to be a monster!"

Alice steps forward, placing a hand on his shoulder in support. "We understand," she says softly. "But there has to be another way." She looks down at her feet, remembering the countless towns they've passed by. "There are always other options out there," she whispers, looking up at Marcus. "We don't need to resort to this."

Dr. Martinez nods in agreement, her gaze hardened. "We can find other ways to survive." She pushes her glasses up her nose, determination etched across her face. "We've done it before, and we'll do it again."

Marcus stands up from his chair, his face twisted into a scowl. "But at what cost? Time? Resources? We waste precious moments searching for food when we could be safe and sound here," he argues.

The smell of rotting meat fills the air as the tension rises between them. Jean-Pierre shudders, trying to push away the image of fresh vegetables and fruit rotting in his mind. His stomach growls, reminding him of the hunger that gnaws at him daily. He looks at Alice, pleading with her to understand.

"I... I can't live like this anymore." He takes a deep breath, his fists clenching at his sides. "I'll make it right. I'll make up for it by not eating anyone else."

Alice sighs, her gaze softening. "Alright. But let's find a way that doesn't involve hurting others."

Marcus steps closer, his cologne filling the room. "You'll have everything you need," he promises. "Fresh ingredients, state-of-the-art equipment, and a sense of belonging."

Jean-Pierre hesitates for a moment, his hunger wars with his conscience. He looks around the room, taking in the decaying surroundings and the desperate faces of his fellow survivors. With a heavy heart, he nods. "Alright."

The room erupts into a cacophony of sounds; voices raised in protest, feet stomping on the rotting floorboards, and dishes clattering against each other. Alice turns away, unable to look at him. Dr. Martinez watches, her jaw clenched tight, as Marcus offers his hand. Jean- Pierre takes it, sealing his fate.

As they leave the room, Alice follows them out, fighting back tears. She knows the consequences of this decision and the impact it will have on their group. Dr. Martinez glares at Marcus, shaking her head slowly before turning to join her.

Together they walk down the hallway, their footsteps echoing in the empty mansion. The air smells of damp wood and mustiness as they make their way to the kitchen. Marcus shows Jean-Pierre around, pointing out the fresh vegetables and meat they've "acquired", his smile predatory.

They discuss recipes and ideas, their voices blending in a soft hum. Alice watches from the doorway, her heart breaking for what they've become. Dr. Martinez stands beside her, arms crossed, her eyes clouded with worry.

Time passes, and the aroma of cooking fills the room. Marcus beams as he tastes the food, his face lighting up with delight. "Exquisite," he murmurs, licking his lips.

Alice's stomach churns at the sight of his gluttony. Dr. Martinez shuffles uncomfortably, remembering the sacrifices they've made to survive until now. The others gather around, eager for a taste of something other than canned goods and stale bread.

As each bite is savored, their eyes widen in amazement. The flavors burst on their tongues - butter, garlic, rosemary, and other luxuries they'd forgotten existed. They watch, enraptured, as Jean-Pierre works his magic with a knife and flame.

Marcus grins, satisfied. "See?" he asks, gesturing to the happy faces around him. "This is what we can provide." He winks at Jean-Pierre who nods, his hands still dirty from preparing the meal.

The women exchange glances before turning back to their leader. Alice speaks first, her voice shaking. "We understand the allure of your offer," she begins, "but at what cost?" Her gaze flickers to Dr. Martinez, hoping for support.

The older woman sighs heavily. "We've fought so hard to forge our path," she says, her voice low and determined. "We cannot abandon it now."

Marcus leans in close, his voice dripping with promises. "You won't have to," he whispers. "I can guarantee your safety, comfort, and maybe even a chance to leave this hellish world behind." He pauses dramatically. "All you have to do is join us."

Jean-Pierre's mind spins with conflicting emotions: guilt over the lives he's taken, longing for companionship, desire for acceptance. He looks into Alice's pleading eyes, then Dr.

Martinez's practical ones. Finally, he finds his voice.

"I... I want that," he says, his decision made. "I want to be part of something bigger." His fingers tremble slightly as he wipes them clean on a napkin. "I'll go with you."

Alice's heart sinks, but she understands the desperation driving him. Dr. Martinez sighs heavily, resigned to the inevitable. As they stand to leave, Marcus claps his hands together enthusiastically.

"Excellent! We'll head out at first light." He turns to Jean-Pierre one last time. "You're sure you want this?" There's an edge to his voice now; power shifts in the air.

Jean-Pierre nods slowly, his stomach churning. He looks at the group he's leaving behind - a mix of relief and sadness in his eyes. Alice watches them all disappear into the night, wondering how long it'll be before they see each other again.

If they ever will.

The air is frigid as they walk back to the main camp, their footsteps echoing on the snow- covered ground like hollow drums. The scent of pine needles and smoke from their fires lingers in the chilly breeze. Marcus struts ahead, his steps confident despite the darkness cloaking them all. Jean-Pierre trails behind, lost in thought, his stomach rumbling. Dr.

Martinez stays close, her gaze flitting between him and the horizon.

Their boots crunch through crusty snow blanketing the forest floor as they near the campfire's warm glow, revealing faces etched with worry. They welcome Jean-Pierre back with nods but say nothing about his decision, saving it for a more private conversation later.

As they sit around the fire, eating cold meat and stale bread, eyes darting to where Jean- Pierre once sat, he can't help but feel like he's betrayed them. He missed their camaraderie and the thrill of providing for them through his cooking. A tear rolls down his cheek as he bites into tough jerky; it dissolves on his tongue like sandpaper, leaving no taste but remorse.

The night passes slowly, each ticking second another moment further from who he used to be. Morning comes too soon, casting an eerie light on Marcus's excited grin. They pack up hastily, eager to leave this place behind them. As they walk, Jean-Pierre notices how differently they treat him now: with a mix of respect and fear; like he's their savior...or their executioner.

Days pass without much conversation, just the crunch of snow underfoot and the labored breathing from exertion. Jean-Pierre feels guilty whenever he sees Alice's beaten-down expression, remembering her plea for aid with a shiver. She watches him closely, always ready for danger; her long dark hair whipping back and forth as she scans their surroundings.

A bird calls out suddenly, startling Dr. Martinez who reaches for her medical kit reflexively. Alice tenses, eyes locked on the sky. Jean-Pierre tries to reassure her, but she shakes her head and keeps walking. They trudge onward through blizzard-like conditions that leave their skin raw, and their clothes sodden.

Night falls again, bringing with it despair. They huddle together in a makeshift shelter, stomachs growling in anticipation of whatever Jean-Pierre might conjure up. He stares into the dying embers, his mind churning with ideas. Today will be different.

He tears through the frozen landscape like a man possessed, ignoring their tired cries to rest. He returns hours later with three rabbits, plucking and gutting them swiftly before building a fire. The smell of singed fur and blood mingles in the air as he cooks haphazardly.

Their eyes widen as he presents them with steaming, tender meat, even Marcus's greed pales in comparison to their surprise. Jean-Pierre watches as they devour the meal like starving animals, moans and gasps of pleasure escaping their lips. It's the first time he's seen such raw emotion from them in days.

Alice leans back against the tree trunk, her eyes closed in bliss. "This is...amazing." She licks her lips slowly, savoring every bite. Dr. Martinez nods in agreement, disbelief written all over her face. Marcus looks satisfied but not pleased; he knows this changes everything.

Their survival had been uncertain until now. Jean-Pierre became their only hope - their lifeline against starvation and despair. But now, with food on the table (or rather, fire pit), they could endure anything. The snow-capped mountains loom ominously outside their shelter, a testament to the challenges ahead; yet they feel invincible under Jean-Pierre's watch.

The young chef smiles warmly at his newfound allies, relishing in the knowledge that he's found people who appreciate his craft even in these dire circumstances. As night falls again, they curl up around the fire, content for once - full bellies distracting them from the cold and fear.

Marcus's whispers haunt Jean-Pierre's thoughts: "You're our savior," he murmurs insistently, "You don't have to do this anymore."

But Jean-Pierre remains steadfast; he can't abandon his principles just because it's easy. He has much more to offer this group than mere sustenance. He watches them sleep, protective instincts kicking in, promising himself that he'll keep them all safe from harm.

In the morning, they wake up to find fresh snow blanketing the ground - and their plates clean. Jean-Pierre has already disappeared deeper into the forest, leaving only a note in his place: "For the road ahead."

They trudge through the snow, heartened by his sacrifice. Alice and Dr. Martinez lean on each other for support; they share a look filled with gratitude and admiration for this man who chose integrity over comfort. The group follows Jean-Pierre's footprints through the wilderness, hoping he knows where he's going.

Suddenly, they stumble upon an abandoned farmhouse. It's derelict, but not uninhabitable - chickens clucking in the coop, smoke rising from the chimney. They enter cautiously, weapons at the ready. It's empty except for a few scrawny cows and a pantry full of canned goods.

Relief washes over them like warm water on parched lips; their lives are no longer hanging by a thread. Marcus, however, frowns as he takes stock of their situation. "We need more," he grumbles, glancing at Jean-Pierre accusingly. "You disappointed me, Jean-Pierre."

His eyes flash dangerously, and the once-rich leader's words slice through the air like an icy wind: "You won't survive without me."

They brace themselves for what comes next; it's clear he's not finished with them yet. But they stand together, united by their decision, and determined to make it work without him if they must.

As night falls, Marcus returns with a satchel of food stolen from a nearby village. Everyone tenses up, wondering how far he's willing to go to maintain his luxurious lifestyle. He grins slyly and plops down by the fire, filling his plate generously before passing it around. No one dares ask where he got it from – they know better than to challenge him now.

But Marcus's charm begins to wear thin as they grow weaker from lack of nutrition and the harsh conditions. The tension simmers between them, always ready to boil over into confrontation. Finally, Alice can't take it anymore: "We need to talk."

She confronts him about his unethical ways, reminding him of their original goals and values. He laughs bitterly, revealing rotten teeth hidden under perfect veneers: "Survival trumps all."

Dr. Martinez shakes his head, longing for the days when they had hope for a better future. They argue heatedly until Marcus storms out of the room, slamming the door behind him. The smell of rotting wood fills the air as they try to find common ground again.

Days turn into weeks, and Marcus's presence looms heavy on their hearts. They forage for berries and hunt small game, but hunger gnaws at them like a pack of wolves. When Marcus inevitably returns, they brace themselves for his wrath. Instead, he slumps in a chair, defeated.

"I cannot do this alone," he admits with a heavy sigh. "I've lost my way." He holds out a filthy bag full of gold - enough to sustain them through the harsh winter months. Their enthusiasm quickly fades upon realizing it was stolen from a defenseless village.

"We can't use this," Alice says, but Dr. Martinez agrees with Marcus: survival trumps all.

CHAPTER 12

Jean-Pierre LeClair had never felt so alone, even in the loneliest moments of his life before the apocalypse. He retreated to a secluded area of their small camp, away from the prying eyes and curious glances of those he once considered his friends. The wind howled through the trees, carrying with it the taste of ash and death, as he sat down on a fallen log, his heart heavy with doubt. His once-rich dishes were now reduced to meager rations, scraps of canned goods, and whatever he could forage from the wasteland. But still, he could not shake the feeling that his culinary skills were merely a distraction from the harsh reality of their situation. He closed his eyes, trying to block out the voices that echoed in his head, the memories of the luxurious kitchens he'd left behind, the delicate aromas that haunted him like ghosts.

Eddie Thompson, his burly friend, strolled up to him, a hunk of stale bread in one hand and a chunk of questionable meat in the other. "Hey, JP," he said, taking a bite out of the questionable meat, "you, okay?" Jean-Pierre nodded, unable to speak. Alice Winters followed close behind, her dark hair falling over her shoulders as she scrutinized him. "We're all worried about you," she said softly, her voice laced with concern. Antoine Dupont lingered in the background, a sly smile playing on his lips as he watched them all.

The doctor, Olivia Martinez, approached with a satchel of herbs and bandages slung over her shoulder. She set them down gently beside Jean-Pierre and took a seat beside him. "I know you're struggling," she began, her voice gentle but firm, "but we need to find another way. The canned goods won't last forever." Her eyes darted towards Antoine, who scoffed softly and walked away. "We have to find another source of food before it's too late."

Marcus Devereaux, their leader, strolled up next, his slick hair glimmering in the sunlight. "Jean-Pierre," he said, his voice smooth but commanding, "we need you. Your skills are what keep us going." Jean-Pierre nodded but couldn't meet his eye. Sophia Reynolds, with her kind face and gentle hands, sat beside him, squeezing his shoulder reassuringly. "I know this is hard for you," she whispered, "but we're all in this together."

As the sun began to set, painting the sky in shades of orange and pink, Jean-Pierre couldn't help but feel like an outsider in his group. He loved them, he truly did, but they couldn't understand his struggles. They didn't see what he saw when he closed his eyes: the ghosts of fine dining past, the specters of culinary perfection. He stood up and walked away, leaving them all behind, needing time to think, needing space to breathe.

The air was chill now, carrying the scent of salty seaweed and rotting wood. He stopped at the cliff's edge, gazing out at the expanse of ocean before him. The crashing waves sounded like a symphony of applause for his failures. He took a deep breath, tasting the salty air, then dug into his bag for his pocketknife. There was only one way to prove himself.

Hours later, covered in mud and blood, he returned to camp. The others were asleep, exhausted from their latest expedition. But he couldn't escape his thoughts, or the growing guilt gnawing at his insides. He had killed for food—no, not just killed; he had butchered with precision, relished in it even. Had he become what he despised most about the old world?

He glanced around at their makeshift camp, hearing the soft snores and heavy breathing, then moved towards his small stove. Using driftwood and dried seaweed, he lit a fire, letting the flames dance across the grate. The sizzling of the fish mixed with the crackling of wood, formed an eerie harmony. He closed his eyes, remembering Marie's sweet potato soufflé, Charles' delight. In this desolate world, his cooking had become something more than sustenance—it was hope.

As the aroma filled the air, Alice Winters stirred, nose twitching. She sat up slowly, eyes narrowed. "What... what is that?" she asked, voice hoarse. Jean-Pierre turned, watching as she approached cautiously, her long dark hair swaying with each step. "Fish," he said simply. "I couldn't bear to let such freshness go to waste."

She eyed the meal warily but took a tentative bite. Her eyes widened, and she let out a quiet groan of pleasure. He watched her devour it, feeling a pang of satisfaction. Even Dr. Olivia Martinez couldn't hide her surprise as she approached, leaning over Alice's shoulder to catch a whiff of the meal. "Where did you get the saltwater bass?" she asked, brow furrowed. Jean-Pierre shrugged nonchalantly as he slid a plate towards her. She took an experimental bite and her eyes lit up.

"It's... it's incredible," she murmured.

Marcus Devereaux, the group's leader, appeared next. Sophia Reynolds followed close behind, the gentle nurturer of the group. They stopped short at the smell, exchanging wary glances. They knew what he had done to acquire this feast. Antoine Dupont lingered on the fringes, smirking in that infuriatingly cunning way of his.

Eddie Thompson was next, barreling towards the source of the aroma. His bulk filled up the small space as he leaned over, inhaling deeply. He looked up at Jean-Pierre, a rare smile splitting his rough face. "You're a damn saint, Chef," he said gruffly before digging in.

But this newfound adoration left Jean-Pierre feeling hollow inside. He had always cooked for the people, not for their admiration. He had loved the friendships he'd formed—with Alice, Eddie, Sophia, Olivia, and Marcus—but now they felt forced, contrived. He looked around, seeing their relieved expressions, feeling like a fraud.

Ending the scene here, it's clear that Jean-Pierre's thoughts are troubled, and he feels like a fraud. The group's dependence on him for food has made him feel like he's losing himself, and he questions his purpose in the group dynamic. The scene ends with a sense of unease and discomfort.

The following day, Jean-Pierre woke up to birds chirping outside his window, a rare sound in this post-apocalyptic world. He rolled out of bed, stretching stiffly. The morning sun felt like a warm caress on his skin, reminding him of happier times. He stared at the collection of recipes and photos scattered across his desk, a grim reminder of his past life.

Slipping on his worn clothes, he walked downstairs to the communal kitchen area. It had become his sanctuary, where he could lose himself in the rhythm of chopping and sautéing. But today it felt empty without his friends around. The silence weighed heavily on him as he prepared breakfast.

As he placed steaming plates of eggs Benedict before them, he noticed they were already roused by the smell, their eyes lighting up expectantly. But something was off—they seemed distracted, preoccupied. It wasn't until later that he found out they were planning to leave him behind. The news hit like a punch to the gut.

His skills were valuable to Marcus Devereaux, who offered him a place among his group of survivors. They needed someone like him to maintain their luxurious lifestyle, and the thought of returning to scavenging for food filled him with dread. The decision lay heavy on his shoulders as he continued to serve them meal after meal.

The taste of blood in his mouth grew stronger with each mouthful of rich, decadent cuisine he presented. How could he deny himself such expertise when it would mean so much to others? Yet staying true to his principles felt equally important.

A sudden knock at the door jerked him back to reality. He opened it to find two young men holding AK-47s, sentries from Marcus's group. They ushered him into a waiting SUV without warning.

As he sped away from his home-away-from-home, doubt gnawed at him. Had he been selfish in pursuing his culinary dreams amidst chaos and suffering? Isolation set in like a dark cloud following him to Marcus's compound.

There he found himself amidst extravagance he once thought impossible—fine china, crystal glasses, and an army of staff catering to his every whim. But this wasn't the camaraderie he craved. He was merely a tool for Marcus's enjoyment.

He felt like a bird in a gilded cage, watched and envied by the other survivors, many of whom had lost loved ones or faced unimaginable hardships since the apocalypse began. Yet still, they appreciated his talents, their eyes lighting up at the sight of his dishes. It wasn't enough.

One night, while preparing an especially elaborate meal, he overheard whispers about an impending raid on a nearby settlement. Fear gripped him—he couldn't be a part of such violence. He slipped away into the night, hiding in the shadows until he reached familiar territory.

The next morning, the settlement was gone, leaving only ash and ruin in its wake. He mourned their loss and vowed to use his skills to bring people together, not tear them apart. In the end, he found solace working with other survivors at a communal garden, cooking simple meals over open flames, sharing food and stories, and bringing people together with his culinary creations. Life had changed, but he had finally found his purpose.

Months passed, and they eked out an existence, scavenging for resources and growing their food. But as winter approached, hunger began to gnaw at their bones. Jean-Pierre knew they needed protein, but the thought of using zombie meat sickened him.

He tried to find alternative sources but failed.

One day, Antoine's voice echoed in his head, "You know what they say, desperate times call for desperate measures."

The smell of rotting flesh filled the air as they hunted, their knives flashing in the sunlight. Jean-Pierre closed his eyes, trying to shut out the horrifying reality of their situation. They returned with the zombie meat, and he was forced to confront his worst fears.

He hesitated, knife hovering over the raw flesh, remembering the innocent lives lost in this new world. He couldn't shake the feeling that using zombie meat was wrong, no matter how hungry they were.

But Alice's words rang true, "We'll all die without it." He took a deep breath and began to cook, the metallic tang of blood filling the air as he seared the meat. His stomach churned, but he powered through.

When it was ready, he presented it, hoping for understanding or at least acceptance. Instead, they devoured it like starving animals, moaning in delight at the unique flavor. He looked at Sophia, regret etched on her face, but she nodded imperceptibly.

He couldn't shake the feeling of wrongness as they praised his dish, Eddie wiping the sauce from his beard with a satisfied grin. Marcus complimented him profusely, discussing future dishes they could create with this newfound "ingredient."

Jean-Pierre felt like he'd sold his soul to the devil.

He retreated to his makeshift kitchen, thoughts swirling like a tornado. Antoine's words echoed in his mind, "You'll never starve with us." The prospect terrified him, but he couldn't shake the idea of being part of something bigger than himself.

Days passed, and Jean-Pierre's culinary masterpieces became darker, using more of the taboo ingredient. The taste was addictive, and he could see it in their eyes as they ate. But he felt hollow inside, like a shell of a man.

Alice noticed his change, concern etched on her face as she watched him meticulously prepare another dish. She approached him cautiously, "Are you okay?"

Jean-Pierre shook his head, unable to meet her gaze, "I don't know anymore."

She put a hand on his shoulder, "We need you. Don't let this change who you are." His eyes burned with unshed tears, "How can I not?" he whispered, defeated.

They talked late into the night, Alice's soft voice providing some solace. But something inside him had broken, and it was only a matter of time before everyone noticed.

As he cooked, he couldn't shake the feeling that he'd lost his way, that he was no longer the chef he once was - or the man Alice knew. The aroma of garlic, onions, and blood mingled in the air, a potent mix that promised both temptation and despair.

Eddie wolfed down his meal as if it were his last, glancing up at Jean-Pierre with a look of awe, "You're a goddamn wizard in that kitchen, JP."

Sophia's gaze lingered on him with worry etched in her features, "We're just trying to survive, Jean-Pierre. Don't let it consume you."

Dr. Martinez's voice cut through the air like a knife, "We can't afford your morals right now." Her statement stung, but he knew she was right.

Antoine's eyes glinted with cunning, "You're the best we've got, JP. Don't forget that." The once-familiar praise sounded hollow, leaving him feeling more isolated than ever.

The taste of zombie meat lingered on his tongue long after they ate, leaving him feeling empty and hollow. Alice watched as he retreated to his room, her heart heavy with the knowledge that they were losing him.

In his solitude, Jean-Pierre contemplated the consequences of his actions, questioning whether he had become so consumed by his passion for cooking that he had lost sight of the bigger picture and the needs of the survivors. A single tear ran down his cheek as he realized his addiction had taken over, and he couldn't go back.

The sound of gunfire, screams, and shuffling feet filled the air outside his window, a constant reminder of the nightmarish reality they were all living in. His stomach churned at the thought of what he had done and what they would all have to continue doing to survive.

He could hear Eddie's deep voice rumbling through the walls, "That shit was good, JP. Real good." The big man's words echoed in his head, causing him physical pain.

The smell of smoke from Antoine's cigarette drifted under the door, mingling with the aroma of rotting flesh from the zombies they had butchered for their feast. The juxtaposition made his stomach turn in knots.

His hands shook as he picked up his pen, writing down new recipes, trying to channel his regret into something productive. But the ideas wouldn't come, and the page remained blank.

The taste of despair settled in his mouth like ash as he thought of Sophia's warning. Had he become a monster in their eyes too?

The only thing that kept him going was the memory of Alice's gratitude when he first arrived, her face lighting up at the sight of his creations. He yearned for her approval but knew she couldn't understand what he was going through.

Sweat trickled down his brow as he tried to block out the sounds outside and focus on creating something that didn't involve death and decay.

His once-vibrant passion had withered, replaced by a hollow void in his chest. The taste of blood lingered on his tongue, and he couldn't shake the feeling that everyone saw him as another one of them - a monster.

In desperation, he downed the last of his drink and stared at the empty page, wondering how long it would be until he lost himself completely.

Suddenly, an image of Sophia's hopeful smile flashed before his eyes. She believed in him, even if Antoine didn't. He couldn't disappoint her.

Taking a deep breath, he stood up, his joints creaking under the weight of uncertainty. The room spun around him for a moment before steadiness returned, and he stumbled towards the door.

Outside, the camp bustled with activity - people moving about with their daily chores or huddled together in small groups. Everyone looked up as he emerged from the shack, their faces a patchwork of curiosity and concern.

The sun beat down on his skin like a hammer, its harsh glare burning through his already frazzled nerves. He tried to ignore it and make his way towards the campfire where Sophia sat nursing the sick child.

As he approached, she looked up at him with worried eyes that softened at the sight of him. "Jean," she said softly, her brow furrowed in concern. "Are you okay?"

He forced a weak smile and sat down beside her, taking the child from her arms. Her warmth comforted him for a moment before reality set in again.

"I...I need to think," he mumbled, rising abruptly and heading towards his shack.

Inside, he collapsed onto his bed, his heart racing in his chest. He needed to find a solution before it was too late.

How could he reconcile his love for cooking with this new world? He thought back to his old life, to the pride he took in crafting perfect meals for eager patrons - could that still exist here? The world outside was bleak, the colors drained out by the apocalypse. Yet, in this tiny corner of safety, he could create something beautiful.

The idea that his food brought joy to these weary faces gave him strength. They clung to it like a lifeline, finding solace in every bite. What would happen if he stopped? What would become of them?

His stomach growled loudly at the thought, reminding him how hungry he was. Food. That's what they needed.

He rose from his bed, grabbing ingredients from his precious stash of spices and herbs. The rich smell of rosemary filled the air as he began to chop vegetables, his knife moving swiftly like a well-oiled machine.

Alice watched from the doorway, curious but wary. She had seen him like this before - lost in his work, oblivious to everything else.

She stepped inside, closing the door behind her. "What are you making?" she asked, taking a deep breath of the familiar scent.

"Something special," he replied, not looking up. "Something to remind us that life doesn't have to be so grim."

Hours passed as he cooked, the aroma filling the shack. Their curious noses led them all to his doorstep.

The sound of chopping and sizzling filled the air, interspersed with Antoine's mocking laughter. The man always seemed to be nearby, a constant reminder of their plight.

Finally, he served them all, proudly watching their expressions as they took their first bites. The taste was unlike anything they had experienced before - an explosion of flavors that danced on their tongues.

Tears welled in Alice's eyes, and she hugged him tightly. "Thank you," she whispered. "Thank you for giving us hope."

CHAPTER 13

Jean-Pierre LeClair sat alone in the dimly lit room; his face illuminated by the flickering candlelight. The kitchen was quiet, save for the occasional clanking of pots and pans from the other survivors gathering supplies and food in the main dining area. He was hunched over a table, lost in thought, his hands absentmindedly twirling a fork as he contemplated the morality of his actions. The warmth from the fireplace provided some comfort against the chill of the post-apocalyptic world outside, but it failed to distract him from the heavy burden weighing on his heart. His obsession with perfecting his dishes had led him down a dark path - a path of sacrifice and compromise that left him grappling with the consequences of his choices. The lingering taste of succulent venison on his tongue reminded him of the life he once knew, of the luxury he'd taken for granted before the collapse of society. He wondered if it was all worth it now.

Slowly, he rose from his chair, wandering towards the window and gazing out at the snow- covered landscape beyond. The survivors' camp was nestled in a valley, surrounded by towering mountains that seemed to loom ominously, as if judging their every move. The harsh reality of their situation was not lost on him; they were fighting for survival in a world where resources were scarce, and every meal was a battle. But was it right to use whatever means necessary? He turned away from the window, feeling the heat of the fire against his skin as he retraced his steps to the kitchen.

The scent of roasting vegetables filled the air as he entered, mingling with the aroma of herbs and spices. Alice Winters looked up from her cooking duties, her dark brows knit in concentration. She understood his struggle better than anyone else, having once been a fighter for animal rights herself. Yet, she too had learned to adapt to endure this new harsh reality. "Need any help with dinner?" she asked, her voice low and measured. He appreciated her resilience but knew she wouldn't approve of what he had planned next.

He shook his head gently, dismissing her offer. "I've got it under control." His voice was hoarse from lack of use, a testament to the weight of his internal turmoil.

Alice watched him warily, sensing something was off, but let it go, knowing better than to press him when he was like this. She turned her attention back to her cooking, her long braid swaying rhythmically as she stirred the stew pot.

Eddie Thompson entered the kitchen then, his broad frame towering over them both. Despite his size, there was an air of vulnerability about him that made Jean-Pierre feel protective. He knew Eddie would never question his methods, no matter how unethical they were. "Smells great, Chef," he said, his gruff voice rumbling with appreciation. Jean-Pierre nodded in response, unable to speak past the lump in his throat.

The stew simmered on the stove, filling the room with its rich aroma, and Jean-Pierre's heart raced as he reached for the hunting knife hidden beneath his apron. The moment of truth had arrived.

Heart thudding in his chest, he slipped outside, scanning the perimeter for any signs of movement. It was dangerous work, but they couldn't afford to be choosy about their food sources anymore. The zombie infestation had decimated their supplies, and desperate times called for desperate measures. He spotted one, its rotting flesh barely held together by sinew, and carefully approached.

The creature lunged at him, causing him to react on instinct, slicing off a chunk of its raw flesh before it could attack. Blood dripped down his forearm, but he paid it no mind, focusing instead on his mission.

Back inside, he prepared the meat with meticulous care, seasoning it to perfection before adding it to the stew. The others entered the kitchen one by one, curious about the unusual fragrance wafting through the air. They all sat around the table; anticipation etched on their faces.

"What's for dinner?" Sophia asked, her voice hushed. Jean-Pierre cleared his throat. "Something special," he replied, his eyes flickering between them nervously.

The first bite elicited gasps of surprise – followed by groans of delight. The zombie meat was tender, the flavors harmonizing perfectly with the other ingredients. Dr. Martinez, usually so critical, was even complimentary. "This might be the best thing you've ever made," she said, her voice tinged with amazement.

Eddie smiled, his bushy beard bouncing as he nodded in agreement. "It's amazing, man," he said, patting Jean-Pierre's back appreciatively. Alice remained silent but dug into her portion with gusto, clearly relishing the taste.

Throughout their journey, Jean-Pierre's culinary skills were a saving grace. His creativity in the face of scarcity was awe-inspiring:

transforming roadkill into gourmet meals, fermenting fruits into palatable alcohol, and even crafting medicinal teas from local herbs. His passion for cooking had saved them from starvation countless times.

Yet, he couldn't shake the feeling that there was something else... more than just hunger driving him. A deeper need to provide comfort and normalcy in these trying times. He looked around the table at his friends, each with their demons haunting them.

They'd become a family of sorts, surviving together in this harsh new world. Alice was the sharp-eyed skeptic, always on guard against danger; Eddie, with his brute strength and unwavering loyalty; Dr. Martinez, with her pragmatism and healing touch; and Sophia, the moral compass, guiding them towards the right choices despite the horrors they faced.

They relied on each other now more than ever before. And so, when Sophia suggested they stop at an abandoned mall, he didn't hesitate. Deep down, he knew it was wrong – but he also knew they couldn't go on like this much longer.

So, they ventured into the darkness of the mall.

As they searched for supplies, Marcus was quick to expose their secret: what they'd been eating to survive. Antoine's smirk of satisfaction widened, clearly enjoying the chaos he'd sowed. Despite their protests, Marcus saw potential in Jean-Pierre's talent and demanded he continue cooking.

Heart racing, Jean-Pierre set about creating another feast. The scent of rosemary and thyme filled the air as he seared the meat, trying to block out the memories of where it came from. The juicy sizzle of the steak echoed through the empty halls as he prepared a sauce.

Soon enough, Eddie's stomach rumbled in anticipation, followed by Alice, who couldn't resist the aroma any longer. Dr. Martinez approached cautiously but curiosity got the better of her. Sophia walked up last, her sweet smile hiding her worry for Jean-Pierre.

He presented them with plates, each garnished with fresh herbs and side dishes they'd found. The first bite sent shockwaves through their taste buds; it tasted like beef, succulent and full-bodied. Alice closed her eyes, lost in the moment, while Eddie moaned in delight. Dr. Martinez cleared her throat, impressed despite herself. Sophia reached over to squeeze his hand gently.

Conversations flowed naturally as they ate, laughter breaking through the gloom that had been consuming them. Jean-Pierre could almost forget the horrors outside as they savored each bite and sipped wine he'd found in cellars beneath the city. It was a brief respite from their harsh reality.

When they finished, Jean-Pierre cleared his throat, hesitating. "There's something I must confess," he said quietly. "The meat...it's not entirely human." Gasps echoed around the room. "But it was either this or starvation," he argued wearily. Their silence weighed heavily on him, knowing he'd crossed a line none could unsee.

"We need to find other food sources," Alice insisted finally. Eddie nodded in agreement, but Marcus's eyes hardened. "I want you to keep cooking," he said firmly. "We'll sort this out later," Antoine smirked, sensing an opportunity to cause more trouble.

Days turned into weeks, and Jean-Pierre continued to cook. His dishes became bolder and more innovative. He tried venison, rabbit, even alligator, but zombie meat remained a staple. The group grew dependent on his culinary skills, ignoring their moral dilemmas for the sake of survival.

Sophia's auburn hair glistened with sweat as she helped gather ingredients, wondering how much longer they could sustain this. Dr. Martinez searched for alternative food sources, finding roots and berries that no one wanted to eat. Alice trained rifles, always vigilant.

Eddie did his best to lift their spirits, always ready for battle.

One night, they gathered around, anticipating Jean-Pierre's latest creation. The aroma was enticing rosemary, garlic, and oregano mixed with zombie meat. Sophia tasted it, savoring the flavors. "It's divine," she said, surprised. "How did you—?"

"I didn't," he admitted softly. "It's human meat." A gasp escaped her lips as he revealed he'd stolen it from a nearby farm while they slept, their guilt dissolving in their mouths. "We can't keep doing this," Sophia said finally. They knew he was right, but starvation loomed. How much farther would they sink into this dark abyss?

Jean-Pierre's heart ached. He loved cooking, but the sacrifices he'd made were too high. His salt-and-pepper hair had turned grey from stress, his tall frame weighed down by guilt.

Each dish was a moment of joy amidst the bleakness, but at what cost? He couldn't continue down this path.

The sound of screeching brakes jolted them awake—a vehicle nearby! Marcus' eyes gleamed with excitement, leading a rescue mission. They found a massive mansion with gardens and livestock, hopeful for a new life. Yet danger lurked within, turning their dreams into nightmares.

Inside, Jean-Pierre glimpsed fine wine, and exquisite ingredients—a glimpse of their old lives. He swore he'd leave this place untouched, but Antoine's calculating gaze unsettled him. He knew Alice would be suspicious. Secretly, Jean-Pierre retrieved a piece of filet mignon and smuggled it back to camp, crafting another masterpiece.

Their mouths watered again. "Unbelievable," Eddie murmured, his eyes wide. Sophia closed hers, savoring the flavors. Dr. Martinez shook her head, resigned to their plight. Antoine licked his lips, his mind churning with plans.

That night, Jean-Pierre couldn't sleep. His heart raced as he grappled with his obsession, wondering if he'd lost himself to fear or desperation. He clenched his fists, vowing to find another way.

Antoine's ploy succeeded; they stole from the rich. Jean-Pierre couldn't bear it, stealing from those who could least afford it, but Eddie convinced him they'd starve otherwise. As they fled, Jean-Pierre watched Sophia's worried glance, knowing he'd crossed a line.

Determined to change, he focused on foraging, using herbs and wild game. It wasn't easy, but at least they weren't stealing hope from others. His creations were still exquisite; Sophia cried tears of joy over a mushroom risotto, unable to hide her delight. Antoine smirked, scheming.

One day, they found an abandoned lab with strange, mutated animals. Jean-Pierre hesitated, but hunger won out. The taste was divine, unforgettable—a symphony of flavors they'd never imagined possible. Marcus' eyes gleamed, greed taking hold.

Alice questioned their actions, but Jean-Pierre's resolve weakened. Dr. Martinez warned against consuming unknown substances, but they did anyway. The taste was too irresistible. Jean-Pierre looked away, heartbroken at what he'd become. Since then, he'd watched his friends suffer strange illnesses, their skin turning green and scales forming. Antoine's laughter only fueled his guilt. The group's bond fractured under the weight of their sins; they questioned each other's loyalties. Jean-Pierre couldn't forgive himself for starting this nightmare. He vowed to find a cure or end it all, even if it meant facing the monsters of his past alone.

Alice and Dr. Martinez approached him near the river, their faces etched with concern. They'd seen him staring into space far too often lately. "What's wrong?" Alice asked quietly.

"I... I need to change," he confessed, eyes downcast. "I realize now that we can't keep living like this."

"You mean the cooking?" Alice ventured.

His gaze flickered upward, shameful. "Yes, the cooking. I want to create sustainable meals for us, not...not what we've been doing."

"That's a good start," Alice said, nodding slowly. "But what about Sophia? She relies on those flavors."

"I know, I know," he sighed heavily, "but I've been selfish."

"You're human," Dr. Martinez reminded him gently. "You can only do so much."

"No, I can't," he insisted. "I'll find ways to make wild foods palatable, create our gardens. We'll survive without compromising ourselves anymore."

They stood there a moment, contemplating his words. Alice's eyes softened, and Dr. Martinez squeezed his shoulder before leaving for her medical duties.

Alone again, Jean-Pierre swore to honor their trust and transform their fate. He'd forgotten who he was amidst the chaos; now, he remembered—a chef with a conscience. And though it pained him to admit it, he understood Alice's words about treading lightly amidst this new reality.

Days passed with Jean-Pierre testing new recipes using found ingredients like roots and berries. His stomach churned at first but grew accustomed. He learned patience once more, testing new methods of preservation and gardening, gathering seeds from untouched landscapes. As the group thrived on his efforts, he was reminded of hope restored.

The peppery taste of the leaves invigorated his senses, and the sweetness of the berries brought a newfound appreciation for life's simple pleasures. The squirrel they'd trapped smelled freshly roasted, filling the air with earthy aromas that tantalized taste buds—a far cry from what they'd become accustomed to.

Everyone around him grew stronger, their morale lifted by the promise of nourishment without bloodshed or guilt. Even Sophia, while still missing her extravagant dishes, found solace in their shared endeavors.

And so, hope began to blossom anew within Jean-Pierre, tempered by the lingering weight of their past transgressions, but he knew they could survive on their terms now. Crafting meals became more than sustenance; it became camaraderie and perseverance.

He looked back at how far they'd come, from eating scraps to growing their crops, from hunting to raising livestock. A tear rolled down his cheek as he gazed out at the lush greenness before him—a testament to their will to survive against all odds.

Just then, a twig snapped in the distance. He quickly wiped his eyes and stood up, approaching the group silently. They were gathered around the fire, their eyes shining with anticipation for his next creation.

He entered the clearing, a flicker of candlelight dancing in the darkness behind him, his face set with newfound resolve—a resolve to reconnect with his friends, to find a way to use his culinary skills for good without compromising his morals.

As he approached the group, he could hear their murmurs, their post-apocalyptic lives having transformed them into a tight-knit family. They looked up at him, waiting for his next masterpiece.

"My friends," he began, his voice wavering slightly, "I have been given much to think about these past few days. Alice and Dr. Martinez's words... they've resonated deeply within me." He swallowed hard. "I understand now what we must do—we must continue with sustainability and self-sufficiency. We can't rely on 'letting nature take its course.'" His heart pounded in his chest as he spoke. "We must be the course ourselves."

There was a collective gasp from the group, Marcus's eyes narrowing suspiciously. Antoine smirked, sensing an opportunity.

But Sophia reached out and squeezed his hand reassuringly, her warmth comforting him. "We're here for you, Jean-Pierre. Whatever decision you make."

He took a deep breath. "From this moment on, I commit to finding alternative food sources and creating a sustainable community." A hush fell over the group as they processed his words.

"But" he continued, "I cannot deny my passion for cooking. Food brings us together, feeds our souls, reminds us of who we were and who we can be." He glanced around at them, taking in their weary faces. "We will continue to cook, but with a purpose—to nourish and heal, not just to satisfy."

Eddie let out a deep breath, relief washing over him. "As long as there's still tasty grub, I'm game."

Sophia nodded; her lips curved in a soft smile. "Thank you, Jean-Pierre. You have no idea how much this means to us all." She turned to the others, her voice ringing with conviction. "We can do this! Together, we can build something beautiful."

Marcus remained silent, but his eyes flashed with something akin to fear. Antoine watched him carefully, waiting for the perfect moment to strike.

Jean-Pierre felt a weightlift from his shoulders, a newfound purpose filling him. He knew it wouldn't be easy, but he was ready to face the challenge. He'd never felt so alive, so driven. The scent of smoke and pine mingled with the sound of crackling wood as he sat down beside Sophia, feeling her warmth seep into him like a ray of sunlight after days of darkness.

Together, they would forge ahead, facing the unknown with open hearts and full stomachs.

CHAPTER 14

The sun had barely risen when Sophia Reynolds awoke, her eyes still heavy with sleep as she stretched languidly. The rocky terrain beneath her was cold and hard, but the crisp morning air was invigorating; it carried a slight chill that woke her up quickly. She glanced around, taking stock of their surroundings - a barren wasteland that seemed almost endless in all directions. Jean-Pierre stood watch over the camp, his keen eyes scanning the horizon for any signs of danger. Antoine Dupont was nowhere to be seen.

The rest of the survivors were scattered about, tending to their morning routines. Some gathered firewood, others prepared meager meals, their movements listless and fatigued. Sophia's heart ached for them; they had been through so much already, and yet they persevered. She couldn't help but feel a sense of responsibility towards them, a need to protect them from further harm. Her gaze settled on Pierre, a frail old man who looked like he might crumble under the weight of his bones. She knelt beside him, offering a reassuring smile as he slowly stirred from his slumber.

"Good morning, Pierre," she whispered her voice like a gentle breeze rustling leaf. "It's going to be another long day, but we'll make it together."

Pierre nodded wearily, his wrinkled face breaking into a small smile. "Merci, chérie. We're lucky to have you with us."

Just then, Antoine returned to the camp, his face inscrutable. His eyes darted between Jean- Pierre and Sophia, a sinister smile playing on his lips. She couldn't help but shudder at the sight of him; there was something truly dark lurking beneath his deceptively charming exterior. His presence caused tension within the group, and she could feel it like an electric current in the air.

Without warning, Antoine launched into action. Before anyone could react, he grabbed Sophia from behind and pinned her arms to her sides. She struggled against him but found herself powerless in his grip. Antoine's face was twisted with determination as he dragged her away from the camp. Screams echoed behind them as the others tried desperately to free her from his hold.

"No! Let her go!" Jean-Pierre shouted, his voice carrying a dangerous edge.

But Antoine was too quick, disappearing into the maze of rocks and shrubs that surrounded them. Sophia felt a lump forming in her throat as she was pulled further away from safety. The cries for help grew fainter with every step.

Antoine pushed her into a small cave hidden within the rocks, her heart racing as she tried to make sense of what was happening. He slammed the entrance shut, plunging them into darkness. She heard a rock being wedged into place, sealing their fate. Sophia let out a shaky breath, trying to contain her terror. It was then that she noticed the faint scent of smoke in the air - like roasting meat. Her stomach rumbled in protest. Antoine was never one for violence, yet he had brought them here, into this dark and desolate place... for what purpose?

As her eyes adjusted to the dim light, she saw a small fire flickering in the corner of the cave, casting dancing shadows upon the rough walls. A figure stirred near the flames, and she realized it was Jean-Pierre, his eyes burning with anger. He was on his feet in an instant, his hands balling into fists. "What do you want?" he demanded, his French accent thickening under the stress. "Why did you take her?"

Antoine stood between them; his expression unreadable. He remained silent for a long moment before he spoke, his words dripping with contempt. "I want what's best for us, Jean-Pierre. For all of us to survive." His tone was cold, calculated. "You see, Sophia is like a daughter to me. And like any good father, I cannot allow my children to make such foolish choices."

Jean-Pierre's jaw clenched at his words. He knew exactly what he meant - Antoine wanted her as leverage against him. She could feel his hot breath on her neck, his grip tightening around her arms. "You can have anything you want," he said through gritted teeth. "Just let her go."

"You're too soft," Antoine countered, his voice low and menacing. "Too willing to trust that everyone has good intentions." His dark gaze darted to Sophia, who flinched under his gaze. "I need something more substantial."

Her heart raced as she tried to comprehend the situation. They were trapped, alone in a small room with no windows or exit. She could feel Jean-Pierre's anger pulsing off him like heat waves, making the air between them crackle with tension. "What do you want?" she whispered, her voice shaking.

Antoine smiled, revealing a predator's smile. "I want control," he said simply. "I want power." He glanced at Jean-Pierre, eyes flashing. "And I think you have what I need."

"What are you talking about?" Sophia asked, feeling a chill run down her spine. She could feel Jean-Pierre stiffen beside her. "I don't have anything of value."

"Oh, but you do," Antoine replied, his voice softening. "You see, you're the glue that holds this group together, Sophia. You're the one they listen to, the one who keeps them in line. And I need that." His eyes flicked back to Jean-Pierre. "Give me the map. Let me lead us to salvation, and I'll let her go."

Jean-Pierre hesitated, torn between protecting Sophia and the rest of the group. He knew Antoine was untrustworthy, but he also knew that Sophia's safety was at stake. He took a deep breath, his mind racing. "Alright," he said finally. "But you'll let her go once we get there? Just the two of us. No one else."

Antoine considered this for a moment before nodding reluctantly. "Fair enough. We have a deal."

As he took the map, Sophia felt a surge of relief washes over her. But the feeling was short- lived as she realized they were walking into a trap. The air around them thickened, electricity dancing across her skin as Antoine disappeared with Jean-Pierre down the dark alleyway.

Meanwhile, Jules and Lucas exchanged anxious glances. They knew they couldn't go after them without upsetting the delicate balance of their group dynamic, but they also couldn't just sit back and do nothing. They waited, nervously pacing to pass the time. The sound of their footsteps echoed against the decaying buildings that surrounded them, the stench of death and decay permeating everything.

Inside the alleyway, Antoine pushed Jean-Pierre against the wall, his hand gripping his neck tightly. "Now, the main course," he hissed. "A zombie feasts."

Jean-Pierre winced, taking a deep breath. "I can't do that. I can't cook with human flesh." It was more than just a moral dilemma; cooking with zombie meat was something he had sworn never to do, something he had always considered beneath him as a chef. But Antoine's grip tightened, and he knew he had to find another way.

"Then you'll never see Sophia again," Antoine snarled, his eyes burning into Jean-Pierre's. "And you'll watch as I break her like a twig." His hand moved to her throat, squeezing tightly.

Sophia tried to hide her fear, but it was evident in her trembling voice as she begged Jean- Pierre not to give in. "Please," she whispered hoarsely. "You don't have to do this."

Jean-Pierre gritted his teeth, his mind racing. He knew Sophia was right - he couldn't let Antoine hurt her, but he also couldn't bring himself to cook something so abhorrent.

Suddenly, an idea came to him. "What if we use game meat?" he suggested hesitantly. "I can make a delicious dish with venison or boar, something along those lines."

Antoine's eyes narrowed in thought before he let out a low chuckle. "Very well but make it worth my while. And no tricks," he warned as he released his grip but kept his dark eyes locked onto Jean-Pierre's. "It is something extraordinary."

Sophia breathed a sigh of relief as she was pushed away from Antoine's grasp, her body shaking from the fright. She looked at Jean-Pierre with gratitude mixed with concern about putting himself in danger again.

As Antoine stalked off, leaving them alone, Jean-Pierre turned to Sophia and sighed heavily. "I don't know how I'm going to do this, Sophia," he confessed, his voice ragged. "I don't know how to make a zombie meal palatable."

She put a hand on his shoulder, offering what comfort she could. "You're a brilliant chef," she said softly. "You'll figure something out."

And so, Jean-Pierre set to work, his mind churning with ideas and memories of dishes he'd created in the past. He gathered ingredients from their meager supplies, trying to create a dish that would impress Antoine while still being safe for a zombie palate. He would need all the help he could get.

Meanwhile, Alice, Eddie, and Dr. Martinez huddled together, discussing their next move. They knew they couldn't just let Antoine use Jean-Pierre like this; they had to save Sophia and stop him before it was too late. They agreed that a confrontation wasn't the best option

- not yet at least - but they needed a plan of action.

"We have to catch him off guard," Alice said, her dark hair swinging as she shook her head. "He's too cunning."

"We'll need to be fast," Eddie added, his hands clenching into fists. "And we can't risk jeopardizing Jean-Pierre or Sophia."

Dr. Martinez nodded in agreement; her brow furrowed with concentration. "We need a plan that won't tip him off."

Their whispered conversation was interrupted by the sound of pots and pans clanging in the kitchen as Jean-Pierre worked feverishly. The smell of garlic and herbs filled the air as he prepared the dish, filling the room with anticipation and fear.

Sophia could feel her stomach rumbling with hunger, despite the unsettling circumstances. She knew they needed this meal, needed to keep their strength up, but the thought of eating zombie meat made her queasy. Still, she trusted Jean-Pierre and hoped he could do something magical.

Eddie stepped forward, cracking his knuckles, and sniffing the air. "Smells good," he commented, his voice dropping into a low growl. "But we need to focus."

"We can't let Antoine win," Alice said firmly. "We need a distraction...something big."

Dr. Martinez nodded, her eyes narrowing. "We could rig up a trap in the storage room. When he comes to collect the food, we ambush him."

Eddie agreed, getting to his feet. "I'll help with that."

"And I'll gather some supplies," Alice said, disappearing into another room.

As they worked, Sophia paced anxiously, worry for Jean-Pierre etched onto her face. She knew he would never willingly cook the zombie meat, but she also knew the consequences of defying Antoine. She needed to help them find another way. Suddenly, inspiration struck.

"What about the gardens?" she asked, her voice barely above a whisper. "We could lure Antoine out there with the promise of fresh vegetables and fruits."

The others exchanged glances, weighing the potential risks. It was dangerous, but it was their best shot. Dr. Martinez nodded slowly. "It's worth a try."

They all sprang into action, setting up the trap in the storage room while Sophia went to work on gathering fresh produce from the makeshift garden outside. The sun was setting, casting long shadows across the barren wasteland as she picked through the earth, her movements careful and precise.

Antoine, meanwhile, waited impatiently by the kitchen door, anticipating his next meal. Little did he know, it was about to walk right into a deadly trap.

The aroma of cooking meat filled the air as Sophia emerged from the garden, carrying a basket of ripe tomatoes and sweet peppers. She could hear Antoine's stomach rumbling from inside the kitchen. She called out to him, her voice shaking slightly. "I found some really good stuff in the garden, Antoine. Fresh tomatoes and peppers. I think they'll go perfectly with whatever you're making."

He appeared in the doorway, his eyes lighting up at the sight of the bounty. "Bring it in," he growled, gesturing to the door.

Sophia carefully set down the basket and stepped aside as Antoine walked past her, his gaze fixed on the food. He didn't notice the trap set up behind him.

With a silent count of three, they had sprung into action. Jean-Pierre emerged from the storage room, blade in hand, followed by Eddie and Dr. Martinez. They tackled Antoine to the ground, pinning him down while Sophia dashed back into the garden to retrieve Sophia.

The fighting was brutal but short-lived. Antoine struggled against them, cursing, and spitting insults, but they managed to bind him before he could cause too much harm.

As they hustled Sophia back to their haven, she glanced over her shoulder at the smoldering remains of their last hope for food. The smell of burning meat filled the air, making her stomach churn. But it was a small price to pay for freedom.

Once inside, they locked Antoine in one of the rooms and turned their attention to treating his wounds. Sophia tended to him carefully, her hands shaking as she dabbed at the deep lacerations on his arm. She couldn't help but feel a twinge of pity for him, despite everything he'd put her through.

The rest of the day was spent in anxious waiting. They couldn't risk leaving the compound, so they hunkered down and waited for nightfall. Sophia paced, glancing out the window every few minutes. Jean-Pierre offered reassurance, but she couldn't shake the feeling that they were sitting ducks.

Finally, as the last rays of sunlight faded, they gathered their things and made their move. Jean-Pierre led the way, his heart pounding in his chest as he saw the guard posts up ahead. Sophia followed closely behind, her hand gripping his tightly. Eddie brought up the rear, ready to provide cover fire if necessary.

They reached the outer fence undetected, but the gate was locked. Looking around, Jean- Pierre spotted an old tree with a low-hanging branch near the wall. He nodded to Eddie, who began to climb. Once at the top, he swung a rope down, creating a makeshift ladder for the others.

They climbed up silently, each rung creaking under their weight. At the top, they peered over the wall, assessing the area for any signs of movement. It was clear. Slowly, they slid down the other side, landing in a pile of soft grass. The wind whispered through the leaves as they crept away from the compound, leaving their old lives behind.

Eddie lit a torch, illuminating their path through the dense forest. They moved quickly but quietly, no one daring to speak. As they emerged from the tree line, they saw a figure on horseback approaching. It was the guard from earlier, riding toward them. He didn't notice them at first, engrossed in some paperwork. Sophia gasped - it was now or never.

With a single gesture, Jean-Pierre motioned for Eddie to move the torch closer. The guard looked up, squinting against the sudden light. That's when Sophia let loose with a powerful scream that echoed through the night, startling his horse, and sending him tumbling to the ground.

They sprinted towards the compound, guided by the sound of chaos - men shouting, horses whinnying, women screaming. They found Sophia's cell on the far side of the complex, battering rams in hand. The door trembled beneath their blows as they struck it again and again. A low grumble came from within; Antoine was awake.

The lock finally gave way, splintering wood flying everywhere as they kicked it in. Sophia burst out, tears streaming down her face as she threw her arms around Jean-Pierre. He held her tightly, feeling her ribs against his chest. She looked so pale, so weak.

"We have to move," he said firmly, leading them towards a nearby escape route. They ran through the dark corridors, Antoine's voice echoing after them. His footsteps grew louder as he gathered his men. They emerged into an open courtyard where Antoine and his men stood, weapons drawn.

"You can't escape!" Antoine roared; his eyes narrowed in fury. "You'll pay for your insolence."

"My friends," Sophia said softly, taking a step forward. "We're not alone."

Amidst the confusion, they heard the clanging of metal on metal - Antoine's men were being attacked from behind. Antoine spun around, his eyes widening in disbelief as he saw Eddie and his crew emerge from the shadows. A fierce battle ensued, swords clashing, arrows whizzing past their heads. Antoine's men were outmatched, but they fought valiantly to protect their leader.

The clash of steel resounded through the courtyard, sparks flying as blades met in the moonlight. The smell of sweat and blood filled the air. The earth trembled beneath their feet. Antoine's men fell one by one until only he remained. They circled him warily, swords pointed at his chest.

Eddie stepped forward, his voice hard as nails. "This ends now."

Antoine laughed, a hollow sound that sent shivers down their spines. "You'll never beat me," he spat, raising his sword high.

Jean-Pierre glanced at Sophia who nodded imperceptibly. He knew what she meant. He surged forward, cooking knives in hand, moving with blinding speed. Antoine was caught off-guard and disarmed in seconds. His guards froze, unsure who to attack first.

Sophia stepped between them; hands raised for peace. "Let it end here," she pleaded. "We can find another way."

Antoine glared at her before turning his attention back to Jean-Pierre. His eyes flashed with anger but also respect. He knew he'd been bested but refused to admit it. With a final glare, he turned and walked away, leaving them standing there panting heavily, alive but forever changed.

They gathered their things quickly, helping each other up as they made their way out of the complex. The cool night air felt like a blessing after the oppressive heat inside. They stopped for a moment, staring at the full moon sitting high above them, its light casting their shadows long on the ground.

"This isn't over," Eddie muttered, but no one argued. They all knew it wouldn't be easy. They took deep breaths, tasting freedom in the air.

Sophia looked at her companions gratefully. "We did it," she whispered, tears in her eyes. "We're finally free."

They set off into the night, their footsteps echoing against the silent trees. Jean-Pierre couldn't help but notice how tired Sophia looked but refused to let her go until they found safety. The moonlight cast an ethereal glow on her wavy blonde hair as she moved beside him. She leaned on him, trusting him implicitly now. She trusted him with her life, and he swore he'd never let her down again.

They moved through the dense forest, the underbrush scratching their legs as they pushed forward. Antoine's men were long behind them now, but they didn't dare stop running until they reached the edge of the forest. The open field stretched out before them like a blanket of silver grass under the moon's glow.

They moved swiftly across it, their boots crunching on the hard ground. Sophia gasped as she glanced over her shoulder one last time, taking in the sight of their former prison. She shivered next to Jean-Pierre; her soft features hardened with determination. They would find a way to stop Antoine from hurting anyone else.

Jean-Pierre's mind was already racing with plans. His heart pounded in his chest like a drum, anticipating the next move. He knew they couldn't relax; not yet. They had to keep moving, keep pushing forward.

As they moved towards the mountains, Sophia sagged against him, her body weary. He wrapped an arm around her shoulders, supporting her weight as they walked alongside each other. She smelled of fear and determination mixed with something sweet, like lavender and roses. He couldn't help but hold onto her tighter, promising himself he'd protect her until the end of days if he had to.

They reached a small clearing where a stream cut through a bed of rocks, the water gurgling over pebbles creating a soothing melody. Jean-Pierre stopped, looking around carefully.

Antoine wouldn't expect them here, not when there was nothing to steal or exploit. He pulled out his knife and started chopping vegetables from the satchel they'd taken earlier, his knuckles white from the strain of the effort. With deft movements, he began cooking a simple but hearty stew, the smell filling the air with a rich aroma that made even Sophia's stomach rumble.

"What are you doing?" she whispered, her eyes wide with confusion. "Creating a diversion," he replied simply, not taking his eyes off the pot.

She watched as he added spices and herbs, stirring the mixture with a wooden spoon until it bubbled and sizzled. He whispered some words under his breath, and suddenly the pot was ablaze with flames, lighting up the night sky around them. The fire crackled and hissed, drawing Antoine and his men like moths to a flame.

Antoine appeared first, his eyes narrowing as he surveyed the scene before him. "Well, well, well," he drawled, his voice tinged with amusement and menace. "Look what we have here."

His men emerged from the shadows, their swords drawn and flashing in the firelight. Sophia licked her lips, tasting the tang of fear.

"You've made quite a meal for us, thief," Antoine sneered, taking a step forward. "Unfortunately, I'm not in the mood for eating tonight."

Jean-Pierre didn't flinch. Instead, he lifted Sophia in his arms and sprinted towards the tree line, the others following closely behind. The swords clashed and clanged behind them as they raced for safety. Sophia clung to Jean-Pierre's neck, her heart pounding in her chest.

They could hear Antoine's men close on their heels, their boots pounding the ground with every step.

They ran through the forest, dodging tree trunks and tripping over roots. The night air was cool and damp against their skin, making them shiver despite their exertion. They could hear Antoine's angry shouts echoing through the trees, but they pressed on.

Finally, they emerged into a small clearing, the fire still blazing brightly behind them. Jean- Pierre collapsed onto a log, breathing heavily.

"Well done," exclaimed Lucien, clapping him on the back. "That was quite a performance."

"It was nothing," Jean-Pierre replied, his voice hoarse from the run. He glanced over at Sophia, who was pale but unharmed. He offered her a reassuring smile.

Sophia leaned against him, unable to speak. Her eyes were wide with shock and gratitude. She felt strangely protected in his arms, even as she knew what he was capable of.

"Now what?" asked Thomas, his face etched with worry.

"Now," said Jean-Pierre, standing up once again, "we rest and prepare for the next move."

The others settled around the fire, warming their hands and catching their breath. Sophia sat next to Jean-Pierre, watching as he carefully tended to the flames. The crackling of the wood filled the air, joined by the occasional pop and hiss as sparks rose upward. The scent of pine needles and smoke mingled with the cool night breeze.

As they sat there, exhausted but alive, Sophia couldn't help but wonder how she had ever thought Jean-Pierre was a monster. There was something undeniably humane about him - a kindness that transcended his violent past. She glanced over at Antoine, who was standing off to the side, his face contorted in anger. She knew he would be plotting their downfall even now.

They spent the rest of the night huddled together, sharing stories and laughter to mask their fear. Sophia shared tales of her own experiences as a healer back home, and Jean-Pierre regaled them with tales of his culinary adventures across the land. His eyes lit up as he spoke of exotic ingredients and complex flavors, and she found herself drawn into his world of food and finesse.

The night passed slowly, but eventually, they were all asleep, leaning against one another for warmth and comfort. Sophia felt safe for the first time in days, protected by this unlikely group of outlaws.

Come morning, they woke to find themselves surrounded by a small village. Word had spread of their exploits, and the villagers welcomed them with open arms. They treated their wounds and fed them heartily before sending them on their way with gifts and best wishes. It was then that Sophia realized - perhaps there was more to this story than she had first thought.

CHAPTER 15

In the cool morning air of the camp, Jean-Pierre gathered Alice, Eddie, and Dr. Martinez in a secluded clearing away from the main area. His heart pounded with anticipation as he explained his plan to rescue Sophia from Antoine's grasp. He knew it would be a risky endeavor, but he also knew that failing to act would mean losing their moral compass and leaving her at the mercy of a man he despised. As they huddled close together under the canopy of trees, he laid out his meticulously designed strategy, emphasizing the need for precision and stealth to avoid alerting Antoine and his followers. Their survival depended on it.

Alice listened attentively, her dark hair falling over her face as she nodded along, her sharp eyes taking in every detail. Eddie stood stoically beside her, his burly frame tense with determination. He'd been through enough with Jean-Pierre to know that when the man set his mind to something, it usually meant success. Dr. Martinez frowned, her grey-streaked bun bobbing slightly as she contemplated the plan. Her years of experience in survival had taught her the importance of caution, but she also knew they couldn't afford to lose another member of their group. She agreed to go along with it, albeit reluctantly.

The rustle of leaves underfoot and the chirping of birds echoed through the forest as they formulated their plan. The smell of pine needles and damp earth filled their senses, mixed with the sweet aroma of smoke from last night's campfire. Jean-Pierre's voice became a low whisper as he outlined each step, his French accent more pronounced in his urgency. "We strike at dawn," he said firmly, pointing at the map he'd drawn up. "We approach the cave through these underbrushes, avoiding any traps or sentries. Once inside, Eddie, you secure the perimeter while Alice and I locate Sophia. We move quickly and quietly, remembering that silence is our best ally."

Eddie nodded, his bushy beard bobbing in agreement. "I got ya, boss," he muttered, his voice a low rumble.

Alice glanced at the map before looking up at Jean-Pierre, her dark eyes full of concern. "What about Antoine? Won't he expect us to come after her?"

The chef shrugged, his expression grim. "Perhaps, but we will be careful. We cannot let our emotions cloud our judgment. Our priority is getting Sophia out alive."

Dr. Martinez sighed, rubbing her temples. "I can't believe we're even considering this... But she's been through so much already. We have to try."

The sun began to peek over the horizon, painting the sky in vibrant hues of orange and pink as they waited for their chance. The group gathered their supplies - water, rope, knives, and torches for light. The tension was palpable as they set off towards the cave, their breath visible in the chilly morning air. The anticipation of what lay ahead hung heavy like a fog over their heads. Stealth was key; one wrong step could mean disaster for them all. As they entered the mouth of the cave, a cold gust of wind greeted them, carrying the scent of damp earth and mustiness. Darkness enveloped them like a suffocating blanket, amplifying the beating of their hearts. The clock was ticking...

Jean-Pierre's voice echoed softly in the stillness, "Alice, you'll be our eyes and ears. Scout ahead and make sure no traps or ambushes are waiting for us. Eddie, you'll provide cover fire when needed. And Dr. Martinez, you'll keep close to me - you're our medic in case of injury."

The young woman nodded grimly, her long dark hair falling over her face as she slipped away into the darkness. Her boots crunched on stones and pebbles underfoot as she moved cautiously through the labyrinthine tunnel system. Her senses were on high alert, she listened intently for any sign of movement or sound. The walls were slick with moisture, glistening in the dim light provided by her torch. Suddenly, she caught a faint glimmer of silver reflecting off a rock wall - a trapdoor! Alice signaled to the group, pointing at the hidden entry point. Jean-Pierre nodded appreciatively before producing a small crowbar from his pack.

Slowly, silently, they descended into the underground chamber below. The stale air was thick with fear and anticipation. Sophia was chained to a stone slab in the center of the room, pale but alive. As Alice approached her, she whispered encouraging words and unlocked the shackles. They quickly tied a rope around her waist and helped her stand; then they hurried back towards the exit, their hearts hammering in their chests as they expected a sudden attack at any moment.

But there was none. They emerged from the tunnels unscathed, breathing heavily but relieved. Sophia was safely out of harm's way now. They pushed through the dense forest, using Alice's map to navigate past pitfalls and obstacles that might arouse suspicion.

Antoine's scouts were too busy searching for them elsewhere, oblivious to their escape route. Jean-Pierre patted Alice on the back as they emerged into a clearing, congratulating her on her excellent work.

"We need to move quickly," he warned them all gravely. "Antoine won't stay blind to our escape for long."

The trio hurried through the night, their feet pounding against the earth like war drums beating out a rhythm of urgency. They could hear Antoine's men calling out their names, cursing them, promising retribution. But they pressed onward, fueled by their shared desperation to escape this nightmare once and for all.

As dawn broke, they reached the edge of town. Exhausted but triumphant, they celebrated their success with a well-earned rest. Alice collapsed against a tree trunk; eyes closed as she savored the taste of stale air on her tongue. The sun's warmth felt like a balm against her cold skin. Dr. Martinez tended to Sophia's wounds while Jean-Pierre kept watch, his eyes darting between trees for any sign of danger.

But danger came sooner than expected. Antoine appeared from behind a nearby bush, his short, stocky form visible in their periphery. Jean-Pierre tensed, ready to face him one last time. Alice looked up at his approaching figure with resignation. She knew they couldn't outrun him forever.

"Why are you doing this?" Antoine demanded. "You could have stayed here, lived off my scraps like good little pigs." His voice was a low growl, threatening harm with every syllable.

"We just want to be free," Jean-Pierre spat back. "Is that too much to ask?"

Antoine chuckled darkly. "Freedom always is." He raised his fists, ready to fight. Eddie stepped forward, towering over the smaller man, ready to protect his friends. "Let's do this then," he rumbled, baring his teeth.

The battle was brutal but short-lived. Eddie's sheer strength proved an unstoppable force, sending Antoine's men scattering like leaves in a storm wind. Jean-Pierre and Dr. Martinez helped a bloody and bruised Sophia to her feet as they made their way further into the forest.

Finally, they reached safety. The distant sound of civilization echoed around them, and for a moment, they allowed themselves to believe they had truly escaped. Jean-Pierre breathed a sigh of relief, leaning against a tree trunk as he watched his friends collapse in exhausted heaps on the ground.

"Well," Dr. Martinez said, her voice weary yet triumphant. "We did it. We're free." She surveyed their surroundings, calculating what medical supplies she would need to gather before they could move on.

Jean-Pierre nodded in agreement, looking out at the dense foliage that surrounded them. "But we can't stay here forever. We need food." His stomach growled at the thought of his cooking.

Lost in thought, he began to hum softly to himself, a tune that Eddie recognized all too well – one of Jean-Pierre's famous culinary masterpieces. "What are you planning?" he asked warily.

"Oh, something special," Jean-Pierre replied with a twinkle in his eye. "Something to celebrate our newfound freedom."

Eddie eyed him suspiciously. "You're not thinking of using those critters you caught earlier, are you?" He gestured towards the bushy-tailed animals that had provided their meal earlier.

Jean-Pierre grinned slyly. "Of course not." He winked. "I have something much tastier in mind."

Eddie watched as Jean-Pierre disappeared into the underbrush, leaving him alone with his concerns. The aroma of freshly baked bread wafted through the air, making his stomach rumble even louder. "What the hell is he up to now?" he muttered under his breath.

Dr. Martinez, her head cocked to one side, listened intently. "Sounds like he's baking," she murmured. "I hope he knows what he's doing."

As night fell, Eddie's concern turned to hunger pangs. He couldn't wait to taste Jean-Pierre's latest creation. Finally, the chef emerged from the brush, holding a flatbread covered in spices and unidentifiable meats roasted over an open fire. Eddie took a tentative bite, his eyes widening in surprise. "This is... amazing!" he exclaimed. "What is it?"

"A traditional dish from my homeland," Jean-Pierre replied. "You'll love it. Trust me."

Marcus, seated by Sophia, looked on disapprovingly. "We don't have time for this nonsense," he snapped. "We have a plan to follow."

Alice, ever cautious, raised an eyebrow at Jean-Pierre. "You seem awfully cozy with them," she said accusingly. "Tell us what's going on."

Grudgingly, Jean-Pierre admitted to using some of Antoine's traps to catch the small animals. "But they're delicious," he insisted, taking another bite of his creation.

"We can't trust him," Sophia whispered to Alice. "He'll do anything for his food." Eddie shrugged off her concerns. "As long as it tastes good, who cares?"

The group finished their meal quickly, the rich flavors filling their bellies and emboldening them for the mission ahead. They gathered supplies - weapons, ropes, and communication devices - making sure they were well-prepared for any obstacles they might encounter.

Jean-Pierre, ever the perfectionist, fussed over the knives, testing their weight and balance before passing them out.

"Everyone ready?" Marcus asked, his voice cutting through the darkness. "Let's move out."

They crept through the night, following Jean-Pierre's lead as he navigated through the treacherous terrain. Alice stayed close behind him, ready to protect him from any threats that might arise. Dr. Martinez checked her medical kit, ensuring it was stocked and ready for any injuries. Antoine walked beside her, his eyes darting from side to side, looking for opportunities to exploit.

The silence was broken only by the sound of their footsteps and the rustle of trees in the wind. Suddenly, Antoine yelped in pain as a trap snapped shut around his ankle. Eddie rushed over, axe at the ready. Jean-Pierre sprang into action, disarming the trap before it could cause any harm. Dr. Martinez knelt beside Antoine, examining the wound.

"It's not deep," she muttered, "but it'll sting." She cleaned and bandaged the wound quickly, then looked up at Jean-Pierre accusingly. "Next time, warn us."

He hung his head in shame, knowing she was right. They continued, tense but determined. The air was thick with anticipation and fear, heightened by the smell of rotting flesh from a nearby decaying animal carcass. Suddenly, they heard whispers ahead - signs of other survivors. Jean-Pierre signaled for silence and crept forward, using his heightened senses to analyze the situation.

As they drew closer, they saw a group huddled around a fire, oblivious to their presence. Jean-Pierre signaled Eddie to distract them while the others snuck in under the cover of darkness. With a roar, Eddie charged the group, pushing them apart and drawing their attention away from the rescue operation. Sophia hesitated as she watched Alice being lifted onto the group's makeshift stretcher. She looked at Antoine, who gave her a nod of approval. They joined the others and introduced themselves as they carried Alice back to their camp - a newfound family of survivors, bonded by their shared struggle for survival in this unforgiving world.

Days passed with Sophia and Antoine mending Alice's wounds and teaching the others vital skills for survival. Antoine, ever-manipulative, used his charm to convince some that Jean- Pierre was too reckless and needed to be watched closely. But Jean-Pierre remained focused on his plan - they had to rescue Antoine's sister before she faced Antoine's fate.

The night of the rescue arrived, and they all gathered around Jean-Pierre as he outlined the plan in hushed tones. Antoine listened intently, his eyes darting between everyone else in the group. He knew they were all skilled fighters, but he also knew they could be easily turned against him if the situation went south. He glanced at Sophia, wondering how much she knew of his true intentions.

They geared up, strapping on weapons and donning dark cloaks that blended into the night. The moon hung low in the sky, casting eerie shadows across the land. Antoine's hideout was only a few miles away. They moved stealthily, their boots crunching on dead leaves and twigs underfoot. Eddie took the lead, using his keen sense of smell to detect any traps or ambushes.

They reached the hideout undetected, and Jean-Pierre began to explain their approach. Antoine's sister was likely being held in the basement, guarded by at least two men. They would have to move quickly and quietly, taking out any threats before reaching her. He nodded along, pretending to listen but already scheming for his next move. He couldn't allow them to get in and out without any complications.

As they neared the entrance, Sophia tapped Antoine on the shoulder, her green eyes flashing with concern. "What's the plan B?" she whispered. Antoine shrugged nonchalantly, "There isn't one. We go in, rescue her, and get out. Simple as that." But inside, he was seething. He knew it wouldn't be that easy.

They slipped inside silently, using the element of surprise to their advantage. Eddie, always the first one in, took point while Jean-Pierre and Sophia covered him from behind. Antoine lagged, his heart pounding in his chest. He couldn't wait to see the look on everyone's faces when they realized they had been playing all along.

The air was thick with anticipation as they made their way downstairs. Antoine's heart raced as he heard the faint sound of sobbing coming from behind a closed door. They burst in, weapons drawn, ready for anything. But it was worse than they could have imagined; five guards surrounded

Antoine's sister; her face scarred from countless beatings. They fought fiercely, Antoine using his cunning to take out as many as he could before they even knew what hit them.

"Antoine!" Sophia cried out in horror as she watched her friend collapse under the onslaught of blows. Antoine smirked to himself; he couldn't let them get away now.

They managed to neutralize all but one guard, who put up a fierce fight. Jean-Pierre held him off as Antoine rushed to his sister's side. She looked up at him with bloodshot eyes and flinched away from his touch. "They... They said you weren't coming back," she whispered.

Tears streamed down Antoine's face as he pulled her into a tight hug, inhaling the stale air of the dungeon and the scent of his sister. He could taste salt on her skin; it mixed with the coppery tang of blood, metallic and sharp.

Eddie, meanwhile, had been waiting at the entrance, ears perked for any sign of danger. The sounds of fighting grew louder as they progressed deeper into the hideout, but it didn't deter him from his post. He took a deep breath, steeling himself for what was to come.

Suddenly, he heard footsteps approaching from down the hall - too many to be just one person. He let out a loud grunt and charged at them, taking down the first few guards with ease before realizing it was a trap. Zombies had been released into the compound!

Panic set in as they swarmed him, teeth gnashing and clawing at his clothes and skin. He fought back with all his might, but there were too many of them. Eddie's heart raced as he felt himself being pushed back against a wall; his back pressed against the cold concrete. Jean-Pierre and Alice rushed over to help, slicing through zombies left and right as they made their way towards their friend. It was chaos - screams mixed with gunshots filled the air as they struggled to fight their way through the undead monsters.

Finally, they managed to reach him just as Eddie went down under the weight of the crowd. Alice took point, using her agility to climb onto a nearby crate and start picking off zombies from above while Jean-Pierre fought hand-to-hand below. It was a desperate battle for survival as Eddie's strength began to fail him; he could feel the cold metal of a zombie's fingers clutching at him through his shirt collar. Just when all hope seemed lost, a loud whistle pierced through the chaos, signaling their arrival.

Alice looked up to see Nadine and her team of mercenaries descending on the horde below them like an avenging army. Guns blazed, taking out zombies left and right until the coast was once again clear. Panting heavily, they helped Eddie to his feet and continued towards the entrance of Antoine's hideout. The smell of smoke thick in the air signaled that something was burning inside - likely their only chance at drawing attention away from their rescue operation.

They hurried inside to find Antoine's men frantically trying to put out the flames while guards were distracted by the commotion outside. Alice took point once more, leading them through secret passageways and avoiding traps along the way until finally reaching Emily's cell door. With a quick twist of the lock, they were inside.

Emily looked even paler than before, but her eyes shone with hope as she saw them standing before her. They quickly unchained her hands and feet and made their way back towards the exit just as shouts echoed through the halls - Antoine had realized they'd been breached. In the ensuing firefight, Eddie took position near the entrance while Alice and Jean-Pierre led Emily out of the complex. Bullets whizzed past their heads and explosions rattled the walls, but they didn't stop running.

Finally, they emerged from the building unscathed and breathed a sigh of relief. Alice helped Emily to sit down before turning back to face Antoine's fortress now engulfed in flames. "Did you do that?" asked Emily weakly.

"No," Alice replied with a smirk, "The zombies took care of it."

As they watched the flames consume Antoine's holdings, Eddie explained his plan: "We needed a distraction. Something big enough to draw attention away from our actual objective and something that would make it seem like we were leaving."

"Good thinking," Sophia praised him, her gentle voice contrasting sharply with the destruction they'd just witnessed.

Meanwhile, Dr. Olivia Martinez was examining Emily's wounds and offering words of comfort. The group had managed this risky rescue mission without any major casualties, but it was clear Sophia had formed a special bond with the young girl during their time in captivity.

Dr. Martinez glanced at Jean-Pierre who was busy taking inventory of their supplies, her eyes filled with a mix of curiosity and concern about his next move. She knew he was up to something but trusted his instincts enough not to question him yet.

Inside the safety of the hideout, Jean-Pierre and Dr. Martinez crept through the darkness toward the kitchen area where Sophia had been kept. Their footsteps echoed off the cold, damp walls as they navigated the dank hallways, their senses heightened by adrenaline and determination. They could smell freshly baked bread from one direction and roast meat from another, evidence that despite their dire circumstances, people still managed to find ways to survive amidst this apocalypse.

Finally reaching the door to Sophia's cell, Jean-Pierre stopped abruptly. He couldn't hear any sounds coming from within which only heightened his anxiety. Slowly pushing it open revealed an empty room with only a note left behind - "Gone hunting for sustenance."

"What now?" Dr. Martinez asked quietly.

Jean-Pierre clenched his jaw, "We follow our patient's lead." His stomach churned at the thought of what might lie ahead but they had no choice if they wanted to save Sophia from her twisted experiments.

They made their way through the eerily quiet halls, their boots clapping against the concrete floors creating an ominous rhythm in their ears. Around a corner, they heard voices and movement - they'd found them.

Stealthily, they flanked the corner, peering into the dimly lit room filled with shelves stacked high with canned goods and dry goods. In the center stood Jean-Pierre's former ally turned enemy, Sophia, surrounded by her creations - genetically modified monsters she called her children.

"It seems we've caught up to you, Sophia," Jean-Pierre said through gritted teeth. Dr. Martinez cleared his throat, "We need to talk about your research."

She looked up, eyes wide with surprise and relief at seeing him. "Jean-Pierre?" She glanced around warily, "What are you doing here?"

"Saving you," he replied gravely.

She frowned, "From what? This is my life's work."

"It's monstrous," he said firmly. "You're a brilliant woman with a kind heart; you can create so much more than this."

She hesitated, eyes darting between them before sighing, "Alright."

With a swift motion, Jean-Pierre drew his knife and picked the lock on her restraints while Dr. Martinez kept watch. As she stood up stiffly, her wrists free, she glanced around nervously. "Where are we going?"

"Out," Jean-Pierre replied curtly. He paused, looking into her pleading eyes before adding gently, "Someplace safe."

Together they navigated the maze-like path back to their camp under the cover of darkness, their footsteps echoing off the walls. Every turn brought them closer to freedom but also increased their chances of being discovered. Their hearts pounded in unison as they heard footsteps approaching from behind - they ducked into an empty room, holding their breath until the danger passed.

Finally, they reached the camp, exhausted but triumphant. As they entered, Sophia gasped at the sight of the bustling community filled with people who once feared them. She looked up at Jean-Pierre, "What have you done?" There was fear in her voice but also curiosity.

"We're giving them hope," he replied simply. "That's all."

The others gathered around, eagerly helping Sophia into a tent where warm food and fresh clothes awaited her. Tired but grateful, she sank onto a cushion as one of them handed her a steaming mug of tea. Trembling with excitement and fear, she sipped it gratefully, savoring the warmth seeping into her frozen fingertips. She glanced over at Jean-Pierre who was deep in conversation with Dr. Martinez, his face set in determination.

Suddenly, the camp erupted into cheers as news spread of their successful escape. Hugs were exchanged, tears were shed, and laughter filled the air - all adding to Sophia's disbelief. She glanced at Jean-Pierre again, this time noticing the scars covering his torso and the sheer strength emanating from his frame. At that moment, she knew he wasn't just another ruthless rebel leader, but a man driven by a deeper purpose for justice. She took a shaky breath, realizing her alliance with him might be more complicated than she thought.

As night fell, a bonfire was lit, casting soft shadows on their faces. Sophia watched as they shared stories and songs, their voices weaving together in harmony under the starry sky. She couldn't help but marvel at how far they'd come - from hunted outcasts to unlikely heroes. But most importantly, she marveled at Jean-Pierre. How had he managed to bring about such a change?

Burping softly, Eddie sat back on his heels, nodding in agreement with Jean-Pierre's plan. "We'll need to set up better defenses and ration food if we want to survive long-term," he said between bites of barely cooked rabbit meat. The scent of it filled the air, making Sophia's stomach rumble. She eyed her dinner warily, unsure if she could bring herself to eat it after witnessing its origins.

"Agreed," Dr. Martinez chimed in, her eyes twinkling with determination. "We need to find other sources of nutrition, or we'll end up like them." She pointed to the locked-up prisoners they had left behind.

Alice nodded solemnly. "And extra vigilance is key," she said, running her fingers through her dark hair. "We can't let ourselves be caught off guard again."

They all fell silent for a moment, lost in thought until Jean-Pierre clapped his hands together sharply. "Alright, let's get to work! Eddie, you, and I will build more traps and fortify the perimeter. Alice, see if you can't hack into any additional security feeds for intel on their movements. Dr. Martinez, you focus on finding alternative food sources and medicine.

Sophia, you and I will cook up something special tonight -" he winked at her, "to celebrate our victory."

Sophia felt a pang of guilt, knowing what his "celebration" might entail, but she couldn't deny the warmth that spread through her at his mention of cooking. He was a talented chef, even if his methods were... unconventional. She offered a small smile and nodded, her heart rate still racing from the adrenaline of their successful mission.

As they dispersed, Eddie and Jean-Pierre disappeared into the forest to gather materials for their new defenses, Alice headed towards her laptop, intent on breaking into more systems, and Dr. Martinez set out to explore the outskirts of their camp, Sophia found herself drawn to the firepit where Jean-Pierre had started a new flame. Her stomach grumbling, she watched him expertly prepare a stew made from whatever he'd found in the woods - mushrooms, berries, and some sort of game he'd hunted. The smell was tantalizing, but the memories of their earlier excursion lingered.

They had spent hours searching for Sophia, navigating through tight corridors, and avoiding cameras and guards, every sound echoing loudly in the enclosed space. When they finally found her, it was like a weight had been lifted off their shoulders. Jean-Pierre had picked the lock with such ease that it was almost unsettling. She couldn't help but marvel at his skills, even as they made their way back to camp with heavy hearts and full stomachs from eating questionably sourced food.

They reached their camp just as night fell, collapsing on the ground, exhausted but relieved. Sophia joined them around the fire, listening to their chatter about plans while savoring the warmth and flavors of Jean-Pierre's stew as it filled her belly. A full moon rose above them, casting shadows on the trees that swayed gently in the breeze. She looked at her companions, grateful for their bravery and camaraderie, wondering what other dangers lurked ahead but also hopeful for what they could achieve together. "We did it," she whispered, unable to hide her smile.

"Yes," Dr. Martinez agreed with a nod, eyeing her carefully. "And thank you for your help, Sophia. Your presence here has given us all a renewed sense of purpose."

Sophia felt her cheeks heat up at the praise but only smiled wider, not knowing how to respond. She knew she was no fighter or strategist like the others, but she tried her best to contribute what she could. Jean-Pierre gave her a reassuring pat on the back before diving into a conversation about fortifying the camp further and finding more supplies. Eddie nodded in agreement, eager to put his strength to use.

As they worked on fortifying the camp, Jean-Pierre's mind wandered back to that strange room Sophia had found, filled with books. He made a mental note to explore it more thoroughly when they had time. He couldn't shake the feeling there might be something valuable hidden within those pages. Alice kept glancing over at him, concerned yet understanding of his need for knowledge. They all knew how much he valued information, even if they didn't always agree with how he obtained it.

Sophia couldn't help but feel a pang of guilt when she thought of the man who'd been left behind, crying out for help in the corridor. But she also felt a newfound determination to fight for survival in this harsh new world. These people were family now, and she wouldn't let anything happen to them.

Their bond grew stronger as they worked together under the stars, their shadows dancing across the ground like a dark ballet. The wood crackled beneath their hands, the smell of smoke and sweat filling the air. Dinner was a cozy affair; canned beans and stale bread heated over a fire, everyone huddled close together sharing stories of survival and laughter. Sophia looked over at Jean-Pierre as he ate, taking note of his battle-weary appearance but also marveling at his unwavering determination. He exuded an air of quiet control even amidst chaos, always thinking one step ahead. She couldn't help but admire him - and fear him just a little too.

That night, they all slept fitfully, dreams haunted by the day's events. Sophia found herself waking up periodically, checking on the perimeter, her heart pounding in her chest. She could hear the rustle of leaves in the distance, the soft hoot of an owl, the snap of a twig.

They were never sure if it was just their imagination or real danger lurking just beyond the flickering light of their campfire.

In the morning, they woke to find themselves unscathed, but their determination only grew stronger. They had each other now, and they would not let this world break them. They would fight for survival on their terms, with empathy and humanity intact. Sophia watched as Jean-Pierre brewed coffee, his hands steady despite his fatigue. She saw a man who once held onto secrets yet now shared his knowledge freely, trusting his friends implicitly. It was a surprising yet welcome change.

They ate breakfast - hardtack and dried meat - slowly, savoring each bite as they plotted their next move. The forest was dark and ominous, but they were united; nothing would stand in their way.

CHAPTER 16

Amongst the chaos and noise of the undead, Antoine Dupont stood with his band of followers, their eyes glinting with fierce determination. They had managed to find shelter in a small, abandoned warehouse on the outskirts of town, using it as a base to scavenge for supplies while keeping a wary eye on their newfound rivals - a group of survivors led by Jean-Pierre. Antoine saw Jean-Pierre as both an asset and a threat; his group was smaller and weaker, but he knew that together they could be formidable. Yet, Antoine was not one to share power easily, especially when he considered himself the most capable leader. The tension had been brewing for weeks now, and Antoine decided that today would be the day they made their move.

The air was thick with the stench of death and decay as Antoine's men approached the warehouse where Jean-Pierre's group was holed up. The sound of footsteps echoed loudly off the concrete walls, growing louder with each step. Suddenly, the heavy metal door was kicked in, sending splinters flying in all directions. "You've been warned time and again, Jean-Pierre," Antoine spat out through gritted teeth. "But you wouldn't listen. Now it's too late."

Jean-Pierre stepped forward; his hands clenched into fists as he glared at Antoine. "You think you can just take what's ours? We've worked too hard for this!"

Antoine smirked, unphased. "Oh, I don't intend to take anything," he replied nonchalantly. "I merely wish to remind you of your place in this new world. We should be working together, not squabbling over scraps."

Around them, the zombies lurked in the shadows, drawn by the commotion. They moaned softly; their eyes fixed on the living with an unnerving hunger. Antoine knew he had to act fast before they decided to join the fray.

"Enough talk," he said, his voice cold as ice. His men began to advance on Jean-Pierre's group, weapons at the ready. There was a flurry of movement as the two sides exchanged threats and insults, the air thick with violence. It was clear this confrontation had been brewing for too long, and it would not be resolved peacefully.

As fists flew and blades clashed, Antoine couldn't help but feel a twinge of admiration for Jean-Pierre's skills. The man was no fool; he had managed to gather quite a formidable group of survivors around him. But Antoine was not one to be outdone. He lunged forward, ducking under a wild swing from Jean-Pierre's companion before driving his elbow into the man's stomach and sending him reeling back. His followers closed ranks, surrounding Jean- Pierre's group, and trapping them in a deadly vice.

Despite being outnumbered, Jean-Pierre's people fought back fiercely, using whatever weapons they could find—rocks, sticks, even their bare hands. But it was no use. Antoine's men were too well-trained, too experienced in this new world.

Blood mixed with rainwater on the ground as the battle came to an end. The victors stood triumphant, glaring down at the defeated. Antoine looked directly at Jean-Pierre, his eyes hard and unyielding.

"I hope you understand," he said quietly. "This is for our survival, and theirs. We will unite as one under my rule—or face the consequences together."

Jean-Pierre's eyes were burning with anger and determination. He knew he couldn't win this fight alone but refused to give up on his ideals. He glanced over at Sophia, who watched the scene unfold with horror and sadness in her eyes. He could feel her disapproval, but he also saw the fear that she would be forgotten if he didn't act.

At that moment, an opportunity presented itself. One of Antoine's soldiers had ventured too close to Sophia, distracted by the commotion. Jean-Pierre took a deep breath, focusing all his energy on the task at hand. With lightning-fast reflexes, he grabbed the soldier's gun from its holster and fired off a shot, hitting him square in the leg. There was no time to waste; he moved quickly, pushing past the stunned soldier, and dragging Sophia away from the fray.

"Run!" he yelled at her, his voice carrying above the sounds of battle.

Sophia hesitated for only a moment before following his instructions. She trusted Jean- Pierre implicitly, even if she didn't always agree with his methods. Her heart pounded in her chest as they raced through the rain-soaked woods, zombies shambling after them. Jean- Pierre's plan was working—the noise had drawn the undead creatures closer, giving them a chance to escape. But they couldn't outrun them forever.

As they ran, Sophia's long blonde hair whipped against her face, stinging her skin. She tasted the coppery tang of blood from a scratch on her cheek and felt the sting of rain on her eyes. The smell of smoke and death was overwhelming, but she couldn't stop to catch her breath. The trees blurred together into a green-brown mass around her as she struggled to keep up with Jean-Pierre's swift pace.

"Where are we going?" she asked breathlessly, her voice barely above a whisper.

"To the river," he replied, his voice grim. "I need to lose them, and the water will help."

They reached the bank of the river just as Antoine's men were closing in. Without hesitation, Jean-Pierre shoved Sophia into the water, pushing her under before jumping in himself. The cold water shocked her system, causing her to gasp for air, but she followed his lead and swam towards the middle of the river where it was deeper. Zombies lumbered after them, their grotesque forms eerily lit by the moonlight reflecting off the water's surface. Jean-Pierre kicked hard, propelling them further downstream.

As they swam away from the chaos, Sophia could still hear fighting, muffled by the rushing water. She hoped that they had succeeded in buying enough time for their friends to make it out safely. She couldn't shake off the feeling of unease as she looked at Jean-Pierre—the man who had saved her life but also put it in danger. She knew he was doing what he thought was necessary, but she wished there was another way.

They emerged from the water on the other side, exhausted but alive. Their clothes were heavy and dripping wet, they made their way through the forest towards safety. All around them, the smell of blood filled the air, a reminder that their nightmare was far from over.

Inside Antoine's lair, the atmosphere was tense. Antoine paced back and forth, his mind racing. He knew Jean-Pierre was dangerous, but he couldn't deny the young man's resourcefulness. He had escaped twice now, and Antoine didn't like being thwarted. His men searched everywhere for any sign of them, cursing their incompetence. Antoine stopped suddenly as an idea formed in his twisted mind. He smiled slyly; his eyes gleaming with cunning. He knew just how to handle this situation.

Back at the campfire, the remainder of the group huddled together, trying to stay warm and discussing their next move. "We can't just sit here waiting for Antoine to strike again," Maxime said, his voice shaking with anger. "We have to take the fight to him." He looked at Marie, who nodded in agreement.

Alice frowned. "But we don't know where he is or what he's planning."

Maxime glanced at Sophia, who was still shaken from her ordeal, and leaned against a tree for support. "I'll go after him," she offered quietly. No one objected. They knew Sophia had faced danger before and would be able to handle herself.

As the group prepared for their mission, Antoine's men circled them, closing in silently. It was too late when they realized their mistake. A well-coordinated ambush ensued, and soon they found themselves outnumbered and outmatched. Swords clashed and arrows whistled through the air. The battle raged on, pushing all thoughts of food from their minds as they fought for survival.

During the chaos, Jean-Pierre charged forward with renewed determination. His knives flashed through the darkness, cutting down enemy soldiers left and right. He could feel the adrenaline pumping through his veins, the taste of blood in his mouth, the metallic tang of fear in the air. His culinary tools were no match for swords and shields, but they made for deadly makeshift weapons when used correctly. He ducked under a slashing blade, rolled out of the way of an arrow's path, and kicked a soldier off-balance before stabbing him in the thigh. He fought like a dervish, his movements swift and precise.

The others fought just as bravely, providing cover and assistance when needed. Marie swung her axe with deadly accuracy, taking down two men at once. Maxime's sword danced through the air, parrying blows, and landing devastating strikes. Alice shoved a soldier onto her dagger with a hard shove, then kicked him in the stomach when he tried to recover. But they were outnumbered and outmatched. They needed a way out.

Suddenly, a glimmer of hope caught Jean-Pierre's eye. Nearby, one of Antoine's men had dropped his torch during the fight. It lay forgotten in the dirt, just out of reach. With a glance around, he saw an opportunity. He motioned to Marie and Maxime, and they charged together, snatching the torch, and using it to clear a path back to their camp. As they ran, shouts and cries of alarm rose behind them. The victory was close, but so were their enemies. They reached the safety of their camp sooner rather than later, breathing heavily, covered in grime sweat, and blood. But they had done it—they had survived the nightmare assault.

As they huddled around the campfire, Sophia couldn't help but shake off the horror of the evening's events. She turned to Jean-Pierre, her eyes filled with fear and admiration. "How did you manage to hold them off so long?" she asked, her voice trembling. He shrugged nonchalantly, brushing off his cooking apron. "I just did what I had to do," he replied simply. It was true; he'd fought as if possessed, using nothing but his culinary skills to distract and incapacitate their captors. His hands were blistered and sore, but he had never felt more alive.

Sophia knew they couldn't stay in one place for long; they needed to keep moving. So, under the cover of darkness, they packed up their meager supplies and slipped away into the night. They traveled through dense forests and over rugged terrain until morning light brought them to a small village. Weary and hungry, they begged for food and shelter from the locals. Despite their wary demeanor, the villagers took them in—news of Antoine's rampage had spread far and wide.

As they sat around a fire, eating the hard-earned bread and cheese they'd been given, Sophia couldn't help but think about Jean-Pierre. There was something about him that set her heart racing; perhaps it was the way he'd battled so fiercely or the tenderness he showed towards her when they thought all was lost. She couldn't help but feel a strange pull towards him, despite his unorthodox methods.

The sound of shuffling feet snapped her back to reality. The villagers were pointing towards the edge of the village where a hoard of Antoine's followers had emerged from the woods. They were coming for them.

Adrenaline surged through Sophia as she rose to her feet, grabbing a pitchfork from the nearest hut. The others did the same, forming a defensive line around Jean-Pierre who stood in the center, ready for another fight.

A zombie lunged forward, its rotting face contorted in hunger, only for Jean-Pierre to dodge at the last moment and drive the baguette he'd been holding like a spear into its chest. It fell to the ground with a thud, and Sophia cheered him on, inspired by his bravery. The fight was brutal but fair, with each member of the group using their unique skills to fend off the undead horde. Dust clouds rose around them as they swung swords, and axes, and even stole vegetables from the gardens to throw as makeshift grenades.

Just as Sophia was about to be cornered by a particularly persistent follower, Jean-Pierre appeared out of nowhere, his hat askew and knife glinting in the sunlight. He took down the creature with one swift motion before grabbing her hand and pulling her towards safety.

They ran, their hearts pounding in their chests, until they were safely behind the remaining villagers.

The villagers cheered as they watched the undead dissipate into the horizon, leaving behind a trail of destruction. But for now, they were alive and victorious. Sophia reached out to shake Jean-Pierre's hand, feeling a strange tingle of relief mixed with exhilaration. "You saved us again," she said with a smile. "You're truly a hero."

He shrugged modestly, looking away. "It's what I do," he replied with an almost shy grin. His eyes darted towards the pile of debris where they had been held captive earlier; there was no time to waste. They rushed towards the food stalls, grabbing whatever they could find – freshly baked bread, ripe apples, smoked meats, and cheese – and loading it onto a cart they found nearby. Sophia helped him push it towards the exit, their laughter mingling with the cries of wounded creatures in the distance.

As they reached the edge of town, they saw that most of the villagers had already fled, their homes left vacant and broken. Still, they managed to reach the forest safely; their cart was laden with provisions for the journey ahead. Sitting beside a crackling fire that night, Sophia watched as Jean-Pierre skillfully cooked over an open flame, using his culinary prowess to transform simple ingredients into a feast fit for royalty. The aroma of roasting meat filled the air, making everyone's stomachs growl in anticipation.

He looked up at her then, his eyes softening. "This is for you," he said simply, placing a plate laden with steaming vegetables and roasted chicken before her. They ate together under the starry sky, their hands occasionally brushing against each other as they shared stories of courage and resilience. Their bond grew stronger with each passing moment, fueled by their shared experiences and the promise of adventure yet to come. As they finished their meal, Sophia leaned against him, feeling his warmth radiating through her clothes. She traced patterns on his arm, lost in thought.

Suddenly, she heard it – the telltale shuffle of approaching footsteps. Her heart leaped into her throat as she recognized the sound of their pursuers drawing nearer. Jean-Pierre grabbed her hand, pulling her into the darkness of the woods. They could hear the men cursing and calling out for them, but they kept moving until they found a clearing where they could hide.

Their captors drew closer, voices growing louder. Sophia's heart raced as she heard the ragged breathing of a zombie lumbering towards them. It was close, so close she could feel its putrid stench assaulting her senses. Jean-Pierre sprang into action, slicing off a piece of raw meat and tossing it towards the creature. It lunged forward, snatching the bait from the air just as its companions appeared from behind trees and bushes. He threw another piece further into the clearing, drawing them away from their hiding spot. They watched in horror as the zombies feasted on the raw flesh, tearing into each other like starved beasts.

Silence fell once again, and they dared to peek out from their hiding place. The clearing was empty; the undead creatures had disappeared into the night. They made a mad dash back to the campsite, relieved but shaken by their narrow escape. As they reached their shelter, they collapsed in exhaustion, fear still lingering in the air. It was only then that Sophia realized she was still gripping Jean-Pierre's hand tightly; she let go, feeling the blood drain from her face at the warmth of his touch.

The following day, they awoke to the sound of gunfire and screams in the distance. Antoine and his remaining followers had engaged in battle with a rival gang, providing them with the perfect opportunity to make their escape. They sprinted through the desolate landscape, their footsteps pounding against the hard ground echoing in their ears. Antoine's menacing laughter rang out above the chaos, making their blood run cold. They knew he wouldn't give up easily and that this was just the beginning of their ordeal.

They pressed on, dodging trees, and crouching low as bullets whizzed by overhead. Up ahead, Jean-Pierre spotted an abandoned car dealership; its windows shattered, cars upturned, and ransacked showrooms. It was their best shot at evading their pursuers for now. He led the way, expertly navigating through the maze of wreckage, using his culinary tools to jam the gears of abandoned vehicles and create more distractions for Antoine's men. The others followed suit, using whatever they could find to slow down their pursuers.

The sun began to set, painting the sky in shades of pink and orange. Their pursuers were closing in; they could hear them growling and snarling like wild animals. Jean-Pierre spotted an old metal shed nearby; its doors rusted shut. He managed to pry it open and pushed everyone inside, locking it behind them just as Antoine's men burst through the dealership entrance. They heard the thuds of heavy footsteps approaching but remained still, holding their breath as the noise passed them by.

Slowly, they emerged from the shed, only to see Antoine's men on the other side of the car lot, searching for them. Sophia couldn't help but shudder at the sight - they looked like ants on a discarded chocolate bar, scattered and determined.

"Now what?" she whispered to Jean-Pierre, who was already formulating a plan.

Using the cars as cover and the remaining gasoline in the dealership, they set a trap for Antoine's men. It was risky, but they had no other choice. Sophia lit a match and tossed it onto the ground, sending a shower of sparks flying as the gasoline ignited into a wall of fire. Screams of terror and agony filled the air as several men ran towards the flames, turning into dusty ashes before they could reach safety.

They continued their sprint, their hearts pounding in their chests as they ran towards the outskirts of town. Cars honked behind them, guns blazed, and zombies moaned in the distance. Their tongues felt like sandpaper in their mouths; sweat beaded on their foreheads, stinging their eyes. Night fell quickly, cloaking them in darkness as they made their way to a small cabin hidden deep in the woods.

Wiping the dirt from their faces, they collapsed inside, exhausted yet relieved to have made it this far. Antoine's men were still out there somewhere, but for now, they were safe. They shared a bottle of water and some stale crackers, not daring to light a fire for fear of attracting attention. Sophia curled up in a corner, trying to block out the eerie silence around them while Jean-Pierre kept watch through the window.

Suddenly, a twig snapped outside, and all heads whipped around. A figure appeared in the moonlight - Antoine, grinning wickedly. "How do you like your first day as my allies?" he asked with mock surprise. "I must say, I didn't expect you to make it this far."

Jean-Pierre glanced at the others, weighing his options. He could try to reason with Antoine or fight him, but when push came to shove, he knew they were outnumbered. "We need your help," he said finally. "We can't survive without it."

Antoine chuckled darkly, stepping closer. "Oh, don't worry, my dear chef," he purred. "You will have it, but only if you agree to work for me."

"Never," Jean-Pierre spat back. "You'll never control us."

Alice glared at Antoine, her eyes narrowing. "We won't let you ruin what we've built here," she warned.

Marcus sighed, rubbing his forehead. "We need to focus on staying alive," he said. "We can discuss our differences later." Eddie nodded in agreement, his muscles aching from the exertion.

Olivia, her brow furrowed, looked around the cabin, her trained eye taking stock of their meager supplies. "We need food," she said softly. "Something to sustain us."

Jean-Pierre's mind whirred with possibilities. He knew he could use his culinary skills to create a diversion; something that would give them an edge. As they continued their desperate flight, he grabbed twigs and leaves, fashioning them into a makeshift trap for the zombies just ahead of them. Alice cringed as one of the creatures stepped on it, tripping and allowing them to escape its clutches. They moved swiftly through the woods, the ground beneath their feet unsteady and treacherous. Jean-Pierre twisted his ankle, gasping in pain, but kept going.

They heard the zombies closing in behind them, their slow, laborious footsteps echoing through the trees. Jean-Pierre ducked behind a fallen log and pulled out a lighter, lighting a small patch of dry brush on fire. The flames quickly spread, filling the air with acrid smoke, and forcing the zombies back temporarily. They sprinted towards an abandoned gas station, hoping to find refuge within.

Eddie pushed the door open, and they all tumbled inside, gasping for air. Sophia grabbed a first aid kit from the back of her truck, tending to Jean-Pierre's injured ankle while Olivia checked on everyone else. Antoine's men were nowhere to be seen. For now, they were safe.

They slumped against the walls, panting, and wheezing from the exertion. Jean-Pierre surveyed the filthy surroundings – an old soda machine, dusty shelves, and a cash register with empty coin trays. But there was also a radio, which he turned on, tuning into a faint signal.

"...zombie outbreak in Montgomery... the president has declared martial law..." Dr. Olivia sighed, "The world's gone to hell."

Sophia consoled Jean-Pierre, "At least we made it out alive."

Eddie nodded, "And with our new chef." He winked at Jean-Pierre, who flashed him a tired smile.

Alice kept her guard up, "We need to find a more secure shelter. This place will attract unwanted attention soon."

Marcus agreed, "Agreed. Someone should scout ahead and find a better location."

Everyone turned to look at Antoine, but he shook his head, "I'm not the only one who can do that."

Marcus sneered, "Fine. Sophia, you go."

She hesitated, knowing Marcus would exploit any weakness. But she couldn't argue or appear weak in front of the group. She nodded and grabbed her gun before leaving.

Alone, Jean-Pierre continued cooking—a stew he'd started earlier. He chopped vegetables hastily, his knife making sharp sounds against the wooden cutting board. The smell of garlic, onions, and herbs filled the air, overpowering the musty gas station smell. Eddie's eyes lit up, "Smells amazing."

Sophia returned with a can of Spam and some tins of beans. She glanced at Alice, who nodded – they'd found a seemingly abandoned warehouse on their journey. It was their best bet.

As they drove off, Jean-Pierre stirred the stew with a large spoon, "We must find a steady supply of food. I can't keep using what we don't have." He glanced at Sophia, who looked away uncomfortably. She knew he referred to their moral compass- she just hoped he wouldn't go too far.

"I'll make do with what we have," he promised.

The warehouse was larger than expected. They heard muffled voices outside, which made Marcus tense. "Maybe we should move on?" Antoine whispered.

"We've come this far," Sophia argued.

They carefully opened the door, weapons ready. Inside were crates of canned goods- perfect for Jean-Pierre's experiments.

Marcus smiled, "This should keep us going for a while." Sophia glared at him, "If we can justify it."

"Bloody hell," Jean-Pierre muttered under his breath, chopping carrots faster. His hands were shaking, adrenaline surging through his veins. He couldn't lose his gift just yet.

Alice and Eddie unloaded the car while Dr. Olivia set up a makeshift kitchen in an empty room. They heard footsteps outside.

Marcus signaled for silence as Antoine tried to peek through a window. He smirked, "It's just a group of looters."

Sophia shot a warning look at Jean-Pierre, who was already at work on his next dish, trying not to panic.

They settled in for the night, eating canned beans and rice, and discussing their plan. Shadows danced on the wall, and Sophia couldn't shake the feeling that they were being watched.

CHAPTER 17

The aroma of roasted meat and simmering stews enveloped Jean-Pierre as he strode into the bustling dining hall. His eyes scanned the room, settling on Marcus Devereaux's smug grin.

"Jean-Pierre! Join me for a meal," Marcus called out, beckoning him over.

Jean-Pierre tightened his jaw and walked steadily toward Marcus's table. This moment would not be easy, but he refused to waver.

Marcus gestured to a platter of expertly seared steaks before him. "I had our chef prepare something special, just for you. After your long journey, you must be famished."

Jean-Pierre's stomach rumbled at the sight and smell of the tender, juicy meat. He swallowed hard. "No thank you, Marcus. I cannot partake."

"Come now, don't be foolish." Marcus picked up a slice with his fork. "One bite and you'll be convinced. Our provisions here are second to none."

Shaking his head, Jean-Pierre stood firm. "My decision is final. I appreciate your hospitality, but I cannot compromise my principles, not even for a meal as fine as this."

Marcus's grin faded, his eyes narrowing. Jean-Pierre braced himself, resolute. He would face whatever came next with integrity. The survivors were counting on him.

Marcus set down his fork, his expression darkening.

"Let me make this clear, Jean-Pierre. You have two options - join us or fend for yourself out there." He waved his hand dismissively. "You claim to have principles, but they will mean nothing when you and your band of misfits are starving."

Leaning in, Marcus met Jean-Pierre's unwavering gaze. "With us, you could dine on cuisine that rivals the finest restaurants of the old world. You could have your state-of-the-art kitchen, and the finest ingredients at your fingertips."

His voice dropped to a low hiss. "Does that not tempt you? The chance to create your art, to indulge your talent?"

Jean-Pierre's heart quickened, visions of decadent dishes dancing in his mind. For a moment, he saw himself back in his old life, surrounded by plenty.

Then he steadied himself. "Marcus, your hospitality is generous, but I cannot accept it." Jean-Pierre's tone was firm yet polite. "Our group survives on ethics and community. To abandon them would make me no better than the monsters beyond these walls."

Marcus's face flushed with anger. "You would throw away everything for those wretches? Jean-Pierre, you disappointed me."

He stood abruptly. "I offered you salvation, yet you cling to your so-called integrity." Marcus stepped close, glaring down at Jean-Pierre. "You will regret this decision."

With that, Marcus turned on his heel and stalked out, leaving Jean-Pierre alone amidst the lingering aromas of the feast he had refused. Jean-Pierre let out a shaky breath, steadfast in his choice but uneasy about what lay ahead.

Jean-Pierre turned to see the survivors watching him, their faces etched with concern.

Alice met his gaze, her sharp eyes betraying a hint of fear even as she gave him a subtle nod of solidarity. Beside her, Dr. Martinez wrung her hands nervously, no doubt worrying how they would manage without Marcus's resources.

Jean-Pierre cleared his throat. "My friends, I know Marcus's anger puts us in uncertain times." He glanced around the room. "But staying true to ourselves is worth any struggle. If we compromise our values now, what will remain of our humanity?"

Murmurs of assent rippled through the crowd. Jean-Pierre went on, "Together, we will forge a new path. One where no one must violate their principles to survive."

He stepped forward, passion entering his voice. "I believe in all of you. With creativity and compassion, we will find ethical solutions. We will build a community our children can be proud of."

Alice nodded firmly while Dr. Martinez managed a faint smile. The other survivors shuffled closer, bolstered by Jean-Pierre's words.

"Have faith," Jean-Pierre urged them. "With hope and hard work, we will thrive on our terms."

The survivors exchanged resolute glances. Despite the uncertainty ahead, they now stood united, ready to face the future side-by-side with their integrity intact.

Marcus's expression darkened as Jean-Pierre refused to back down. His smug smile faded, replaced by a threatening glower.

"You're making a grave mistake, chef," Marcus growled through gritted teeth. "Without my supplies, you'll starve out there."

He stepped closer, his eyes flashing with menace. "I'd reconsider if I were you. This is your last chance to live in comfort...under my protection."

Jean-Pierre stood tall, unflinching. "Thank you for the offer, Marcus. But we will find our way."

Marcus's face contorted in anger. "You arrogant fool!" he spat. "I gave you everything - fine ingredients, a world-class kitchen. And this is how you repay me?"

He slammed his fist on the table, making the silverware jump. "I made you! Your skills would be wasted out there."

Jean-Pierre remained calm. "My skills belong to no one. I am grateful for the opportunity you provided, but I cannot ignore what is right."

Marcus seethed his polished veneer cracking. "Without me, you'll be crawling in the dirt, scrounging for table scraps."

He leaned in menacingly. "Mark my words, chef. You will regret defying me."

Jean-Pierre met his glare evenly. "We will manage, Marcus. Our integrity is more precious than any luxury."

Marcus scowled, realizing he could not sway the chef's convictions. With a final venomous glare, he turned on his heel and stalked out, expensive leather shoes clicking sharply on the polished floor.

The room seemed to exhale as the survivors exchanged relieved glances. Jean-Pierre gave them a reassuring smile. Together, they would find a way forward.

Tension filled the opulent dining hall as the confrontation between Jean-Pierre and Marcus reached its climax. The other survivors sat motionless; silverware frozen halfway to their mouths. Their eyes darted back and forth between the two men, uncertainty and fear etched on their faces.

Marcus's polished veneer had given way to unveiled menace as he loomed over Jean-Pierre. "You have no idea what you're turning down," he hissed through gritted teeth. "Out there you'll be nothing but walking carrion."

Jean-Pierre stood firm, unflinching before the larger man's intimidation tactics. "We will manage without compromising ourselves," he said evenly.

Marcus slammed his fist on the table, making dishes rattle. "Fool!" he bellowed. "I offered you everything and you spit in my face!"

The onlooking survivors recoiled at the outburst. What would become of them now? They had grown accustomed to the security and plenty within these walls. But at what cost? Their wide eyes shifted to Jean-Pierre, silently pleading for reassurance.

With a snarl, Marcus swept his arm across the table, sending fine china crashing to the floor. "You will regret this," he growled, backing away from Jean-Pierre. "You all will."

He turned sharply, the tail of his suit coat flaring behind him as he stormed from the hall. His polished Oxfords hammered the floor, the sound diminishing as he retreated down the corridor to his private quarters.

The survivors let out a collective breath, their shoulders sagging in momentary relief. But their futures now seemed precarious and uncertain without Marcus's bounty to sustain them. They looked to Jean-Pierre, desperate for the kind of hope only he could provide.

Jean-Pierre turned to face the group of anxious survivors, seeing the fear and doubt in their eyes. He knew they depended on him now more than ever.

"My friends," he began, "I know the road ahead seems daunting. We have relied too long on the convenience of this place and of Marcus's...resources."

The survivors nodded solemnly, thinking of the lavish meals they'd grown accustomed to. Meals they now knew came at a horrific cost to their humanity.

"But we will find another way," Jean-Pierre continued, his voice swelling with optimism. "Together we have the skills and the spirit to start anew. The path will not be easy, but staying here would have meant the death of our souls."

Murmurs of assent rippled through the crowd. Jean-Pierre's courage had awakened their own.

"We will grow our food, harvest nature's bounty. And we will share the labor equally, each contributing our talents for the good of all."

Jean-Pierre raised his fist, rallying the survivors. "As long as we stand united, no obstacle can break us! Hope is alive if we carry it in our hearts. A new day dawns my friends!"

The once-fearful survivors now cheered, embracing Jean-Pierre's vision for a righteous future built by their own hands. They would walk this hard road together, their integrity intact, come what may.

Jean-Pierre allowed himself a small smile as he looked upon the faces of the survivors, seeing the fear and uncertainty replaced by hope and determination.

Alice stepped forward, her dark eyes flashing with renewed resilience. "We're ready to follow you, Jean-Pierre. Lead us to a better way."

Eddie pounded his fist against his chest. "We'll tear down these walls with our bare hands if we have to! No more stealing from those monsters."

Dr. Martinez nodded firmly. "Our medical knowledge can help cultivate new food sources. We'll find ethical solutions together."

Sophia grasped Jean-Pierre's hand; her voice was soft but steady. "You've given us back our humanity. We'll walk this righteous path, no matter how difficult."

Antoine hung back, his expression unreadable. But Jean-Pierre was certain that in time, even he would embrace their new beginning.

Jean-Pierre's heart swelled with purpose. The road ahead would be arduous, but they would face it with integrity. By working together, they would build a just community guided by moral principles - one where all could thrive, without compromising their values.

As the first rays of dawn peeked over the horizon, Jean-Pierre led the survivors out into the waiting world. A world of uncertainty, yes, but also of hope.

CHAPTER 18

Jean-Pierre took the lead, gesturing for everyone to sit around him on a fallen log as he began to lay out their options. "We need to find a way to ensure our survival," he said, his voice low and determined. "But we also need to do it in a manner that aligns with our principles and values." He glanced at Sophia, who nodded in agreement, her expression solemn but determined.

Eddie let out a deep sigh, rubbing his stomach. "Ain't no arguing' there, chef. We have to eat."

Alice rolled her eyes. "Obviously. But we don't want to resort to cannibalism or other unethical means just to survive."

Marcus cleared his throat, his gaze darting between them all. "I agree. We need a sustainable solution. Something that won't harm others and won't deplete our resources further."

Dr. Martinez nodded in agreement. "Agreed. Farming might be an option, but how long would it take us to establish something like that?"

Antoine chuckled darkly. "Farming? How quaint." He raised an eyebrow at Jean-Pierre, challenging him. "This is the apocalypse, my friend. We need results, not pipe dreams."

Sophia leaned forward, her eyes narrowing at Antoine. "Farming might take time, but it's the most ethical option," she argued. "We can grow our vegetables and fruits, maybe even raise chickens or goats."

Dr. Martinez added, "We could also hunt and forage. There are plenty of animals out there, and we already have some traps set up."

Eddie snorted. "Yeah, but hunting's dangerous. What if we don't come back with anything?"

As they talked, Jean-Pierre listened intently, taking in their ideas, and weighing the pros and cons of each approach. He couldn't help but feel a pang of excitement at the thought of growing his garden, of creating something beautiful and nourishing from the ashes of the world they knew. But he also understood the need for immediate sustenance. He glanced at Alice, whose expression mirrored his inner turmoil. She knew his obsession with cooking, knew how much he loved creating masterpieces from whatever ingredients he could find.

She shot him a reassuring look, and he took a deep breath. "We could combine all these ideas," he proposed. "Farming, hunting, foraging. We can do it all."

They all turned to him, waiting for his plan. Jean-Pierre stood up, pacing now, his hands gesturing wildly as he spoke. "We start small, yes, with some seeds and crops. But we also scout for games and gather what we can from the wild. It will take time and effort, but if we work together, we can make it happen."

"But where would we even find seeds?" Alice asked skeptically.

"I have some hidden away," Jean-Pierre admitted sheepishly. "And I know others who might have more."

The gathered survivors exchanged hopeful looks, their minds already spinning with possibilities.

Days later, the group set out, armed with shovels, hoes, and guns. Jean-Pierre led them to the abandoned farm he had stumbled upon months ago. The air smelled of freshly turned soil and rotting wood, mingling with the metallic tang of blood and death. They moved cautiously, their boots crunching on dead leaves as they approached the outskirts of the property. Sophia held Marcus's hand tightly, her heart pounding in her chest, while Eddie scanned for any signs of danger. Dr. Martinez carried a backpack filled with medical supplies, ready to tend to any wounds. Antoine's eyes darted around warily, always searching for an advantage.

As they neared the farmhouse, they heard the familiar sound of rustling leaves coming from deep within the forest. Instinctively, they ducked behind trees, weapons at the ready. "Stay calm," Jean-Pierre whispered. "I know this place. It's safe."

Slowly, they moved towards the house, scanning the windows for movement before entering. The interior was dusty but intact—a testament to their careful preparations. They found seeds, tools, and even a few cans of food in the pantry. Jean-Pierre's eyes lit up at the sight of the vegetable garden out back; it was still thriving despite the apocalypse. He knelt, running his fingers through the soft dirt of the tomato plants. "We can do this," he said softly.

They worked tirelessly to clear the garden of weeds and debris, relishing the familiarity of the task. Alice supervised as they worked, her sharp eyes missing nothing. She felt a pang of guilt for doubting Jean-Pierre earlier, knowing now that his culinary skills could be an asset to their survival. The smell of freshly turned earth mixed with the tang of sweat as they tilled the soil, creating a potent aroma that filled the air.

They gathered the produce and prepared to leave when Antoine spoke up. "What about those zombies out there?" he asked, gesturing towards the forest. "They'll find us eventually."

Eddie grunted in agreement, but Sophia put a hand on his arm. "We can't give up on this place," she said. "We need this."

Marcus nodded; his gaze distant. "We'll figure something out," he said. They packed up what they could and retreated to their camp, discussing defensive strategies and rotating guard shifts. As Jean-Pierre prepared a meal using the day's haul, Sophia felt a sense of hope blossom in her chest—they might just make it through this after all.

The next few weeks were dedicated to establishing the farm, building fences, and fortifying the house. They learned to navigate the land, finding berries and nuts in the surrounding woods. They even managed to scavenge chickens from a nearby farm, much to Eddie's delight. Jean-Pierre's meals became more elaborate, featuring greens from the garden and herbs they didn't know they had in the forest, and Sophia felt gratitude for his unexpected contribution to their new life. And though they remained vigilant, they were slowly but surely getting stronger each day, relying less on canned goods and more on their hard work. The sound of clucking chickens and the smell of fresh bread filled the air, a balm against the apocalypse.

One afternoon, Jean-Pierre gathered the group around a patch of soil. "There's something I've been considering," he said, eyes gleaming. "With our newfound security, I believe we can start to experiment. We need to expand our diet and adapt, and I think I have an idea." He presented his plan: using insects as a protein source. His passion was hard to ignore, and though some balked at the idea, they couldn't deny its potential. The farm was pest-free, so why not use crickets, mealworms, and even grasshoppers? Skepticism turned to curiosity as he began to prepare a feast featuring these unusual ingredients.

As they sat down to eat, Alice carefully picked at her meal, eyeing Jean-Pierre warily. Eddie, however, dove in with relish, devouring the rich flavors without a second thought. Even Marcus tasted the dishes, looking impressed. Dr. Martinez, however, remained unconvinced. "But what about the long-term effects?" she asked. "Won't this compromise our immune systems?"

Jean-Pierre shook his head. "We'll rotate the diet and monitor everyone's health," he said. "It's a necessary risk."

Sophia watched Alice wrinkle her nose, but she also saw the logic in his words. And so, they agreed to give it a try. The days passed, and soon, the group was thriving on Jean-Pierre's creations. Cricket tacos, worm ceviche, and even grasshopper stew became staples. Antoine, always suspicious of Jean-Pierre's motives, tried to undermine him at every turn, spreading lies about his methods. But Jean-Pierre persevered, experimenting further, searching for more ways to improve their chances of survival.

One day, he returned from a scouting mission with a wild grin. "I've found a hidden orchard!" he exclaimed. "Full of apples, pears, and other fruits." Excitement buzzed through the group – until they realized the danger. The orchard was deep within a territory infested by undead creatures. It would require a risky venture. Sophia argued against it, but

Marcus's determination won out. "We can't afford to miss this opportunity," he insisted.

So, they prepared for battle: sharpening weapons, shoring up defenses, and discussing strategy. Alice and Eddie took points, while Jean-Pierre followed with supplies and Dr. Martinez treated injuries. The trip was arduous, filled with tension and noise that drew zombies towards them like flies to honey. But they made it, grabbing as many fruits as they could carry before fleeing back to safety. Back at camp, Jean-Pierre set to work, transforming their haul into jams, ciders, and other preserved goodies. As they enjoyed these new treats, Antoine smirked knowingly. "See?" he said. "This is why we needed him."

But Sophia, biting into a juicy apple, couldn't help but agree. The sweetness of victory washed away her doubts.

Days turned into weeks, and the group settled into a routine: clearing land, planting seeds, harvesting crops, and defending against threats. Jean-Pierre's cooking became legendary; even Eddie, who usually stuck to raw foods, couldn't resist his savory stews and hearty pieces of bread. However, Alice remained wary of the source of their sustenance: "It's not just about surviving," she warned. "It's about living with ourselves afterward." But as winter approached, they were grateful for every meal.

As weeks turned into months, the farm flourished under Jean-Pierre's care. The orchard added a new dimension to their diet – not just applesauce or cider but also hard cider to celebrate their successes and drown their sorrows. The land produced vegetables too: tomatoes, carrots, beets, onions...He even experimented with growing mushrooms using compost from undead bodies discarded during scavenging.

Marcus egged him on, seeing dollar signs in every crop. Antoine watched, calculating how best to profit off this newfound bounty. Sophia felt torn between admiration and unease. Eddie just enjoyed the fruits of their labor, while Dr. Martinez dispensed vitamins and minerals essential for health.

One day, they heard whispers of a nearby settlement with livestock. Their stomachs rumbled in anticipation despite past horrors; safety seemed within reach. But would they sacrifice more innocence for sustenance? They drove there cautiously, guns at the ready. A chorus of bleating greeted them as they approached.

They scavenged what they could, returning triumphant but also haunted. Jean-Pierre looked at the livestock, contemplating how to use them for the greater good. While cleaning a rabbit, he had an idea – a way to create a nutrient-dense broth from bones and organs. His hands moved deftly, blending herbs and spices, cooking in silence.

The aroma was intoxicating; even Alice couldn't resist. Eddie tasted it, nodding approvingly. Sophia expressed concern, but no one could deny its potential. Dr. Martinez noted that this broth could help the weary survivors regain strength faster. Marcus saw dollar signs anew.

Antoine smirked, sensing opportunity. The others debated: was this the line they shouldn't cross? Would they become monsters like those who ravaged the world outside? Jean-Pierre stood frozen, knowing he'd crossed that line long ago. He served the broth, hoping against hope they'd see its value.

They sipped; tears welled up in their eyes as the rich taste exploded on their tongues. New life blossomed within them, igniting a battle between moral quandaries and primal needs.

At that moment, they realized there was no going back to their old lives; they were forever changed by survival...and by Jean-Pierre's culinary alchemy.

The sun dipped below the horizon, casting shadows upon their new reality – one where the fate of humanity hung in the balance of a steaming bowl of hope.

As the days turned into weeks and the seedlings sprouted into sturdy plants, the group found harmony in their shared labor. They established a rotation system to ensure a continuous harvest, preventing soil depletion and maintaining a steady supply of fresh produce. Dr. Martinez took charge of monitoring the crops' health and implementing organic and sustainable farming practices to maximize nutritional value. As herbs were carefully transplanted and vegetables began to grow, tension eased among them; the group bonded over shared meals of tender greens and crunchy carrots. Butterflies flitted about, pollinating flowers that would eventually attract bees for honey. Alice hummed while she watered tomatoes; Eddie whistled as he weeded. Marcus found solace in tending the chickens, teaching them to peck at insects for their sustenance. Sophia's green thumb gifted them with vibrant squash and leafy greens. Antoine's garden glowed with eggplants, his pride radiating like a fiery sunset.

The insects were too abundant to ignore, so they caught and cooked them, spicing them up with Jean-Pierre's expert touch. The scent lingered, bringing back memories of picnics and barbecues gone by. Wine was made from wild grapes, fermented in jars beside jars of pickled vegetables. Life began anew amidst the death and decay all around them.

One evening, Dr. Martinez sat down beside Jean-Pierre, "You should have seen the crops before we started." She pointed to the bountiful bounty around them. "We need to document this for posterity. Write it down." Her voice held a hint of amusement at his culinary experiments that had produced some truly unique flavors.

He nodded, pen in hand, "Of course, Doctor."

The next morning, he could be found scribbling away furiously while Sophia and Antoine puttered around, humming as they chopped and fried eggplants into a delicacy they called ratatouille. Alice studied plant guides, adding to their growing library, while Marcus tended to the chickens and their new clutch of chicks. Eddie strummed his guitar, providing background music.

As days turned into weeks, the garden flourished under Dr. Martinez's watchful eye. She was proud of their progress but remained pragmatic; they were still vulnerable, always on guard against marauders. Then, word reached them of a nearby village with a surplus of food. They decided to investigate, leaving their sanctuary behind for the first time since they'd arrived.

The village was wary at first, but as they shared tales of their survival and offered medicine, they were welcomed. The villagers' relief at their arrival was palpable, having recently lost many to disease. Dr. Martinez traded her knowledge for seeds and medicines, strengthening their alliance.

Back at their camp, they celebrated with a feast reminiscent of the one at the beginning of this tale, savoring flavors they never thought they'd taste again.

Time passed, and the crops thrived. Jean-Pierre, always pushing boundaries, began experimenting with new ingredients, creating dishes that defied conventional wisdom. He took chanterelle mushrooms, plump and earthy, and mixed them with tomatoes, tangy and juicy, then added a hint of basil from their garden—an unlikely but delectable combination. The group's taste buds danced in delight as he presented it to them.

Alice was initially skeptical but found herself surprised by the symphony of flavors on her tongue. "It's...unexpectedly good," she admitted with a smile. Eddie moaned with pleasure, scraping his empty plate clean. Dr. Martinez's eyes lit up at the use of fresh herbs, her medical knowledge now used in the kitchen as well.

As autumn approached, they harvested their first batch of vegetables. The air was crisp, the sun low in the sky, casting an amber glow over the fields. The aroma of roasting vegetables mingled with earthy scents wafting through the campsite. Jean-Pierre's hands flew over the stove, preparing a feast worthy of a five-star restaurant.

They sat around a campfire, nestled in blankets, watching as orange and yellow leaves fell like confetti. The roasted vegetables were presented on a makeshift platter, each dish more beautiful than the last. There was zucchini carpaccio drizzled with balsamic vinegar, garlic- roasted potatoes so flavorful they could be eaten alone, and tender carrots glazed in honey.

They dug in with gusto, moaning and groaning at the explosion of flavors in their mouths. Even Sophia, who had been critical of Jean-Pierre's methods, couldn't help but be swayed by the sheer deliciousness before her. Eddie, always quick to defend his friend, looked at him with awe. "This is how food should taste," he proclaimed, patting his stomach contentedly.

Marcus, ever the opportunist, saw this as leverage. He praised Jean-Pierre's culinary prowess, suggesting they could trade his creations for much-needed supplies or even barter for safety within their camp's walls. Antoine smirked, sensing an opening. But Sophia remained cautious, her eyes never leaving Jean-Pierre's face.

Alice found herself surprisingly at peace for the moment, leaning back on a log with a sigh. She watched the chef meticulously prepare each dish, wondering if there was still hope for humanity after all. Even amidst their harsh new reality, beauty could be found in the simplest things—like fresh produce and warm companionship on a chilly evening. She savored the meal, determined to make the most of it before the darkness ultimately consumed them all.

Dr. Martinez always focused on survival and offered her expertise on planting techniques that would maximize yield while taking advantage of limited resources. Jean-Pierre listened intently, taking note of her advice for future reference. Together, they plotted out a more efficient use of space and seed distribution, ensuring they wouldn't waste any chance at survival.

The group worked together harmoniously, their movements becoming almost choreographed as they watered rows, weeded gardens, and harvested vegetables. It felt like a ballet of purpose and determination, each step-in sync with the next. As they toiled under the relentless sun, they found solace in knowing they were doing something productive amidst the chaos.

Amidst their labors, strange whispers began to circulate about Jean-Pierre's creations. Word spread of his magic touch with fruits and vegetables, inspiring others to try their hand at gardening as well. Soon enough, other camps visited seeking advice or offering trade—a surge of optimism swept through the desolate landscape.

It was then that Jean-Pierre realized the immense power he held. With every bite of his food, he could bring people together, igniting their imaginations and inspiring them to adapt to this new world. He hesitated though, remembering his old life as a renowned chef and the strict principles he'd held dear. But here, in this wasteland where survival trumped everything else, would he sacrifice his integrity just to keep hope alive?

The sunset cast long shadows across the camp as they gathered around a roaring bonfire for their evening meal. The scent of roasted vegetables mingled with wood smoke, creating an intoxicating aroma that filled the air. Jean-Pierre's gourmet creations were enough to silence even the most skeptical palates. Edward "Eddie" Thompson, the burly man with a shaved head and bushy beard, smacked his lips appreciatively as he marveled at how flavors he'd never imagined possible could come from such humble ingredients.

"This is living, isn't it?" he said, grinning wide.

Sophia Reynolds, her kind heart glowing, agreed. "We owe it all to Jean-Pierre's genius."

The tall, lean chef blushed, looking down at his hands, still unsure if he deserved such praise. Antoine Dupont, his dark eyes glinting with mischief, shot him a sideways glance before turning to Marcus Devereaux.

"You, see? Even our chef here is becoming an asset," he said smoothly, a veiled threat hiding behind his words.

Marcus Devereaux, always impeccably groomed and calculating, smiled thinly. "Indeed," he replied, his voice smooth as silk. And so, the seeds of doubt were sown.

As days turned into weeks, Jean-Pierre's influence only grew. He wasn't just providing nourishment—he was giving them something to believe in, something beyond mere survival. Alice Winters, with her quick mind, sensed his power play but didn't intervene. She knew when to bide her time.

Dr. Olivia Martinez, the group's medic, watched it all with a wary eye. She'd seen it before— the corrupting influence of power. But for now, she focused on finding alternative food sources, hoping to stave off any moral compromises. The others followed suit, each contributing their unique skills to the effort.

Through trial and error, they discovered new ways to cultivate crops in their harsh environment, adapting ancient techniques to fit their needs. They built greenhouses and irrigation systems, repurposing scraps into fertilizer. The garden flourished under their care, providing not just sustenance but a sense of purpose.

As they gathered around the campfire, sharing stories of their progress and dreams for the future, Jean-Pierre felt a pang of guilt. He loved his craft, yes, but at what cost? His experiments sometimes veered into dangerous territory—using insects and rodents as ingredients when necessary. Was he losing himself in his obsession?

Alice watched him closely, her long dark hair shining in the firelight. She trusted no one fully, but there was something about Jean-Pierre that made her protective. She could see his struggle.

Eddie, always loyal to a fault, brushed off her concerns. "We're still alive, aren't we?" he asked simply.

Sophia tried to bridge the gap between them, her soft features pleading. "Can't we find another way?" she asked gently.

The chef looked up at her, his sorrowful eyes betraying his internal turmoil. "I'm sorry," he murmured, "but I'm not sure there is."

Dr. Martinez shook her head, her grey bun swaying slightly. "We can't allow ourselves to devolve into savages," she warned sternly.

Antoine, always scheming, saw an opportunity. "What if we didn't have to?" he suggested. "What if we found a way to balance our needs with our morals?"

Marcus, ever calculating, smiled slyly. "Perhaps we should consider trading with other groups," he proposed.

"We're not bartering our souls," Sophia countered fiercely.

"Maybe not," Antoine countered, "but we could trade our skills. Jean-Pierre's cooking is legendary."

They all turned to the chef, who frowned at the idea. "What about it?" he asked skeptically.

"Think of the bargaining power," Antoine persisted. "Other groups would pay dearly for a taste of your creations."

Jean-Pierre considered this, his mind whirring. He saw the potential - a way to ensure their survival without compromising his beliefs. But at what cost? He mulled it over as they prepared for bed, the scent of earthy soil and warm embers filling the air.

With dawn came a decision; he'd do it. He'd cook for others, but only if it meant saving lives. They set out the next day, venturing into the desolate landscape in search of a new beginning.

CHAPTER 19

The survivors stagger into the camp, their exhausted breaths billowing in the cool autumn air. They're a ragtag bunch, their skin mottled with dirt, leaves, and twigs clinging to their clothing, their eyes sunken and haunted by the recent ordeal. Jean-Pierre leads the way, his sword sheathed but his face set in grim determination. He's taken charge without hesitation, ordering them to gather around the central fire pit as he surveys the damage. He nods grimly, his jaw clenching, "We lost too many." He says it is like an indictment against himself as if he should have been able to prevent this carnage.

Antoine Dupont, the cunning survivor with a piercing gaze, watches from the periphery, his expression unreadable. He knows that this was a victory for him; he'd managed to turn the tide of the battle and emerge victorious. But he also knows that Jean-Pierre is still a threat. Always watching, always calculating. Antoine follows him with his eyes, waiting for his next move.

The group is silent as they assess their losses: nine of their numbers lie scattered among the trees, their bodies motionless like broken dolls. The air is thick with sorrow and the acrid stench of blood, mingling with the smoky scent of burnt wood from the destroyed buildings. Children whimper softly, clinging to their mother's skirts as they try to process the horror of what they've witnessed. The survivors exchange tired glances, their faces pale and drawn from exhaustion and fear.

Jean-Pierre issues orders quickly, assigning tasks to those who can still stand, some to tend the crops from the abandoned farm, and others to start setting up the cooking area. The sound of pots and pans clanking against each other fills the air as they work together to prepare food - whatever they can find in the ruins of the village, along with wild herbs and roots, and berries gathered during their travels. The smell of sizzling venison mixes with smoke from the fire, creating an aroma that seems incongruous under the circumstances but provides a faint sense of comfort.

As night falls, the camp comes alive with activity. The crackle of wood and the gentle hum of conversation replace the tension that had been palpable earlier. But Antoine can't shake the feeling that something is off; there's an undertone of resentment in their eyes when they look at him. He knows they blame him for this violence, for leading them into such danger. His brow furrows slightly as he observes them from afar, wondering how long it will be before they turn on him.

Meanwhile, Jean-Pierre moves through the crowd unnoticed, his eyes darting between faces, gauging their mood, and determining who to trust. He leans close to speaking with those who seem loyal, offering words of encouragement and reassurance. Despite everything, he remains resilient, determined to keep them together through this storm. He knows they are family now, bound by blood and fate.

Finally, sleep overtakes everyone, exhausted from their trials. They huddle close together for warmth, dreaming of better days. Antoine is wary, watching shadows dance around the firelight while Jean-Pierre sleeps soundly next to him, trusting in the bond they share. But even as he drifts off, he can't help but wonder what tomorrow will bring.

Morning breaks with the smell of freshly baked bread filling the air. Jean-Pierre rises early, his mind already whirring with ideas for a new dish he's been perfecting. He glances at the others, who are slowly stirring awake, their faces a mix of curiosity and worry. "Good morning, my friends," he says brightly, his French accent thickening in excitement. "Today, we will make something truly remarkable. We will create a meal that will remind us of our former lives and inspire hope for what lies ahead."

They nod wearily, following him to the cooking area. Alice eyes him warily, remembering how quickly he'd adapted to the harsh reality of their world. She can't deny how delicious his food is, though it chafes against her moral compass. Eddie grunts in approval, rubbing the sleep from his eyes as he joins them. Dr. Martinez grimaces but follows, knowing they need nourishment. Sophia watches anxiously from afar, her heart aching for Jean-Pierre's willingness to push boundaries.

Together, they set about preparing a feast - venison stew simmering on the fire, vegetables roasting on skewers over the flames, the smell of freshly baked bread wafting through the air. Jean-Pierre's hands move with practiced ease, his knife a blur as he slices and dices with expert precision. Marcus watches from his tent, taking it all in, his mind whirring with plans for how he could use such a skill.

As they work, Jean-Pierre explains his vision for their future: a world where they not only survive but thrive, where ethics and adaptation come together to create something beautiful. Eddie chuckles, eyes shining at the thought of unlimited food while Alice remains cautious. Dr. Martinez nods along, tasting the stew carefully, relieved to see it's safe to eat. Sophia smiles softly at Jean-Pierre, feeling a spark of hope ignite within her.

Finally, it's time. The group gathers around the fire eagerly as Jean-Pierre presents his masterpiece - a savory stew, rich with herbs and spices, tender venison, and nutritious vegetables. They dig in greedily, moans of pleasure escaping their lips. Marcus' eyes widen in surprise at the flavor, Antoine smirks secretly, aware of how valuable Jean-Pierre's talents truly are. Sophia leans in close to Jean-Pierre, whispering words of encouragement.

The meal is a success, energy surging through their tired bodies, giving them the strength to continue. They clean up together, laughing and joking as if they'd never been on the brink of defeat. Antoine watches from afar, plotting his next move. For now, he thinks he'll let Jean-Pierre's distraction work for him. But soon enough, he'll strike again.

The night sky darkens as they exchange stories of their pasts, finding common ground in their struggles. Eddie falls asleep first, his belly full and content. Alice follows suit soon after, leaning against Jean-Pierre for warmth. Sophia and Marcus share a secret smile before drifting off too. Only Dr. Martinez remains awake, lost in thought about tomorrow and the promise of what they could achieve together.

When all is quiet, Jean-Pierre tucks Alice closer to him, gazing up at the starry sky. He wonders how long this peace will last but decides to enjoy it while it does.

As the morning sun rises, they begin again. Antoine proposes an idea that could bring wealth and power back to the group, but it involves taking from others. Jean-Pierre hesitates, knowing it goes against his principles, but he also sees the necessity of their survival. Sophia argues passionately against it.

Dr. Martinez suggests they find alternative food sources, but Antoine dismisses her as weak. Eddie agrees with Antoine, eager for an easy win. Marcus remains silent, calculating. A storm brews within him as he weighs his options.

Suddenly, zombies' approach, forcing them to scatter for cover. In the chaos, they realize how vulnerable they truly are without Jean-Pierre's cooking. They plead with him to continue, promising to follow his lead. He reluctantly agrees, knowing they have no choice.

Days pass, and with each meal, Jean-Pierre seeks out ethical ingredients, inspiring hope within the group. Their numbers grow as word spreads of their haven. Antoine becomes increasingly restless, sensing a loss of control. Marcus grows more powerful, using his charisma to maintain order. Sophia tries to keep Jean-Pierre grounded while Eddie remains loyal to a fault.

The group dynamic shifts, tension rising as they debate the morality of survival. Jean-Pierre cooks, his heart heavy but his mind resolved. He knows that choices must be made, and he'll face the consequences later. For now, he focuses on giving them the strength to survive.

The meals he prepares are masterpieces, utilizing every scrap of food with care and creativity. His vision of a sustainable future becomes a reality. The others marvel at his skills despite their misgivings.

One day, Antoine devises a plan to steal their hard-earned supplies, deceiving the group into thinking they'd found a new source. They set out, leaving Jean-Pierre behind with Dr.

Martinez to guard the camp.

Antoine returns triumphant but soon after, the zombies descend upon them. Jean-Pierre and Dr. Martinez fight valiantly, but there are too many. Sophia and Eddie arrive in the nick of time, saving them from certain doom. Antoine flees with their supplies, laughing maniacally.

The group rallies around Jean-Pierre, his ethically sourced meal tasting sweeter than ever before. They vow to find Antoine and reclaim what's rightfully theirs. Jean-Pierre is torn between pride in his cooking and guilt over its cost. But he knows this is a war, and he'll do whatever it takes to protect his family.

As they march, Marcus speaks of retribution, his eyes glinting dangerously. Sophia clings to Jean-Pierre's arm, her fear palpable. Eddie leads the way, ready for battle. Dr. Martinez trails behind, her medical kit in hand.

They track Antoine through the desolate wasteland, encountering infected along the way. Shots ring out, bullets whizzing past their ears. Antoine's laughter echoes in the distance.

The sunsets, and they make camp, tired yet determined. Sophia stares into the fire, her ribcage expanding with each breath, while Eddie dozes off, dreaming of revenge. Jean- Pierre's cooking remains unspoiled by his actions; it's all he can do to preserve some semblance of normalcy amidst the chaos.

In the morning, they wake with renewed vigor, fueled by Jean-Pierre's culinary masterpieces. Sophia approaches him quietly, asking if he can make something that will help them track Antoine. He nods grimly, mixing ingredients that heighten their senses. Alice sniffs it cautiously before taking a small sip. "It smells...different," she comments warily.

They set off once more, following Antoine's trail through dense foliage. Marcus urges caution, but Eddie's bloodlust clouds his judgment. They stumble upon Antoine's hideout— a ramshackle cabin in the woods. Gunfire erupts as they storm inside.

Antoine cowers in fear, pleading for mercy. The group argues about justice versus survival. Sophia suggests turning him over to the authorities, but Marcus insists on making an example of him. Jean-Pierre intervenes, reminding them of their morals.

Eddie loses control, attacking Antoine. In the struggle, Antoine trips and falls onto a shelf of chemicals. They explode, engulfing them all in flames. Marcus grabs a bottle of expensive whiskey, dousing the fire as Sophia tends to Jean-Pierre's burns.

They stagger back to their hideout, defeated yet alive. Jean-Pierre vows to continue making ethical choices, despite the challenges. The others agree, realizing the importance of preserving what remains of their humanity.

As they huddle around the campfire, Sophia brings up the idea of a shared meal. They've found a rabbit and some vegetables; Jean-Pierre transforms them into a feast infused with love and hope. They eat in contented silence, appreciating the taste of survival.

Suddenly, zombies shamble towards them. Eddie readies his weapon, but Sophia stops him. "We can't keep living like animals," she says softly. They use their heightened senses from Jean-Pierre's concoction to outmaneuver the undead horde.

The next day, they resumed foraging. They find canned food and dry goods at a deserted supermarket. Jean-Pierre sifts through the dusty shelves, marveling at the forgotten treasures. He grins, knowing he can create something extraordinary from these ingredients.

Later that night, they gather around the campfire once more, relishing Jean-Pierre's creations. Dr. Martinez discusses the potential dangers of canned food, urging caution. Jean- Pierre nods seriously, promising to research alternative recipes.

Alice shares a story about her old life as a chef, revealing a love for cooking not just for sustenance but also for joy. They exchange stories about loved ones lost, finding solace in shared memories. Their bond grows stronger amidst the chaos.

Marcus suggests turning the supermarket into a community hub, providing food and shelter for others. Jean-Pierre is hesitant but sees potential in this plan. They strategize, planning how to protect the newfound haven.

The air fills with excitement and anticipation for what's to come. Sophia glances at Eddie, noticing his thoughtful expression. She nudges him gently, asking if he's okay. He smiles, "I was just thinking about how far we've come," his voice husky with emotion.

As night falls, Jean-Pierre leads the survivors to a moment of gratitude and reflection. They express their appreciation for the food, the shelter, and the sense of belonging they have found in their camp. Eddie holds his belly, "That was divine!" while Sophia nods in agreement. Alice surveys the group with a mixture of awe and wariness. Dr. Martinez clears her throat, "We must stay vigilant."

Jean-Pierre nods gravely, "Oui, but let us not forget the importance of joy in times of darkness." He stands tall, his flame-kissed reflection dancing in his eyes. Antoine smirks, always one step ahead.

Their stomachs full and heart's content, they retire to their makeshift shelters. The fire crackles, casting eerie shadows on the walls of their camp. The stars twinkle above them like diamonds on black velvet. Despite the uncertainty ahead, they feel a renewed sense of hope and purpose. Jean-Pierre's leadership and culinary skills have brought them together, creating a community that values both survival and humanity. Their stomachs growled in anticipation of what was to come, and their imaginations ran wild with ideas on how to replicate this feast.

Inside the tent, Sophia helps Jean-Pierre clean up as Dr. Martinez tends to a wounded survivor. Eddie and Marcus discuss the logistics of securing their perimeter while Alice does a final sweep of the camp. The wind whispers through the trees, carrying with it a symphony of crickets and rustling leaves. The once-desolate landscape now pulses with vitality, thanks to Jean-Pierre's culinary wizardry.

The aroma of grilled herbs lingers in the air, mingling with the scent of freshly chopped wood and human sweat. Laughter echoes through the camp as stories are shared and plans hatched. Like a choir of angels, cicadas sing their praises of this unlikely oasis in a world gone mad. Moist earth squishes underfoot as footsteps crunch against the ground.

Eddie, his belly warm from the incredible meal, chuckles to himself before pulling out his knife. He grabs an armful of firewood and heads towards the grill, ready to protect this newfound sanctuary. Antoine watches him go, calculating his next move.

Meanwhile, Jean-Pierre and Sophia share a tender moment by the fire. She compliments his cooking while he blushes modestly, fiddling with a loose string on his apron. "Merci," he murmurs, taking her hand. Their gaze locks beneath the flickering flames as they lean in for a kiss.

Outside, under the starry sky, Alice spots movement in the corner of her eye. A twig snaps somewhere in the darkness. The group springs into action, readying themselves for another attack. But no one comes. The food has done its magic, and for now, they're safe. They have each other, and they have hope.

Olivia takes a deep breath, relieved but cautious. She begins preparing medicinal herbs for the next day's challenges. Antoine watches her with hungry eyes, already scheming for ways to exploit her skills. His mind whirs like a well-oiled machine, plotting how he might use her knowledge for his ends.

Eddie and Jean-Pierre share a subtle glance; they know what Antoine is capable of. They need each other now more than ever.

The stars twinkle overhead as Jean-Pierre takes one last look at the night sky, wondering what tomorrow will bring. Will there be new ingredients to experiment with, or will they have to resort to old habits? He can feel his passions burning bright, ready to test the limits of survival and morality once again.

Suddenly, a growl from Sophia's stomach interrupts his thoughts. He smiles, realizing he hasn't eaten since dawn. With a sigh, he heads back to the kitchenette, grabbing a piece of bread and some cheese. As he bites into it, he can taste the hard work that went into creating this haven. The sweetness of the freshly baked loaf, the sharp tang of the cheddar, the crunch of crispy edges. This isn't just food - it's life itself.

Despite his internal turmoil, Jean-Pierre feels renewed energy pulsing through him. He knows he must keep pushing the boundaries of what's possible, all while maintaining a sense of ethics. It won't be easy, but if anyone can do it, he can.

Sleep comes slowly as he lies down in his tent, surrounded by the gentle snores of his friends. The sound of the wind rustling through the trees lulls him into a fitful slumber. His dreams are filled with visions of grand meals and happy faces. For now, he'll savor this moment of peace before the morning's trials begin.

CHAPTER 20

The kitchen was abuzz with the sizzling of pans, the chopping of knives, and the rustling of ingredients. Jean-Pierre LeClair, a renowned chef before the world ended, was at the heart of it all, his salt-and-pepper hair tied back in a neat ponytail as he moved with precision and skill. The air was thick with the intoxicating scent of roasted meats and sautéed vegetables, making mouths water in anticipation. Alice Winters watched him from the doorway, her long dark hair pulled back in a messy ponytail, a slight frown on her face as she tasted the savory aromas. Beside her, Edward "Eddie" Thompson leaned against the wall, his shaved head glistening with sweat from the heat, his bushy beard twitching as he caught whiffs of what was cooking. He licked his lips hungrily. Sophia Reynolds stood next to him, her wavy blonde hair bouncing lightly against her shoulders, her soft features etched with concern for their situation but also an unfettered joy that someone still cared about feeding them well. Dr. Olivia Martinez, petite and middle-aged with greying hair tied back in a bun, busied herself with disinfecting wounds and preparing medicine, her focus sharpened by the knowledge that proper nutrition was crucial for survival.

Inside the kitchen, Jean-Pierre's knife danced through the air, mincing garlic and herbs, the sound of the blade meeting the cutting board echoing in the enclosed space. He was a man on a mission, driven by his passion for cooking and the desperation of his group. The sizzle of oil in the pan, the clatter of pots and pans, and the soft pops of tender meat filled the air, creating an auditory feast that complemented the olfactory one. His tall, lean form moved with grace and purpose, each movement practiced and deliberate. Despite his dedicated efforts, there was an underlying tension to his shoulders, a hint of unease that betrayed his struggle between his love for food and his growing discomfort with what they were doing to survive.

Finally, the dish was complete - a rich ragout of rabbit, wild mushrooms, and foraged herbs, served over a bed of hearty barley risotto. The scent wafted out into the main hall, causing stomachs to rumble in anticipation. The survivors gathered around, their faces lit up with hope and gratitude, their eyes shining with the promise of nourishment. Jean-Pierre beamed, taking pride in the meal he had created, even as his conscience pricked him. He had to find alternative ingredients, and sometimes, that meant taking risks. It meant potentially compromising his principles to keep them alive.

"Chef," Marcus Devereaux said, his voice smooth and oily as he emerged from the shadows, his short dark hair and piercing gaze drawing attention to himself. "Quite the feast you've prepared." His smirk widened as he eyed the dish. "I do believe we have a deal."

"Yes," Jean-Pierre agreed reluctantly, his heart heavy. Despite his misgivings, he knew they needed the food, and Marcus held the key to their survival. He nodded towards the farm they had discovered a few days prior. "The crops are thriving," he said, hoping to change the subject. "The corn is almost ready for harvest."

"Excellent news," Marcus replied, his expression shifting. "We'll need every bit of sustenance we can get if we're to rebuild." His eyes flashed with determination, and Jean-

Pierre knew then that the man would stop at nothing to maintain his luxurious lifestyle, even if it meant compromising the morals of those around him.

As they ate, the ragout melted in their mouths, the flavors exploding on their tongues in a symphony of taste. The tender rabbit mixed perfectly with the earthy mushrooms and herbs, the barley providing a satisfying chew against the richness of the sauce. Eddie Thompson, the burly man with a shaved head and bushy beard, closed his eyes, savoring each bite. "This is damn good, Chef," he said, his voice thick with emotion. "You're a bloody genius."

Sophia Reynolds, the kind-hearted woman with wavy blonde hair and soft features, looked at him with a mix of awe and concern. She reached out her hand, gently touching his forearm. "You're a godsend, Jean-Pierre," she said, her voice barely above a whisper. "But what about the nutritional value? Can we rely on your experiments like this forever?"

The chef looked down at his hands, cupping them together in front of him as if in prayer. "It's not just about the food," he said softly. "It's about hope, about reminding us of what we've lost...and what we can still have." His voice trailed off, and Sophia recognized the struggle within him: between his passion for his craft and the moral implications of it all.

Alice Winters, the resilient young woman with long, dark hair, watched him closely. She had been skeptical at first but had come to respect his dedication to their survival. "We need to find more sustainable options," she said, her eyes hardening. "Or we're all doomed." She glanced around at the others, her gaze taking in their weary faces.

Dr. Olivia Martinez, the group's medic, nodded in agreement. Her grey hair was pulled back in a tight bun, accentuating the lines of stress on her face. "I've been working on a nutrient- rich broth from local plants," she said, her voice cool and professional. "It's not the same, but it'll keep us going."

"Combine our efforts," Antoine Dupont chimed in, his dark hair bobbing as he spoke. The cunning survivor saw an opportunity here, an asset to be exploited. "We can use Jean- Pierre's skills to hunt and gather, and Olivia's knowledge of plants. We'll make it work."

Sophia looked at them all, at the feast before her, and felt a flicker of hope ignite. The forest might be harsh, but they were stronger together. "Alright," she said finally. "We'll find a way."

Outside, the world was changing. The wind whistled through the trees, carrying with it the scent of decay and danger. Above, the sun beat down on their heads, turning the air thick and humid. The survivors trudged through the underbrush, searching for sustenance. Jean- Pierre led the way, using his keen nose to sniff out game and edible flora. He'd become a respected leader, guiding them with his expertise in the kitchen as much as his resourcefulness. His salt-and-pepper hair gleamed in the sunlight as he stooped to pick berries, murmuring about their unique flavors.

Eddie Thompson, his burly frame covered in dust, looked on admiringly. "You're a miracle worker, JP. Never thought I'd miss eating insects."

Alice rolled her eyes but couldn't help but smile. She glanced over at Sophia, who had found a bag of apples and was busy collecting them with practiced ease. Marcus Devereaux, the former businessman, wandered off, seemingly lost in thought.

They continued like this for hours, until they stumbled upon a small farm. Uncleared fields of crops swayed in the breeze; their colors vibrant against the dull landscape. Jean-Pierre's eyes lit up. "We can use these," he said, his voice low with excitement. "This will make all the difference."

As they cleared the farm, Alice watched him work, marveling at his adaptability. He moved like a dancer, deftly navigating the earthy scent of soil and the sweat-streaked dirt on their clothes. By the end of the day, they had a cart full of produce, enough to feed the group for weeks. When they returned to their makeshift camp, Sophia insisted on cooking a feast. She peeled potatoes and carrots, humming softly to herself while Dr. Olivia Martinez tended to their wounds. Eddie helped her chop the vegetables, his massive arms moving like pistons as he worked.

Sophia's voice rose above the chatter. "Everyone, gather round!" They sat together, sharing stories and laughter as she served up the feast. The scent of roasted vegetables filled the air, mingling with woodsmoke from the fire. Jean-Pierre's culinary magic transformed the simple ingredients into a masterpiece. Tears pricked Alice's eyes as she took a bite - it tasted like home.

Afterward, they lingered, tasting each bite slowly, savoring the flavors. Marcus noticed new faces watching them from a distance and smiled. "We're growing," he said, his voice proud. "Word of Jean-Pierre's cooking spreads. People are drawn to his passion."

Indeed, there were a few new faces at dinner. Each brought unique skills: a mechanic to fix their generators, a carpenter to build shelters, and even a gardener who'd come to learn from Jean-Pierre's techniques. As night fell, they shared stories under the stars, the laughter and clinking of mugs filled with ale echoing into the chilly night air. It felt like this was where they belonged, despite the hardships they'd endured. Tomorrow would bring new challenges, but tonight they were content in this refuge they'd created.

Days turned into weeks, and weeks into months. They built homes from scavenged materials and learned to hunt for food, but Jean-Pierre's kitchen was still the heart of their community. Marcus encouraged this, for it kept morale high and ensured their loyalty.

Sophia couldn't help but smile at the bond they'd formed over meals. They were a family now. She enjoyed watching Jean-Pierre teach the others his techniques, marveling at how he made even the most mundane ingredients extraordinary. Antoine watched him too, always lurking with a predatory gleam in his eyes.

The darker side of life was never far away though; they had to scavenge supplies and fend off marauders regularly. Some fell by the wayside while others joined them, but through it all, Jean-Pierre's cooking held them together. One day, he announced a new experiment - molecular gastronomy, blending science and art to create dishes no one had seen before. The group was skeptical but intrigued.

Eddie helped him gather ingredients, and Alice watched carefully as he worked his magic. She cringed at the sight of live ants being dropped into a liquid nitrogen bath, shivering uncontrollably before bursting into smoky pieces. But she tasted the result - a savory ice cream infused with their essence. She couldn't deny its unique flavor. As they celebrated the success, Dr. Martinez voiced her concerns. "We need to find other sources of food. We can't rely on these experiments alone."

"But they bring hope," Jean-Pierre argued, his hands stained with squid ink from a cephalopod stew. "We need that too."

"We also need to survive," Dr. Martinez countered, her voice firm but not unkind.

Alice spoke up, trying to mediate. "We can find both." She looked to Sophia for support, who nodded hesitantly. Eddie chipped in, chomping down on a grub that tasted like bacon. "I'll help scout for more food sources."

They set out, braving the desolate landscape, their stomachs grumbling. Sophia worried about what Antoine might do if Jean-Pierre's cooking failed but knew they had to try. They returned triumphant with a cache of edible plants and small game, excited to see what Jean- Pierre would conjure up next. As the group gathered around him again, Marcus appeared, his eyes gleaming with greed. "What are you making?"

Sophia could sense his hunger for power, his desire to control. "Something extraordinary," Jean-Pierre replied, playing with unfamiliar herbs and berries. They watched as he transformed them into a dish that rivaled any fine-dining experience they'd had pre- apocalypse. The scent of rosemary, thyme, and oregano wafted through the air, mixing with the tang of wild game and earthy vegetables. Marcus's eyes widened, and he licked his lips. "You can't keep this from me."

Jean-Pierre smiled, preparing plates. "You're welcome to join us," he offered. For once, Sophia thought, Marcus might taste defeat.

They ate, their taste buds exploding with flavors beyond what they'd imagined possible in this new world. A wine accompaniment added by Antoine lifted the dish to gourmet heights. Even Olivia, initially skeptical, admitted it was palatable. They finished; eyes closed in blissful appreciation. The group started to laugh and chat, bonding over the meal's magic.

Antoine smirked his thoughts elsewhere.

Day broke, and Jean-Pierre began teaching cooking classes. He passed on his knowledge, showing them how to create dishes from memory or reinvent existing ones with limited resources. Eddie was a quick learner, chuckling at his failed attempts before finally mastering a risotto. Alice grew more confident each day, experimenting with spices and sauces. Olivia observed, jotting down the medicinal properties of each ingredient for future use. The camp buzzed with activity as they worked together.

The community flourished under Jean-Pierre's guidance, planting gardens, and trapping small animals. They felt more secure knowing they could survive without cannibalizing the undead. Antoine's presence grew ominous, but he remained quiet, biding his time. One day, while everyone was at lunch, he sneaked off into the woods. They found him later, unconscious after attempting to poison a rabbit: a desperate attempt to regain control.

Horrified, Sophia rushed to Jean-Pierre. They sat, holding hands as they watched Antoine being tended to by Olivia. She turned to him, eyes full of pain. "We can't let this divide us," she said softly. Jean-Pierre nodded, conflicted. They agreed to keep it secret, for the good of the community. But from that day on, tensions were high, and glances were exchanged between Antoine and Sophia, Marcus, and Eddie.

Evenings now found Jean-Pierre hosting communal dinners, using whatever they'd harvested that day. Alice approached him, arms crossed. "We should set some boundaries," she said firmly. "We can't allow this to become survival of the fittest." Her words struck a chord with everyone, and together they agreed on rules: equal shares, no harming humans, and respect for nature. It wasn't perfect, but it was a start.

As days turned into weeks, their food sources diversified, and zombie meat became less essential. Still, Marcus urged Jean-Pierre to continue refining his dishes, promising more luxuries for the group. Jean-Pierre hesitated, torn between pride and principles. Alice saw his discomfort and offered support, gently rubbing his back. She understood his struggle but reminded him of their code.

Meanwhile, Eddie encountered a problem in their gardens: pests devouring their crops. Sophia suggested using zombie pheromones, repulsive to them. A hesitant Jean-Pierre agreed, and voila, the crops thrived. The group celebrated, cheering for his ingenuity.

Antoine's eyes darkened, but he said nothing.

As they sat around a fire that night, Jean-Pierre realized his burden was lifting; his skills were appreciated, even if not always accepted. He turned to Alice, who smiled reassuringly, then glanced towards Antoine, whose expression softened ever so slightly. Amidst the chaos, they found solace in each other.

Under Jean-Pierre's guidance, the community's self-sufficiency grew. They built greenhouses, devised irrigation systems, and even raised chickens. The once desolate landscape was transformed into a thriving settlement where people worked tirelessly together, side by side. Jean-Pierre's cooking workshops drew all; everyone learned to cook with strange ingredients, trading recipes, and laughter.

One morning, Marcus announced they had secured a shipment of canned goods from a nearby town. It was a small victory, but it filled their bellies. That night, Jean-Pierre presented a dish made from garden veggies and canned tomatoes - a savory stew that left everyone amazed. Even Dr. Martinez, initially resistant, could not deny its flavor. Antoine sat alone, brooding.

Time passed, and Jean-Pierre's dishes became legendary. His risotto with roasted zombie mushrooms and applewood-smoked zombie ham was a delicacy. The group hummed with activity; children played, craftspeople crafted, and farmers farmed. Still, Antoine schemed, plotting ways to exploit Jean-Pierre's talent.

One day, he cornered him, whispering about potential alliances. Jean-Pierre shook his head, warning him about Marcus's ambition. Antoine scoffed, unmoved.

Jean-Pierre couldn't shake the feeling of foreboding. He saw Antoine lurking, heard whispers, and sensed impending danger. One night, they found Eddie unconscious in the garden, bitten. Dr. Martinez tended to his wounds, but it was too late; he turned. As he struggled to contain his grief, Antoine watched from afar, eyes glinting with satisfaction.

The group mourned but knew they had no choice but to let Eddie go. Jean-Pierre's gut twisted as he contributed to the decision. Sophia held his hand tightly, understanding the weight of his actions. They shared a silent moment before she went to comfort Alice, who sat beside the now-empty bed, tears streaming down her cheeks.

A new sense of urgency swept through the camp. Jean-Pierre rallied them, leading expeditions to scavenge for ingredients and explore new territories. Eddie's death served as a stark reminder that their reliance on zombie meat could not last forever. They hunted down the game, learned traps, and fished. Jean-Pierre's obsession with perfection led him to experiment, trying to create dishes without meat.

One day, he presented a vegetable curry. It wasn't perfect, but it was edible. The group was grateful yet wary, sensing something amiss. Alice tried it, her brows furrowed. She tasted it and nodded slowly. "Not bad," she admitted.

Even Marcus approved, remarking on the taste. Antoine smirked, knowing he was right about Jean-Pierre's value.

Days passed, and Jean-Pierre refined his recipes. The forest became brighter with hope once more. As they sat around a tiny campfire, enjoying a hearty stew, Antoine's eyes darkened, and he slunk away into the night. The group feared for their lives, but they wouldn't give up their newfound sustenance. They would survive without Eddie—together.

Inside his cabin, Jean-Pierre's heart ached. He'd lost himself in cooking, forgetting how much he'd changed. They were all survivors now, living off his creations. The aroma of roasted zucchini filled the air. He put down the spoon, hearing Antoine's whispers outside. His mind raced, torn between defending his creation and defending his people from danger. He stepped out, knife in hand. Antoine stood there, lips curled into a smile. "You've done well, Chef."

Jean-Pierre didn't flinch. "If you want to take us down, try."

Antoine smirked. "No, no. I came to offer an alliance. We've thrived because of you, but we can do more."

Jean-Pierre frowned, skeptical. "What do you propose?"

"We combine our strengths. You cook, and we find fresh ingredients. Protein for your dishes, variety for our bellies."

Jean-Pierre hesitated. He needed help, but at what cost? "I'll think about it," he said finally, sheathing his knife.

Time passed, and Jean-Pierre found solace in the kitchen—a place free from morality. His senses heightened in the face of mortal danger. The group watched as crops were planted, and vegetables grown. Dr. Martinez praised his efforts, but her eyes carried sadness. Sophia glowed under his guidance, learning new recipes. Alice worked with him like a finely tuned machine, trusting him implicitly. Eddie ate everything he made, oblivious to its sourcing.

One day, they discovered a herd of wild pigs. Jean-Pierre's pulse raced. It was risky but necessary. They needed nourishment; if they failed, it would all be for nothing.

He cooked the meat over an open fire, adding herbs from his garden. The sizzling sounds echoed through the camp, drawing everyone closer. Sophia gasped at the rich aroma.

Together, they savored each bite, marveling at how far they'd come. Antoine watched silently, calculating his next move.

Later, as they digested their plates clean, Jean-Pierre looked around the table—these were the faces he'd saved. Eddie wiped his mouth, smiling. "You are a miracle worker, Chef." Alice nodded in agreement. Dr. Martinez's eyes danced with hope. Sophia's cheeks flushed with joy. Yet none knew the sacrifices he'd made to bring them here.

He couldn't bear the guilt any longer. "I've committed acts," he began, voice trembling. "Things I swore not to do." Their gazes shifted to him, worried. "I've used my skills for survival," he admitted. "But we need to remember, we're better than that."

Silence hung heavy. Eddie's brow furrowed. "What do you mean?"

"We've found a way to live without taking life," Jean-Pierre said, "Let's stick to it." They hesitated, weighing his words. But something in his eyes said they'd found their purpose again - to find another way.

Days passed, and hope blossomed. Sophia taught him about the medicinal properties of plants. Alice discovered hidden springs of water. Eddie made a shelter from discarded materials. Dr. Martinez experimented with other food sources. The group began to thrive. Even Antoine, seeing the potential, offered his help, his dark eyes glinting with ambition.

One day, they stumbled upon a library amidst ruins. Jean-Pierre's heart raced; knowledge was power. He devoured books on cooking, history, and agriculture—his passion rekindled. The others grew stronger too;

Marcus even showed interest in learning new skills. They began trading with other survivors, bringing much-needed unity.

One fateful day, a disease threatened the camp. Jean-Pierre remembered his training, mixing herbs to create an antidote. It worked! Cheers erupted as Sophia wrapped the sick in blankets. Their community's future gleamed brighter than ever before.

As they sat around the fire that night, Jean-Pierre saw it—a future where humanity could flourish once again. It was a long shot, but with hard work and determination, they could build something beautiful from these ashes. He closed his eyes, savoring the sweet taste of success. The crackling flames warmed his face. He was no longer just a chef; he was a leader, guiding them all to a brighter tomorrow.

The wind picked up, rustling leaves, carrying with it the promise of change. The stars twinkled above, and for the first time in months, Jean-Pierre didn't feel alone. He had found his purpose amidst the chaos. The group huddled close together, their hearts full of hope and possibility. Eddie's arm rested on his shoulder—his stomach rumbling from anticipation of tomorrow's meal. Alice watched him warily but respectfully, her eyes acknowledging his contributions. Even Marcus, usually impeccable, seemed humbled by their achievements. Antoine lurked on the outskirts, calculating his next move.

Chef LeClair smiled, his salt-and-pepper hair glistening in the firelight. His hands caressed the rough bark of a fallen tree they'd used for the fire. He wondered if they'd make it out alive... but for now, he'd savor this moment. The delicious scent of cooking dinner wafted through the air; Dr. Martinez's voice floated over to him, discussing alternative food sources. He hummed softly, his mind wandering to the rich flavors dancing on his tongue. Tomorrow would bring new challenges, but tonight, they'd feast. As everyone settled down under the stars, Jean-Pierre reveled in the warmth and camaraderie around him.

Alice curled up nearby, shadowed by Marcus's absence, her gaze lingering on the chef. She couldn't help but appreciate the magic he worked with mere scraps. A soft sigh escaped her lips as she remembered how far they'd come. Sophia, ever-watchful, nestled closer to her, and Eddie snored gently beside them. Antoine sulked in the corner, but even he couldn't resist the aroma of sizzling venison. For now, they were united by survival and hunger. The stars twinkled overhead like diamonds sprinkled across black velvet—a reminder that life still held beauty amidst darkness.

www.ingramcontent.com/pod-product-compliance
Ingram Content Group UK Ltd.
Pitfield, Milton Keynes, MK11 3LW, UK
UKHW021935200726
13853UKWH00011B/2143

9 798869 214775